Oddity

Sarah Cannon

D0062676

SQUARE
FISH

Feiwel and Friends
New York

MAR -- 2019

SQUARE
FISH

An imprint of Macmillan Publishing Group, LLC
175 Fifth Avenue
New York, NY 10010
mackids.com

Square Fish and the Square Fish logo are trademarks of Macmillan and
are used by Feiwel and Friends under license from Macmillan.

Our books may be purchased in bulk for promotional, educational, or
business use. Please contact your local bookseller or the Macmillan
Corporate and Premium Sales Department at (800) 221-7945 ext. 5442 or
by email at MacmillanSpecialMarkets@macmillan.com.

Library of Congress Cataloging-in-Publication Data

Names: Cannon, Sarah, author.
Title: Oddity / Sarah Cannon.
Description: New York : Feiwel and Friends, 2017. | Summary:
    Eleven-year-old Ada and her friends face zombie rabbits, alien mobs,
    and puppet cartels as they explore their small New Mexico town seeking
    Ada's missing twin sister.
Identifiers: LCCN 2016058774 (print) | LCCN 2017029144 (ebook)
    ISBN 978-1-250-17906-7 (paperback) | ISBN 978-1-250-12329-9 (ebook)
Subjects: | CYAC: Friendship—Fiction. | Supernatural—Fiction. | Missing
    children—Fiction. | Sisters—Fiction. | Twins—Fiction. | Humorous stories.
Classification: LCC PZ7.1.C37 (ebook) | LCC PZ7.1.C37 Odd 2017 (print) |
    DDC [Fic]—dc23
LC record available at https://lccn.loc.gov/2016058774

Originally published in the United States by Feiwel and Friends
First Square Fish edition, 2019
Book designed by Liz Dresner
Square Fish logo designed by Filomena Tuosto

10 9 8 7 6 5 4 3 2 1

LEXILE: 780L

For Will, Rosemary, and Graeme.

Because places are easy, but finding the right people is hard—and I got incredibly lucky.

Chapter 1
Safety Drill

Times like now, as I hide behind a stack of gym mats holding Cayden's head down so he won't get clawed, I wish Pearl was here. I don't know why safety drills have to be so realistic. Everyone knows Cayden just moved here from Chicago. Why not prepare him a little before setting angry leopards loose in the gym, instead of letting him drag down our class's score?

Cayden's our neighbor, and I know I should help him, but he's holding me back. Raymond's going to get more points than me. He dove straight for the weapons locker, like I wanted to. We're finally fifth graders, and there's no one bigger to get there first. On the other hand, I know Cayden hasn't finished his half of our diorama on "The Three Reasons Science Is

Risky." If he gets eaten, I'll have to do all that homework myself.

A bead of sweat rolls down his forehead. He's always pale next to Raymond and me, but right now he's white as a yeti.

"You know what my dad says every time we move, Ada? He says, 'It'll be an adventure!' This time, I told him he was just saying it to make himself feel better. He's getting back at me for complaining, isn't he?"

"Nope. This is pretty normal for Oddity. Do what I say and you'll probably live."

Gosh, kid. Pull it together.

I glance over the stack of mats we're hiding behind. Eunice is doing way better at rope climbing this year. She's got claw marks in her gym shorts, but she's high enough up that the leopards aren't going to get her again.

The fourth graders pulled the bleachers out and are defending the top. Our class tried that, the time we had cassowaries. It didn't work so well. Too easy for whatever it is to run around under there, going after your feet.

The teachers stand outside the grilled doors, waiting. Mr. Bakshi watches and makes notes on his clipboard. Ms. Winters rubs her hands up and down her arms, even though she's got a sweater on and it's about a hundred degrees out. She hasn't been the same since she spent Labor Day weekend in the morgue. (It was an honest mistake. The EMTs thought she was dead.) I heard her tell Mrs. O'Halloran she's so behind on grading now it will be Memorial Day before she's caught up. That's what they get for going to year-round school.

I run a hand through my braids and give the gym a quick once-over. The heavy doors they put in last spring will keep the leopards out of the locker room, at least. Sure enough, most of the big cats are under the bleachers swiping at people's ankles. Raymond tranqed one on his way over here, at close range, I notice. I approve.

He tosses me a gun. "How many minutes you figure we got?"

"I'm timing," I say. "Three and change."

He sends another gun sailing over the stack of gym mats, almost whacking Cayden in the head.

"Aw, Mendez, you know he can't use that."

He vaults over the mats to land beside us. None of Cayden's swingy skater hair for him, just the same old military buzz cut. He's the one thing I can count on.

"Look, he's gotta learn sometime. I'm not giving up a pizza party for the new kid."

That's this year's prize for the highest safety ratings. There's a new place we want to try called Ransom Pizza. They deliver empty boxes with threatening notes inside, and you have thirty minutes to find your pizza, or it explodes.

"He's had three months of small sortie fighting drills. He's ready. Cayden, get up!"

Cayden does. He's still pale, but he's standing. I give him the tranquilizer gun. Raymond also has Betsy, a shotgun, slung over his shoulder, but he won't use her for this. Leopards are endangered, and we're a green school.

I squeeze off a shot over Raymond's shoulder, and the leopard stumbles, sliding to a stop behind him, out. Probably out. The other one's still down. That's a good sign. If they had superpowers, we'd know by now. I head around the side of the bleachers to get a clear view. Wish I had a flashlight. There must not have been any in the locker. Raymond's good about grabbing that stuff.

I use the reflected light in their eyes to aim, and I get one. Then I take out the one Cayden's aiming at and missing. The one behind that is so close I can see the ripple of its spots in the bars of light coming in through the bleachers. I yank Cayden out. It rounds the corner.

"Try again, Cayden," I say, but Raymond puts it down before Cayden's got a clear shot.

"Three for me, two for you," I say, mad that he messed up my lesson. There's only one left out on the floor, but either it's not too swift on the uptake or Mr. Bakshi was taunting them this morning, because it's swiping at the glass of the outside door over and over, and not accomplishing anything. I motion for Cayden to take that one, and he edges over. Still, I'm not impressed with the intelligence of leopards. The raptors were way worse.

WHAM!

Something hits me between the shoulder blades, knocking me flat, and I just know I'm about to get savaged. Figures. Kindergarten through fourth grade, no savagings, then I decide to be a Good Samaritan—savaging. It's got the back of my sweatshirt in its teeth, and it's shaking me. My shoes squeak as they're jerked back and forth across the very, very waxed gym floor. My braids whip back and forth past my face, beads clacking. I don't know where Raymond is, but I hope he's doing something helpful. This thing is going to figure out it doesn't have my head in its mouth eventually. I still have my tranquilizer gun, but there's no way to aim when I can't at least brace my arm.

I imagine the overhead announcement:

"Students are advised during future safety drills to please watch your twenty and keep your head out of leopards' mouths if at all possible. As of today, the safety drill running score total is as follows: Fourth grade, fifty; fifth grade, minus twenty for preventable decapitation; third grade . . ."

There's a shot, and I'm suddenly buried under a very heavy leopard robe.

Someone rolls the big cat off me, and I blink up at Raymond and that Emuel kid. Cayden points his shaking gun at the remaining glass-pawing leopard to cover us. He couldn't hit the broad side of a barn, but at least he's trying.

Cayden finally bags the last leopard, mostly because it's so obsessed with Mr. Bakshi that it's impossible to miss. We're dismissed to wash up and change our clothes, which is good because our gym shorts are ugly as ever.

When I leave the locker room, I'm wearing jeans with the cuffs rolled up and a sleeveless blouse I found at For a Song Secondhand Clothes. That's one good thing about gym uniforms—my favorite clothes don't get shredded. My arms are too skinny, but I like the white blouse against my dark skin, so I wear it anyway. I meet up with Cayden and Raymond in the hall, and we start to head for class, but something is . . . heinous.

"What is that SMELL?"

Cayden's expression is guilty. "What?"

"Someone reeks like a lovesick hyena."

Raymond actually laughs. I'm a bit proud—usually only Pearl can get him to do that—but Cayden's miffed.

"How would you even know what a lovesick hyena smells like?"

Raymond and I start to answer at the same time, and Cayden rolls his eyes. "Never mind. I don't want to know."

"It's obviously you, Cayden." Raymond makes a gag face. "What IS that?"

"It's just . . . this spray kids use at home."

"That's pretty smart," I say. "What does it repel?"

He stares. "It's not supposed to repel anything. It's supposed to smell good."

Raymond unzips Cayden's backpack and fishes out a spray can with a hammer as big as Thor's on the side.

BASH! it reads. IN YOUR FACE! (DO NOT APPLY TO YOUR ACTUAL FACE.)

We burst out laughing, and even behind his hair, I can tell Cayden's turning red. "Shut up," he says.

"It's okay." I pat his shoulder. "You can wash it off at my house after school."

Chapter 2

Scary

When the last bell rings, I scoop up my stuff and make a run for it, before something happens in the bus line to trigger a lockdown. Last week a bologna sandwich in the back of someone's locker developed sentience and busted its way out, attacking bystanders' ankles. It took staff a while to sort out what was blood and what was ketchup. I don't know why things like that never happen during spelling tests.

As I weave and twist my way through the crowded halls, Raymond and Cayden are right behind me. For once we don't have my cousin Mason tagging along. He's going home with a friend.

Cayden lives next door to us, in Aunt Bets's old house. Pearl and I used to hide in its creaky old bathroom and yell down the tub drain, and something down there yelled back. I should tell

Cayden about it so he can try. I swear, though, I've never seen such a special little flower in all my life as Cayden Coates. He can't handle carnivorous slugs, or angry clowns, or anything. It's wearying having him around all the time, but I can't very well leave him alone. He wouldn't last a day without me.

We hoof it down Havasu Hill past Greeley's Groceries, which is creepily, perfectly white no matter how hard the sun beats down on it. Its vast, freshly paved parking lot shimmers in the haze of the New Mexico heat. On the left end of the building, the conveyor belt rolls out of its dark opening. Workers in blue shirts and white pants scurry to load groceries into waiting cars as the latest in a long series of Greeleys gives directions, with his straw hat sitting jauntily on his head and his gray beard neatly trimmed, same as Greeleys have been doing for as long as anyone can remember.

A conveyor belt from the store to your trunk. It's one of those things no one thought to want, but now that we have it, everyone feels like it should have been that way all the time. Like air-conditioning, I guess, or cable TV. But I never liked it. The thing about the conveyor belt is that, between the moment you pick out your groceries and the moment you load them into your car, you don't actually know what's happening to them in there.

When Cayden saw it, he didn't understand what it was. No grocery stores anywhere he lived—and he's lived in Orlando, and Philadelphia, and Chicago—ever had one. If I wasn't still wondering where Pearl went after they led her into the Greeley's Sweepstakes tent in that very parking lot last year, I would be a little bit proud of having an invention he'd never seen right here in my hometown. As it is, every time I look at that conveyor belt, all I want to know is what's at the other end.

Lately I keep thinking that Greeley's is trying a little too hard. The signs are so jaunty and cheery that they insist you're not having a bad day. The carts and parking lot lines are aggressively perfect. It makes me want to shove something really dangerous into that conveyor belt's open mouth. Greeley's doesn't get to tell me to be cheerful.

I remember the brass band playing, and the blue-and-white tent that put the desert sky to shame. I'm supposed to be happy for Pearl. But I never considered being the one left behind. The win-less twin, missing my winsome sister.

Once I'm past, it's better. Main Street is everything Greeley's isn't. Instead of a building full of blue-shirts who follow us around smiling and offering us samples just a little too enthusiastically, there's a row of stores filled with people who knew our parents before they were parents. The brightly painted false fronts remind me of a row of greeting cards, and right now they all read: food!

My stomach rumbles.

"Bakery?" says Cayden hopefully, pointing down the street at Aunt Bets's hand-painted sign and the bright red storefront with the weather vane on top.

"No way. If she gets one look at me, I'll be in there polishing the display cases all afternoon."

Cayden sighs. He never had a bizcochito cookie before he moved here, and now he's addicted to their spicy flavor.

9

"We could hit the co-op," says Raymond. One of his moms is probably in there volunteering, but Raymond's moms are pretty free-range, so he won't get roped into anything like I would. He's kidding, though. I'm banned for life, a consequence of my feud with Scoby, the big kombucha sponge who sits in a jar at the register. He's one of the town's oldest residents, so he's basically running the place, the slimy fungus. Being banned doesn't stop me from getting in there when I need to do something really important, like put tarantulas in the bulk bins, but it's not worth the risk just for a snack.

"Let's go to Bodega Bodega," I say, and Raymond smirks at me but doesn't call me out.

We stop in front of the peeling pink stucco building. You'd think people would learn that the site of a failed bodega is a bad place to open a bodega, but I guess anyone who can't manage to nail up a new sign that fully covers the old one is not the sharpest pencil in the box to begin with. Bodega Bodega survives mostly because us kids spend all our money on junk food and sushi-shaped erasers in there. For me, it offers the bonus of not being Greeley's. I'd beg for Dad and Aunt Bets to get all our stuff here if we could. I reach up to tap the patched-together signs for luck as we go in.

The bell bangs the dusty glass door. Old Joe's behind the counter, which I guess means that his Curtis Clone, Young Joe, is off making deliveries. I browse my way down the dingy aisles as the boys head for the cooler for drinks.

I go for the gummy peach rings, but just as I get there, a squid-chinned alien in a pinstriped suit grabs the last bag.

"Hey!" I protest, but it looks at me with one round yellow eye and walks to the counter to pay, tearing open the bag just to make its point, I guess. Its chin tentacles start fishing out gummy rings and depositing them in its mouth.

Grumbling, I take a bag of gummy cacti instead, slapping my money down in front of Old Joe and joining the boys outside.

We eat while we walk. Lucky for me, Aunt Bets is too short these days to see me as I pass, but we wave at Raymond's mom, who's hanging a FREE-RANGE JACKALOPE sign in the window of the co-op. It's about time to plan another after-hours raid on the place, so Scoby doesn't get too relaxed. I can't take Cayden along, though. Last time, he set off the bear horn Scoby mounted on the wall where the door handle hits. Total rookie move.

I spot my mountain of a father across the street.

"Hey, Daddy," I call. His dark, bald head shines in the sun. He's hauling a centipede twice as long as he is out of an open manhole cover with one of his special capture nooses. That's at least the third one this week.

"Hey, baby girl," he says. He's sweating through his brown uniform.

"Home for dinner?" I ask, keeping a safe distance.

He gives another great heave, getting about half of the scrambling centipede out of the manhole, then shakes his head.

"Sorry, baby. Gotta . . . uh, I gotta work late."

That did not sound super convincing.

"Oh . . . no big. Love you!" I say. I've been trying to be cool about him working so many extra hours. Somebody has to make ends meet. I get it. But the way Mama's been acting since Pearl left, I need him more than ever. Sure, I've got Aunt Bets and Mason to eat with, but they mostly moved in to help us keep it together, and that's hard to forget when I have no parent types at the dinner table.

Is he fibbing to me about what he's doing when he's not home?

I'm distracted from my worries by Cayden hitching his backpack up higher. I roll my eyes.

"You need to think a little harder about how you hold that thing," I say. "You carry it on one shoulder like that, it's going to slow you down if you have to run."

"I figured I could drop it easier if it was only half on."

"Maybe," I say, "but isn't there anything in there you need? I keep waterproof matches in mine, a water bottle, some food. One of those foil emergency blankets NASA traded to the aliens they met on the moon."

He gives me a strange look, and now I feel like he's the one about to roll his eyes.

"I never thought about carrying that stuff. I keep my cell in my pocket."

I had to tell him that, too. His last school made him keep it in his locker. I can't believe that. I know we lose signal during time slips, but . . .

Adults are always asking what you want to be when you grow up, like it's a legitimate question. First of all, there's no guarantee you will grow up, so why borrow trouble? Second,

I kind of dismiss the question on the grounds that I don't have enough information to answer it. After all, it's not like I know what people actually *do* at most grown-up jobs anyway. But the more I watch all of Cayden's missteps as he learns to navigate Oddity, the more I'm sure of one thing:

When I grow up, I want to be scary.

I want people to cross the street when they see me coming. Step one: refuse to cross for anyone else. Even if it's a member of the Protection Committee. Starting right now.

Mr. Whanslaw steps toward us, clicking as he comes. The long, red brocade overcoat he wears can't completely conceal the unnatural rhythm of his movements—as if the brilliant blue hue of his face and hands weren't enough of a clue. Strings brush and part in the air above his white hair as he walks, and above those is the wooden control bar, held in gloved hands by the dark-suited, sunglasses-wearing puppeteer behind him.

The puppeteers are like cardboard cutouts of real people: all the same in some indefinable way, and all supremely uninteresting. I barely spare a glance for this one. He just works the control bar, staring straight ahead. Or at least I assume he is, behind his mirrored shades.

In contrast, the puppets are in full, blazing color, and their presence is larger than their actual selves. They laugh scornfully in the face of danger, and we're lucky they do. For as long as I've been alive, they've led Oddiputians in protecting our town from any number of disasters, and kept strange things that lurk around the edges of town at bay.

Whanslaw turns his head with a creak and looks at me as

he goes by. Under his white, fluffy hair, his blue face wears a faint smile, grandfatherly and mild, but also creepily fixed.

Me and Raymond, we're the top two fifth graders. Everyone knows it, even the Protection Committee. I thrill at Mr. Whanslaw's attention.

Cayden doesn't. He's still twitching half a block later.

"I don't see what the big deal is," says Raymond.

Cayden shoves his hair back out of his face and stares.

"Are you serious? Where I come from, puppets aren't alive. They're inanimate, and the puppeteers control them. And puppets definitely do not run towns."

"Um, yeah," I say. "Because where you come from is boring."

He continues to shiver, in spite of the afternoon heat. The puppets are that scary.

THAT is how it's done.

We climb Grackle Street, and I unlock my door with the key I wear around my neck, under my shirt with my locket.

We've got almost two hours before everyone else comes home.

This is when Pearl and I would have taken the opportunity to make the biggest, most disgusting snack we could come up with, but things have changed. These boys and I have something better to do.

We troop downstairs to the basement, and I start flipping on lights. Cayden cautiously drags the beanbag chairs out of the corner, shaking each one. I grab the old laptop off my dad's desk and collapse onto one of the beanbags, opening the browser and typing in our destination before the Wi-Fi even kicks in.

The shadowy splash page of Nopes.com comes up on my screen.

Chapter 3
Tagalong

"Whose turn is it to pick?" asks Raymond.

"Ada's." Cayden glances at me, then quickly looks away. His relationship with Nopes is complicated.

Nopes is a crowdsourced wiki of stuff Oddiputians should avoid. People being people, everyone nopes out of different things, so the site has a post for basically anything about Oddity, past, present, or future. If you focus on one post at a time, it's wildly inaccurate (and posts vanish constantly, courtesy of the Protection Committee). But the tsunami of conspiracy theories, viewed from a distance, has pointed me in the right direction over and over.

We were using Nopes to pound home truths into Cayden's thick head when it hit me: Nopes is an excellent resource for planning an expedition to check out the exact thing it's warning you away from. It was just what I needed.

The thing is, a vanishing twin is not unlike a vanishing arm. There were two of them for a reason. Losing Pearl? I never saw it coming. As far as we knew, kids couldn't win the Sweepstakes. It had never happened before.

It's been a long time since anything successfully snuck up on me. To say I did not like it is an understatement.

So now, with help from Nopes, I'm poking around in every corner, learning all Oddity's secrets. If I happen to find out where Sweepstakes winners go? So much the better. It beats hanging out in Pearl's room pretending to be her, which I can't do anymore anyway because it was making Mama cry.

"What's next, Ada?" Raymond asks.

"I've got a good one today. Give me a minute. It's taking forever to load."

Cayden sighs. His parents work for Splint, the local cellular and Internet provider (*We'll Patch You Through*). Splint's signal is pretty spotty, and me and Raymond never miss a chance to wind him up about it.

Raymond picked our last expedition. Our search for cursed gold led us to a corner of the junkyard. When we moved the mattresses and dresser a Nopeser described, we found a half-rotten cardboard box with three gold bars inside. No one took one. We all know better, ever since that fog came and carried off Henry Atchison from Atchison Motors. But Nopes's intel was good. I scratched a bar with my fingernail, and it left a mark.

Finally, the page loads.

Raymond's eyebrows go up. He's impressed. "Whoa. The Sunset Six."

Cayden's gray eyes darken with confusion. "Ada, there are hundreds of posts here. How could anybody find anything useful?"

I start pointing out the trends I've spotted, and Raymond grabs a notebook to jot them down. We don't usually bother loading Nopes on our phones, partly because of the signal issues, and partly because paper is easier to destroy. I bragged quite a bit on Nopes the first few times we found something cool, and lately other kids from our class have been mounting expeditions of their own. I don't mind a little friendly competition, but there's no reason to make it easy for people.

Cayden's reading over my shoulder. "This is about missing kids? You think you figured out what happened to them?"

"Neighbor boy, I think I know where they *are*." I pull up my crown jewel, a screenshot I grabbed just before the original post got deleted.

Raymond lets out a long breath and turns to me. "So this isn't a planning day. You want to go out there."

I'm already on my feet. "You know I do. Let's go!"

"Right now?" asks Cayden. "It'll be dark soon!"

I roll my eyes, even though I know I look just like Pearl when I do it. "How often do I have a whole afternoon without Mason? We've got at least two hours before dark. We need to *go*."

18

Cayden looks at Raymond, and I open my mouth again to tell him off. Luckily, Raymond's on my side.

"It'll be tight, but we can make it." He's a ball of coiled energy. Ready to go on campaign.

We dump our school stuff out of our backpacks, and I run upstairs to grab a hat off one of the hooks in the front hall and fill water bottles from the kitchen sink.

Just as I'm screwing the top on the last one, the front door bangs. I freeze. If it's Mama, there's still a chance.

A book bag thumps down in the front hall, and I turn to see Mason headed for the refrigerator, one shoelace dragging. I canNOT convince that kid to keep his laces double-knotted. He's going to trip and get eaten one of these days.

"Is there pudding?" he asks by way of greeting, rummaging for snack cups until all I can see of him is his dark, curly hair. If I were Mason, I'd be careful. Nobody believes me about Scoby putting powdered cheese sauce in that butterscotch pudding Bets brought me, but it happened. Right now, though, I've got bigger problems.

"What are you doing home? I thought you went to the Murphys'!"

"I did, but those big bumps they all got last week turned out to be spider nests. Everybody was screaming and stuff, so I walked home."

"Alone?" I ask sharply.

"No, they got the neighbor to bring me." He starts crunching an apple.

I mentally review the list of Murphy neighbors: flesh-eating-virus guy, blind lady who can see if someone's lying, and . . . well, he's home now. Which is actually kind of a problem.

"Hey, you ready to go?" asks Cayden, appearing in the kitchen.

Mason perks up, craning his head around the fridge door. "Go where?"

Darn it. Cayden has the worst timing on earth. The way he flinched, he knows it, too.

"Uh. We were going to go to . . . the park!"

I gently rest my forehead on the counter.

"What? Kids aren't allowed in the park!"

Great, now we scared him. I shut the fridge, which has been open for an age now.

"He was kidding. Of course we're not going to the park." Mama will be home from work any minute. I can't leave him here with her, though.

Raymond must have heard the noise, because he comes upstairs, assessing the situation like he always does. "Hey, Mason, do you still have my Commander Amazing comic upstairs? Can I have it back?"

"Oh. Yeah, I guess so. Hang on." He pounds upstairs to get it.

"We can take him," says Raymond.

"No way. Aunt Bets will pull my hair out," I say.

"It's not actually that far," he says, in that super-calm tone of his. "We'll be back by dinner, and she'll figure he's still at the Murphys'. . . . Why isn't he?"

"The bumps were spider nests."

"Figures." He shakes his head in disgust.

I fiddle with my braids, pondering. "Okay. We'll do it. But we've got to go now. Mason!" I call, to hurry him. The way he's trashed the guest-room-turned-his-room, he could search for that comic for hours.

There's thumping and a muffled, shouted reply, from which I gather that he's on his way, but arguing.

The front door opens and shuts again, but it's just Mama. She puts her purse on the hall table, all elegant in her skirt and heels with her hair pinned up.

"Hi, Mama!" I say, but it's like tapping on the side of a terrarium to make the lizard move. She doesn't look at me, or speak to Mason when he barrels past her. She just goes upstairs. The floor creaks as she gets to her bedroom, then the bedsprings creak as she lies down, fully clothed, on the bed, like she's done every day since Pearl's been gone. At least now she gets up for work, but I'm starting to suspect that's as good as it's ever going to get.

For a second, I think about going and shaking her. But at least today there's something to distract me.

"We're going for a bike ride, then a hike," I say to Mason. "You can come with us, but you have to keep up! And you can't tell *anyone*. Okay?"

"Okay," he says, eyes wide with excitement at being included.

"Now put your foot on this chair, and I'll tie your shoe."

Chapter 4

The Sunset Six

Raymond's right: it's not far from town. Which makes sense, when I think about it. Six kids, the oldest our age, the youngest littler than Mason. . . . I mean, how far were they going to go on their own steam? On the other hand, the way the story's told, search parties combed every inch of territory within a mile of town, and it was summer, so they had plenty of daylight. But some stories get bigger with time.

We're behind the Sunset Ridge housing development, but not that far. Close enough to be called in for dinner if you're listening for it. It's the kind of place only kids would find, because only kids would bother. There's a trace of a path on the ground, like a deer trail, but I can tell kids made it, because in places it's lined with colored glass and interesting rocks. They probably played out here all the time, created a whole world like kids do, with made-up names and houses and stories that picked right back up every time they returned. Until one night, they never came home. Six kids from four families. Gone.

It was the worst scandal to hit Oddity since the late 1800s, when both the mayor and the sheriff got ridden out on a rail for arson and something called collusion, which as near as I can tell means being deluded with a friend. Thankfully, the puppets and the original Greeley were already here by then. They stepped in and replaced Oddity's former leaders, and the Protection Committee was born.

In the case of the Sunset Six, the culprit turned out to be Mike Hannagan, the owner of Mikey's Market. Daddy said he seemed like a fine, upstanding guy, but maybe not the brightest bulb in the sign. He served alongside Greeley—I don't know if it was the current one or his predecessor; everybody lost count a while ago—on the Committee for Wisdom, Understanding, and Trust, which Greeley created to explain the puppets' point of view to Oddiputians who experience confusion.

The PC told the WUT (and the WUT told everyone else) that Mike murdered the Sunset Six. But he never told anyone where he hid the bodies. Now we're about to find out.

The path winds between tall, spiny black ocotillo bushes and around boulders, following along the back of Sunset Ridge at a distance. If this is where the Sunset Six are, I'm starting to ask myself how these kids never got found until now. Maybe there's a cave? An old mine shaft?

"You stay between me and Raymond," I tell Mason. "Don't you go running off."

In my head, I hear Pearl telling me I'm not his mom. Easy for her to say. Daredevil-may-care, that's what Mama called her. She'd be skipping from boulder to boulder, trying to get Raymond up there with her. He'd probably go, for Pearl. She always could loosen him up.

I bet she's cackling at me someplace right now, because even though she's gone, I still argue with her. You want to know the truth? Sometimes, even when I argue, I don't really disagree.

The thing about Oddity that kids know, but grown-ups forget, is that there's no point in allowing or forbidding us to do pretty much anything. We never know where the danger is. It could come out of the desert, or out of the faucet. Every place is dangerous at least some of the time, which means no one place is really safer than another. It's like rock-paper-scissors. If the other player's good enough, you can't guess their move. You just have to shoot.

But there's a difference between being a smother and being worried about my cousin falling down an actual, factual hole. So he can stay where I tell him to, and the Pearl in my head can hush.

"What now?" asks Raymond, looking back at Cayden even though he's got a memory like a steel trap. This is where he's nicer than me. He gives Cayden something to do, where I'd just shove him around.

"There's a cross path up here," Cayden says. "We need to go left."

We do, and after passing between two more huge boulders, we find ourselves facing a ridge lined with bushy piñon pines. And there, our directions run out.

I'll admit I'm feeling a little foolish. I was the one who insisted we had to come out here, and now what?

"Maybe there's a cave entrance behind these trees," says Raymond. It's not a bad suggestion.

"We can't just go into a cave," says Cayden.

"What the heck do you think we're going to do if we find one?" I ask. "*Not* go in?"

"Of course not!" Cayden says. "There could be snakes in there, or sudden drops, or . . . I don't know, poisonous gas."

"That's only happened to me once," says Raymond. I never know if he's kidding now that Pearl's not here to laugh at him. Maybe he doesn't, either.

"Look," I say, "cave or no cave, there's got to be something here somewhere. If we don't find the Sunset Six now, someone's going to beat us to them." I've got my cell in my pocket, and I am going to be the first person who puts a picture up where people can see it. Though the light's not great for a photo right now. Because . . . the sun is going down. Aunt Bets is going to kill me, and if I don't get a picture, I'm gonna die for no reason at all.

So I look harder.

"I can't see anything behind all the trees," I say. I feel kind of silly, but I get down on the ground and start crawling along the tree line, looking under the branches. I go all the way along the ridge. After a while, Mason starts helping me.

"Are you ever going to tell me what we're looking for?" he asks. He's been pestering me since we left the house, but I made him shut up when we stepped out into the desert. Maybe if I warn him and it turns out to be gruesome, he won't look. Right. Still . . .

"We're looking for some kids who disappeared," I say. He was real little when it happened. I don't actually know if the smaller kids talk about it.

"The Sunset Six? We're looking for the Sunset Six?" he squeaks. I should have known. Some jerk big sister or brother always talks.

"Yeah, we are. We're following some clues that . . . turned up. And we want to find them first. So you just help me look. See if you see a hole or something, along the base of this ridge, behind the trees."

"I saw a drawing. Could that be another clue?"

I sit back on my heels and stare at him. "What, down along the path?"

"No, look!" Pleased to have found something, he pulls me back the way we came. I could have sworn I looked carefully, but sometimes little kids see things no one else does. So I dutifully crawl back along the ridge. Halfway there, I notice two pairs of legs in denim and look up at my . . . friends. Sigh.

"Are you two enjoying this? You wanna get down here and help a girl out?"

"Somebody's got to keep a lookout," says Raymond.

Mason is lying flat on his stomach, pointing. "It's right there."

Forgetting how undignified it is, I lie down flat like him. I do see something, but . . . "I think it's just different colors in the rock, Mase," I say, disappointed.

"No! I see shoes."

I look harder. Then it occurs to me that what I need to do is look less hard. I unfocus my eyes a little, stop studying the rock, and just *see*.

He's right. There, in a gap between two branches that's still letting sunlight through, I see the edge of a high-top, clear and perfect on the ridge.

"I can even see the eyelets where the laces go through," I say, amazed. But—

"Painted on the stone? If this is all some kind of prank . . . ," begins Raymond, coming to see.

But I don't think it's a prank. I stand up and grab the nearest dense, prickly tree limb. "Help me bend these branches, so I can see!"

We all jump to do it, and I can see their heads are buzzing with excitement like mine, even Cayden's.

How could the searchers not have found them? But maybe the trees grew up quickly, to hide them. Stranger things have happened around here. There they are, pressed perfectly into the rock. I remember a movie we watched in class once, about erosion and the Grand Canyon, and it talked about the "Living Rock," like it was capitalized. People shouldn't be allowed to say things like that to little kids, because we were all watching out for rock monsters for weeks, until we found out it was a metaphor. But now, I forgive that stuck-up narrator because I'm staring one of the Sunset Six in the eye and expecting him to blink.

Oh, they don't stick out. And it's not like they're inside a case made of rock, either. Picture the best, most real drawing you've ever seen. Now picture it not done on top of the rock, where you could rub it off, but soaked into the rock, part of it. Except there's no way this is a painting. No one can paint on rock so that you can see the frayed edges on the little gap-toothed girl's shorts, or the shine in the eyes of the boy in front of me. One boy has his hands behind his head, and there's a scab on his elbow. All six of them are staring up at something in the sky, and the thing that stands out most is their happiness, like they won the Greeley's Sweepstakes.

No one found their bodies because there weren't any to find. No one should've found a murderer, either. These kids aren't dead, they're . . . changed.

"I'll tell you one thing," I say. "I don't believe for one second that some grocery store owner did this."

Raymond nods.

It doesn't seem quite right to take a picture of the Sunset Six. Their smiles make me think of Pearl, which makes me think about their families. I don't guess they'd want to find out what happened from a bunch of kids who are treating this like a game. I let go of my branch, and it about takes Cayden's ear off. He yelps.

"What did you do that for?" he asks.

I start to explain that I don't want to take their picture, ready for a fight after I dragged my friends all the way out here, when Raymond lets go of his branch, too. It takes Mason right down.

"Hey!" he says.

"Shhh!"

I turn to look where Raymond's looking, and listen, not too worried because I figure it's other kids. But I'm really, really wrong.

You know that writing on American cheese packages that says PROCESSED CHEESE FOOD? Let's face it, we all know there's probably no actual cheese in there. This thing coming at us is like that.

We call it the Blurmonster, and it might really be a monster, but it's hard to be sure. It's only visible as a sort of blur, like a big, meat loaf–shaped heat haze, so none of us knows exactly what it is, only that it's big and unwieldy, like a parade float wearing an invisibility cloak. It's incredibly strong, but never caused any real trouble. Then, one day, it started smashing up any part of Oddity it could get to. Oddiputians know how to roll with a lot of strange things, but the Blurmonster turning on us was a shock. It was the first thing the puppets ever protected us from, and why they were such a welcome addition to our town.

None of us are supposed to be anywhere near the

Blurmonster. Which is a problem, because once it finds some-one to follow, it doesn't stop. The only way to track it is by the way it scruffs up the ground as it passes, and by the way things seen through it are all blurry and distorted. It's not very fast, but Mrs. O'Halloran would probably take a pay cut to have a student with its attention span.

"Let's go." I'm already grabbing at Mason. This is why I'm not supposed to bring him places like this. The Protection Committee's citizen patrols keep the Blurmonster from com-ing into the middle of town, but out here, I'm all the protec-tion my cousin has got.

"We can outrun it, I think." Raymond is shouldering his pack. "It's big, you know? If we go straight down the hillside, through the brush, I don't think it can follow us."

Cayden's not coming.

"What are you doing?" I ask him. "Come on!" Boy jumps at his own shadow, then totally fails to run from the capital-*D* Danger.

"Help me!" He's shoving the branches out of the way, try-ing to hold down the ones we had with his foot.

"*What* are you doing?" The Blurmonster's still down the path a ways, but not as far as I'd like.

"Getting a picture!"

I shake my head. "It's not right."

"You say that now, but if we don't, you'll be sorry later."

"What kind of girl do you think I am?"

"We can argue about it tomorrow. This is our last chance."

There's sense in that. So even though I feel bad about it,

I help Raymond and Mason move branches. Cayden takes out his phone, and as soon as we've got the Six mostly clear, he shoots one photo. He tries to upload it to Nopes right away, but there's no signal. Figures. That's all there's time for. I reach for Mason's hand and we run, farther away from the Sunset Ridge development at first, because it's that or run back toward the thing. Then I see a piece of slope we could get down without breaking all our legs, and I cut right. Pebbles rush past me as Cayden and Raymond come sliding down behind me.

It's getting dark fast. I don't know if the streetlights turn on out here anymore. How are we going to get away from this thing if we can't see it?

"So," Cayden wheezes, as we blast out of the brush into the open and race for the garage where our bikes are heeled over, "we're going to outrun the Blurmonster on roads, on our bikes. You know that thing does roads, right?"

"Yeah, but slow," says Raymond, shoving his backpack into one of the saddlebags that hang down on either side of our rear wheels. Always be prepared, that's our motto. Storms, Blurmonsters. You know. Whatever.

"Mason's not that fast." I chest pass him his bike helmet. "Mase, put this on."

He's already on his bike, using his feet to push it backward out from between ours. "I'm fast enough."

"You got your light switched on?" I ask. His helmet bobs, so I think he's nodding. Good. We're going to need them. I just hope they work. The Oddity Children's Safety Council handed them out last year. They're manufactured locally by Osmosis Co.

POWERED BY INSPIRATION! it said on the boxes.

What that means is that they're lit by human thought, which sounds great in concept. In reality, if you're doing something really boneheaded in the dark, they shut off. I hope this doesn't count.

I look over my shoulder for the Blurmonster. I didn't think it could manage the brushy slope we came down, but it did, just slow, like Raymond said. It's reaching the bottom now. It's very hard to see in the dark, but the rattle of pebbles tells me where it is.

"Go!" I yell, and we stand on our pedals.

As usual, our biggest challenge isn't what's chasing us. One word: sand. Riding our bikes on sandy roads and sandy paths and sandy everything is how I imagine surfing must be. What I'm moving through is also moving, and I've got to manage the skids without falling over. Sometimes I lean the other way to counterbalance, and sometimes I ride them out. If I pick the wrong option I slow down too much, or tip sideways, and I have to stop and waddle through the big groove I made until I can get going again.

We all know what we're doing, but we're in a rush in the dark. My light's on, though. As the wind begins to sing in my ears and my tires grit on the pavement, I steal a quick glance over my shoulder to see that Mason's is lit up, too. Hopefully that means he's thinking.

The blurry behemoth is still coming. Seems to me we should

have lost it by now. I've never heard of it hanging around at night, so I don't think it's tracking us by sight. Bike tires aren't that noisy. That leaves . . . smell.

Uh-oh.

Cayden's bringing up the rear, as he tends to do, so I slow way down and drop behind him. I hear feet or paws or treads or whatever the Blurmonster has gritting on the sand. Like I said, it's not fast, but it's definitely still coming. I draw a deep breath, then drop back even farther, giving it a chance to notice me. Then, taking my life in my hands, I work my way to the wrong side of the street, listening for it to follow me.

It doesn't. It crunches right past me, following Cayden.

He forgot to wash off the BASH!

I zoom back past the boys, running a stop sign and spinning onto the main road leading out of Sunset Ridge. We're back in the land of finished houses with no shredded tar paper blowing in the wind, and I stand on the pedals some more. Up here on the right, I can shoot up a driveway to avoid the curb, and get onto a trail that'll cut the corner and put us a good piece farther down the main road back into town. The trail goes along it, through the brush. With a little luck, we'll keep ahead of the Blurmonster. Maybe it'll still be slower on the road than we are on the path.

Then I see an armaduino on the driveway, and because only a bonehead would ride straight at one, my bike light cuts out.

Armadillos exist to be hit by vehicles. It's like they wait around for wheels to throw themselves under. But armaduinos

33

are the worst. I don't know who thinks it's funny to use arma-duino kits to strap flamethrowers, surveillance cameras, and really noisy, motion-activated musical instruments to arma-dillos, but the results need labels that say: NOW WITH ADDED DANGER! This one makes a popping noise, and I know we're about to get scorched.

"Hard right!" I shout, and hope its head is still pointed the way I think it is. It isn't. Fire erupts in a long stream, and it's arcing toward us, because instead of running away like sensible roadkill, the armaduino is turning to look at us. It's awfully fast considering how heavy that flamethrower must be. Behind me, everyone screams as they skid to avoid it, but when I have space to look, though there are big tire arcs in the sand, everybody has managed to stay up. That thing is as good as a beacon for the Blurmonster if it's still following us, though, so I push forward as fast as I can go, and as soon as I'm clear, my light kicks back on.

Behind us, the brush crackles as it catches fire. See? This is why flame-throwing armadillos in the desert are a bad idea.

"Ada!" cries Mason. He sounds freaked out. You know I'm the worst cousin ever when our bike ride is scarier than spiders hatching out of his friend's face.

"Keep up with me, Mase!" I holler. "There's the road!"

I stay alongside it, not in it, just to be safe. The path is packed nice and hard here. For a minute, we make up some ground, and I'm exhilarated. It's a straight shot into town, and the Blurmonster won't follow us there. We're almost there when, out of the corner of my eye, I see motion up ahead on the right. It's low and rounded, coming fast, with a blinking light on top. Another armaduino. It's headed right onto the path. Before there's time to react, I'm past it, and behind me Mason yells, "Aaaah!" I steer off the path so he won't hit me if he keeps coming, and squeeze my brakes as hard as I can, as white light washes across me from behind. I turn in horror, to see headlights coming up the road as the silhouette of Mason, still on his bike, jumps the curb and wobbles into their path. Brakes scream, and so do I.

Chapter 5

Crash

Silence. Silence and, when I dare to look, Mason, still upright in the glare of the headlights, his eyes squinched shut, and the armaduino that caused this disaster scuttling by. As it passes, the red light mounted on its back traces a path across Mason's jeans, and as he realizes he's not dead and moves his leg, he trips its sensor and loud salsa music begins to play.

The door of the truck that almost hit Mason creaks open, and a tall, dark figure steps out. My bike light switches back on, and right away I know who we're dealing with.

The man's name is Badri Hassan Khalid, and he claims to be a Somali pirate, though what a pirate's doing in Oddity, New Mexico, I could not say. He's new, but not Cayden's family's kind of new, where you can almost hear the crinkle of the wrapping. He's the kind of person who wanders into town like he's coming home, even though no one's ever seen him before. He tells people he decided to get as far from the Atlantic Ocean as he possibly could.

I like him. As pirates go, he is highly perfect. He's even got a scar, though if Pearl were here, she'd say it's not ugly enough. I only notice it because it's pale pink against his black, black skin. It traces his cheek like the trail of a curious finger.

"What do you kids think you are doing out here? According to the radio, half the emergency vehicles in town are on their way out here to hose down Sunset Ridge before it burns to the ground; this is Blurmonster territory, and here you are in the middle of the road!"

I've never been accosted by a pirate before. In spite of his strong, lilting accent, he sounds like a dad. Even shaking from what almost happened to Mason, I'm a little bit disappointed, but I rally.

"What are *you* doing out here, then?" I ask. (He's not OUR dad.)

He blinks. I bet he doesn't want us to know. I figure he's cooking up a cover story to tell us, but then he surprises me.

"Put your bikes in the back of the truck and get in," he says.

Mason, on grown-up autopilot, moves to obey, but I stick my hand out to stop him.

"We aren't going anywhere with you. We don't know you."

"You spend a lot of time staring at me for kids who do not know me. I'm Badri Hassan Khalid."

In the distance, I detect the wail of sirens.

"Your dad, he works for animal control? I have done work for him before. You can call him on your phones and see. Get in the truck."

That's enough for Raymond, and I guess for me, too. Nobody who's worked for Daddy is likely to mess with us, and no one who knows who he is would lie about it, either. There's something to be said for having a father who's as big as a Porta-Potty and wrangles escaped science experiments. Besides, in the dark there's no way of knowing whether the Blurmonster's still coming. We move. After I lift my bike up over the tailgate, I take a quick peek under the tarp at the heap of stuff already in the bed. Sure enough: pipes and gutters, and what appears to be garage door track. He was out the other end of Sunset Ridge, ripping off empty houses. No wonder he wants to get out of here. And no way he'll rat us out even if he figures out the fire was our fault . . . sort of.

We finish stowing the bikes and cram into the cab, and by the time the first fire truck roars by, we're rolling.

Raymond borrows my phone and calls home right away, because of course now we have full bars for no reason. Lucky for him it sounds like he gets his mom-mom and not his jefa-mom, who takes the job of being "the chief" pretty seriously, and expects him to be home on the dot. But his mom-mom's all focused on being thankful he called, and not tearing his ear off at all. Then I call home, and bad luck me. I get Aunt Bets.

"Do you know," she says, before I even say hello, "what it

does to me when I come home to an empty house, call the family that is supposed to have my young, beloved son, and find out that they brought him home hours and hours ago? Are you aware that if I were not already missing both my feet, I would be using them on your deserving backside right now? Do you understand that I can access your bedroom at any time, without warning? Can you imagine what it would be like to wake up bald?"

I am rendered momentarily speechless. I think she'd actually do it. The good news is that, at this point, I don't think things could get worse. So I brazen my way through it.

"Hi, Aunt Bets. Sorry we missed dinner."

There is a long and deadly pause.

"You seem to be missing my point."

"No," I say, "I don't think so." Mason is looking at me like I've lost my mind, which I clearly have.

"We were out biking," I say blithely, "and it got late. Mr. Khalid is bringing us home, but I'm sure he'll understand if we don't offer him anything to eat." We're pulling into town, and if I'm going to die of hysterical baldness, my last meal is going to be epic.

"Mr. WHO? Little girl, you get back here before I—"

"Okay, we'll see about getting something on the way." In a last and utterly suicidal flourish, I add, "We love you. Say 'I love you,' Mase!" He stares at me wide-eyed as an owl. I smile winningly.

"I love you, Mama!" he sings out, drowning the sound of her shouting.

I hang up and mute the ringer, then point off to the right. "We haven't eaten. Have you? Is it okay if we stop there?"

"Oh YES!" says Mason, finally figuring out my plan. He pumps his fist as Badri, giving me a dark, suspicious look, turns into the parking lot of Crash Diner.

Cayden hasn't called his folks.

"It doesn't matter," he says, when I ask him. "They're probably still at work."

Cayden's parents are here to sort out why cell signals in Oddity are so unreliable. It must be a tough job, because they generally work late and look frustrated. Probably they won't even notice he's gone.

Our shoes hit the ground before the tires have stopped gritting on the sandy asphalt. Pearl would remember this place as Patsy's, but the flying saucer that embedded itself in the chrome roof and now sticks halfway through the sizzling, sparking sign is too funny to ignore . . . at least for everyone who wasn't eating here when it happened. We call it what we want, and I guess Patsy can like it or not. We swing open the chrome-handled doors and breathe in the scent of french fries and chili. "Jailhouse Rock" is playing on the jukebox, and right away I know that Song is here.

Song's my friend, if a grown-up can be your friend. She took over Bob's Cut-Rate Emporium a few years back, and renamed it For a Song. Me and Pearl started bringing our scavenging finds to her right away, though Song did eventually refuse to sell Pearl hat pins anymore. She said nobody needed that many, and it was getting creepy. She gives me store credit or cash, though last time she paid me with a seven-dollar bill that had Princess Leia–looking ladies on it, and they wouldn't take it at Bodega Bodega when I tried to buy candy.

Song's got a really strong accent, but different from Badri's. She's obviously from Asia somewhere, but I can't get a straight answer out of her about where. If I ask about any specific country, she says "Yes" and smiles her sparkly, beauty-pageant smile. If that doesn't work, she pretends not to understand me—which is a bunch of bull, of course. She gets me fine the rest of the time. I guess it is rude to keep asking, but it's like a game for me now. I figure if I surprise her at the right time, she'll slip up.

She's got her back to me when I spot her. She's wearing a blue dress with pink sunglasses printed all over it, and her shiny black ponytail is set in curls and spills over one shoulder. She's plugging quarters into the jukebox, and I know we'll be listening to Elvis all night. Song *loves* Elvis. She waves wildly when she sees us.

I'm still fretting about Mike Hannagan, who died in jail. Doesn't seem fair, him getting punished for something he couldn't have done. I need to relax about the Sunset Six, though. Cayden's right. We've got the photo, and we got away clean. No way anyone else is bold enough to go up there tonight, but to be on the safe side, I look over my shoulder at Cayden. He waggles his hand sideways at me.

"Two bars," he says.

"Try it," I say.

He's got his phone in his hand, and as he hits send on the photo, he flashes me a covert thumbs-up. Let's see how Nopes likes *them* dragon fruits. I still feel a twinge of guilt, though.

The booth under the saucer is open. Grown-ups don't like it for some reason, but I figured the high school kids would have it staked out already. Our good luck continues! I slide all the way into the back corner and don't even bother to open the menu. Our waiter, a black-haired, skinny-jeaned teenager named Duke, of all things, is already writing before he asks, "You all here for the Frito pie?" I point a finger gun of approval at him as I pull my wallet from my pocket with my other hand. I put a ten and two fives down on the table to cover everyone. I'm going to need to do some work for Song soon. I'm officially low on funds.

"I don't understand this town at all," says Cayden. "Why don't they call the state to come deal with the Blurmonster, or the National Guard, or something?"

Raymond shrugs. "They've been here before," he says. "Mostly they get eaten. Not everyone's cut out for Oddity."

"No point having a bunch of nosey parkers around when there are so many things here with an appetite for noses," I agree. "Besides, a lot of the stuff Daddy uses at animal control is not exactly state-issued."

"Like what?"

"The rocket launcher, the flash grenades, the arcane spells he put on the nets—ooh, dinner!"

I love Frito pie. Aunt Bets says it's trash, so call me the Ada Can, because I can eat a whole plate of it. When Duke brings all five plates over at once, laddered up his arms, I take mine and start scooping chili and cheese into my mouth right away, before my Fritos get soggy. Badri carries his plate over to the counter to get the latest gossip from Patsy—she's the one thing here that hasn't changed. She still has the kind of white hair that's almost blue, and knows everything.

"Out where?" I hear her ask Badri. "You got to be careful out by Sunset Ridge. Blurmonster dens up out there pretty regular."

Badri says something I can't quite hear.

"Oh no, it never comes right into town. That is to say, it did once, the way I heard, but the puppets sent it packing. My Gammar said that first Blurmonster attack, way back at the end of the Gold Rush, was when the town realized the puppets were something special."

Patsy's eyes glow with nostalgia behind her rhinestone glasses.

"It was a plain miracle, that's what she said. The Blurmonster always prowled around the edges of things, but it had never come into town. But the morning after Greeley's Medicine Show came to Oddity, and put on the best puppet show anyone ever saw, I might add, here came the Blurmonster, bold as brass and full of wrath. It's not easy to rally a defense against an invisible monster, I can tell you that! The way my old Gammar told it, the Blurmonster seemed likely to knock the whole town down before it was through, and folks were scattering. Then *wham!* goes the door of Greeley's caravan, and out come the puppets, thundering orders and rallying the town.

"Living puppets! Nobody had ever seen such a thing! It took some doing, but they ran that hazy critter right out of Oddity. Nowadays, the Protection Committee keeps it past the city limits. But you go into outlying neighborhoods, you've got to be careful. It still likes to test our boundaries."

I've heard the story a million times, of course. It's nice for Patsy to have fresh listeners now and then. Badri grunts, focused more on his dinner than Patsy, but that's how she likes things anyway, so she smiles down at him like he's her favorite grandkid.

Song slides into my side of the booth to sit by me, tugging one of my braids.

"You kids hear about the spiderface thing?" she asks.

I push my plate between us so she'll know she can help. She takes a chip, much neater than me, and I see that her pink-painted fingernails have blue sunglasses decals on them. "Firsthand," I say.

"You got any new swag for me?"

"Not yet. But I've got the weekend, and some ideas. I'll come see you."

"Good. I'm running low."

This is not true. That store is stuffed to the gills. But she tries to always have something new in the windows to tempt people. Last week they were totally covered with a rainbow array of high-heeled shoes, like butterflies under glass. You couldn't even see inside the store. Song's a wizard with window displays.

"Try to find something blue," she says. "I have a Sweepstakes poster to put up."

The Sweepstakes. I sigh, my last Frito dangling halfway between my plate and my mouth. On the jukebox, Elvis is singing about blue Hawaii, but our booth is quiet as my friends side-eye me. It's hard to get excited about the Sweepstakes this year. As far as I know, there've never been two winners from the same generation of the same family. Of course, I've never seen them choose a kid, like Pearl, either, but it's better not to get my hopes up.

"Hey, Song, you ever seen an armaduino with a flame-thrower on it?" asks Raymond. He's a good soldier even when it means chatting with a pretty grown-up, which makes his brown cheeks red like bricks.

I put my fingers to my locket and finger its raised design. It's all wrapped up in my head with scavenging for Song, because it was my first real find, taken from our house before it was ever ours. Sometimes I think wearing it drew our family to that house from the day I put it on, way back when Pearl and I were little and sending Mama into a panic by exploring where we weren't supposed to be.

Me and Pearl were as sneaky and fast as those new little critters in our yard, the ones I call zombie rabbits. We went straight for every little gap, every untended door—and those grand, deserted houses at one end of our street were way too tempting to avoid.

I remember creeping down the hallway with her, thinking

that this must be what forests were like, because of how still it was, and the way the sunlight slanted across the woodwork. The cabinets were so weathered that the green paint was fuzzy like moss. When I stand in our cheery yellow kitchen now, I can still see the cream wallpaper with little red flowers, glue coming loose, rumpling like a sheet across the wall.

But the locket, that was the best thing. Even better than picking flowers in the upstairs bathroom with the caved-in roof and leaking pipes.

It was where only a kid would find it. I bet it had been there forever, because the bed, the same one I sleep in now, is so massive and heavy that it's like it was built in that room. At the time, I was sure it had grown there.

While Pearl was dancing in the empty rooms, I was kneeling in front of the footboard, tracing my fingers over its carvings. My fingernail fit under the edge of one of the flowers. I wiggled it, and it began to lever its way out of its socket. Tucked into the space behind it was the locket. I held it in my hand and admired the smooth, heavy gold rim, the turquoise enameled scallops along the edge, the matching eleven-petaled flower in the center. The frames inside were empty, but I couldn't muster any disappointment, not when it was so old and heavy and lovely.

If we'd been a little older, we might have worried that it was cursed. Instead, it was a gift left just for me. Not even the ghost that banged the closet door and made us scream could spoil my find.

"Ada?"

I jump, banging my head on the rim of the flying saucer. "What?"

It's Badri, who's dropping a tip on the table in a way that says my time is up. I squeeze Song's sunglasses-covered fingertips as she stands to let me slide out of the booth. Time to face the dragon lady.

Chapter 6

Close Shaves

We drop Raymond at his place, a little one-story adobe, its courtyard festooned with party lights, and head home.

When Badri's truck rolls to a stop in front of our house, Aunt Bets is sitting on the front stoop in her red wheelchair, arms folded, the hall light blazing behind her and making a halo of her hair. She quit braiding on the grounds that she's got enough to do since the accident set her back. She wears a bandanna headband to keep it out of her face while she's baking.

The accident happened not long before Cayden moved in. She was up on a ladder, patching the awning of the bakery, and one of the dumpsters snuck up and got her. Most people lose arms in a dumpster attack, but Bets lost both legs below the thigh.

Cayden says that everywhere he's ever lived, Aunt Bets

would have been fitted for prosthetics by now. I've never heard of such a thing! No wonder he's a baby. I told him, around here, making your own prosthetics is part of your rehab.

He didn't know what to make of that. Unfortunately, Aunt Bets doesn't, either. There are about a dozen wooden legs in a box in the hall closet, but so far she can't get the fit right. I guess no one is good at everything. She bakes better than anyone. She must have used up all her DIY points, or something. In the meantime, she picked out the fastest wheelchair she could find, the kind where the wheels tilt in. She and Mason moved into our house so we could all help one another, and here we are.

When I see Aunt Bets waiting at the top of the ramp that now leads to our stoop, I'm reminded of a story we heard in school about a queen in Africa. A bunch of Europeans were trying to swindle her out of her kingdom. To make the queen feel foolish and inferior when they met with her, they provided chairs for themselves but none for her. She made one of her attendants get down on hands and knees, and sat on her own personal human chair while she conducted negotiations. Aunt Bets is like that. She might not have full-on legs anymore, but she's got a baker's arms and serious wheels, and she will chase you down. She makes that red wheelchair one of the scariest things you've ever seen.

Badri sizes her up from the front seat of his truck before getting out, and when he reaches his conclusion, my opinion of him goes up another notch. Her physical size is not the important thing about her, and he gets it, I can tell. He squares his shoulders and puts his chin up a little, not like he's ready for a fight, but like he's straightening his tie before a business meeting. Even though I know I'm a dead girl walking, I'm proud to have such a scary aunt. I wish Mama was half as dangerous as Aunt Bets. . . . But I feel awful for thinking it.

Mason's already running for the house with a big grin, telling how I bought him dinner. Hopefully Aunt Bets won't ask where the money came from, because she does not approve of me creeping around abandoned houses. I've got a few lies that might pass, but I don't really want to talk about it. Bets pulls Mase down for a hug, then sends him in to bed so she can chew me up and spit me out without interruption. Cayden says a hurried good-night and heads for his house as fast as he can go without running. Coward.

I can see the stairwell through the doorway. Salvation is ten feet and a million miles away. I need a piratical diversion.

"Aunt Bets, meet Badri Hassan Khalid. Badri, this is my aunt, Elizabeth Weathers."

Lucky for Badri, he's not one of those awkward types who act like Aunt Bets lost her hands as well as her feet. He shakes, good and firm, right away.

"You run Fair Weather Bakery."

"That's right. And I'd like to know what a grown man is doing running around with a bunch of kids in the dark of night."

"I was doing some salvage work"—I manage not to snort—"and was on my way back into town when I came across your son and niece and their friends. There had been brushfires in the area, and emergency vehicles were moving through, so I told them they should ride back with me."

"What sort of things do you salvage, Mr. Khalid?" Our aunt's expression is darkly skeptical. He wouldn't be the first person to come back from the desert loaded down with "salvage" not fit for human eyes.

"Scrap metal, mostly. I do a lot of mechanical work, welding, patching."

They keep talking, but I'm hardly listening. It doesn't matter what they say; it matters what Aunt Bets's body language says. Her eyes are on Badri, but she's still got about half her attention on me, and that's at least 30 percent too much. Why can't a pirate say something really attention-grabbing when you need him to?

Then her voice sharpens. He *has* said something interesting, though I'm not sure exactly what. She's talking about her big stand mixer, and she's not touching her wheels. I ought to be able to get through on the right side, the side closest to the stairs. This is my chance. I make a run for it.

She starts at my sudden movement, and swivels to grab me. I've got no chance at all if she succeeds. I leap like a deer, and I'm over her right wheel and scooting up the stairs before she's turned all the way toward me.

"Night, Badri!" I yell, loud as I can.

"You call him Mr. Khalid!" Aunt Bets says, which, as parting shots go in our family, is W-E-A-K. I race to the bathroom and then back to my room, listening all the time for the slam of the front door. Aunt Bets's bedroom is on the first floor, but if she's mad enough, she will army crawl up those stairs to get to me. As I shut my door, though, I see through the railings that they're still down there talking. I lock myself in anyway. Bets made Daddy disable my door lock after I snuck into the co-op and put the fair-trade peyote in the green smoothies, but half an hour of playing around with the knob and a screwdriver took care of *that*. I drag a chair in front of the door for good measure. I might be leaving for school out the window tomorrow. It's no fun, but it can be done—though all my schoolbooks are downstairs, where I dumped them to make room in my backpack.

I contemplate trying to sneak down and get them. Cayden's been loaning me some of his books to read, and one of them's in that stack. They're so weird they're addictive. This one kid rafts down the Mississippi River completely unmolested by monster catfish, and people keep letting him stay at their houses without checking to see if he's a clone or anything. The series about kids at wizarding school is better, but I'm on book three and no one has died yet. I'm starting to get skeptical.

Not worth it, I decide. Aunt Bets is not above running me down.

I reach behind my neck and unhook the locket.

My closet door bangs open just like the day I found the locket, and there's Stella the ghost, all gray and silent, watching me.

I wonder what Pearl would think of Stella now that she actually shows herself. I don't know why she started. Maybe she got bored of clattering the hangers and slamming the door. Maybe the extra attention I gave her after Pearl left helped her focus. We picked the right name for her, though. Visible or in-, day after day, she's Stella-in-the-closet, though she likes to put the toes of her Mary Janes right up to the line of the doorway. Her fat, spiral curls blow my mind. I bet she had to mess with those things all day long to keep them neat, and they're way too easy to grab. I will keep my nice short braids, please and thank you. She's staring at the locket, like she always does, so I hold it up where she can see that I'm taking good care of it before setting it on the dresser. She blinks at me, and says something.

"Girl, I am not a lip-reader," I say, then shut the closet door before changing into one of Daddy's oversize T-shirts. Maybe she can still see me through the door with spectral vision or whatever, but at least I don't have to see her do it. I try to lie awake for a few more minutes, listening for Bets, but I'm ten kinds of bushed.

I'm in a foul mood when I wake up, not because I'm in trouble, but because I actually might not be. Daddy didn't come in to tell me off. According to my phone, Mama left for work an hour ago. Basically, both my parents are falling down on the job. If it weren't for Aunt Bets, I could never come home at all, I bet, and nobody would even notice. I lie there all sorry for myself.

Bets is the only person who might punish me, and she's busy talking Mason through making breakfast. Their cheerful chatter drifts upstairs, but I can't join them. After the way I worried her, I have no business expecting pancakes the next morning. Besides, I'm embarrassed. A year ago we were just an aunt and a niece, and she didn't have to tell me what to do.

By the time I'm tired of staring up at the curlicue pattern of water stains on my ceiling and thinking about this stuff, my stomach is as heavy as if I ate a rock last night, instead of Frito pie. I roll onto my side.

The pillowcase feels weird against my head. Or maybe my head feels weird against the pillowcase. I'm not sure. I reach up to touch my braids.

They're not there.

I sit straight up in bed, running my hands over my head and finding nothing but bare skin.

She did it. I can't believe she really did it.

I look wildly at the door. The chair is still wedged under the handle. I turn to my windows. Shut and locked.

Stella is laughing and pointing at me from the closet, and she's totally right. I lost. My legless aunt pwned me and committed a locked room mystery at the same time. I feel my head all over, hoping against hope that my hair will be there.

Wait.

There, at the base of my skull. An edge. I work my way under it, and pull. The bare surface peels away, and my braids fall into place. I look at what I'm holding in my hands.

It's one of those fake bald caps from a costume shop. She must have been *saving* it for something like this!

I scream with rage . . . and hear mocking auntly laughter from downstairs.

When I pull myself together and head down the hall to get ready, I find the bathroom door shut and locked. I kick it.

"Come ON, Mase!" I holler, exasperated.

There's a lot of scrabbling and scuffling before the door opens.

When it does, there's no one there.

Stella's using the bathroom now? I think, before remembering she can't leave the closet. I look down. Nope. Not ghosts. It's one of those little critters I've been calling zombie rabbits, though they're not really zombies and they're not quite rabbits, either. What they are, apparently, is in our house. Guess that job Daddy did repairing the mortar in the corner of the basement didn't take.

The little vermin looks up at me with his round, wide eyes. Like all zombie rabbits, he's wearing footie pajamas. These have green-and-yellow-flowered ears. After a long, awkward standoff, he thumps one foot impatiently. He's waiting for me to get out of the way. Zombie rabbits are sneaky, and my feet are bare, so I do, but I bet I'll regret it later. Give a zombie rabbit an inch, and he'll take a mile. They're like a bunch of tiny pirates, no disrespect to Badri.

"Move," he growls, pushing past me. Then he slouches down the hallway and disappears into the linen closet. The laundry chute door, which is on a spring, opens and slams. The chute gives a metallic ripple as the rabbit goes down it. I shake my head.

Chapter 7
Sweepstakes Time

When I land in the grass at the bottom of the trellis outside my window, Mason is waiting for me with my books. I load them into my backpack.

"She see you take these?" I ask, shouldering my pack.

"Naw, I don't think so. But anyway, the wheelchair's not so good on grass." He's got a point.

"You get in any trouble?" I know he was jumping to go with us, but still. As the oldest, I'm supposed to be the voice of reason.

He shoves me, which is how he tells me I'm treating him like a baby. "I have to go help at the bakery after school for a week. It was worth it."

As we cut through the hedge to the sidewalk, I notice the newspaper still sitting there. Daddy must have gotten home really late if the paper's still out here. There's a blue insert sticking out above the headline: SOUTH SIDE RESIDENTS COMPLAIN OF BIOLUMINESCENCE, LOST SLEEP.

When Mason and I meet Cayden and Raymond on the corner, there's a cheery blue-and-white sticker on the stop sign. A block later, another on the window of the co-op. I pull a flyer out of my backpack and add it to the glass as I go by. It reads ORGANIC HOMESCHOOLED CHICKEN 50% OFF.

My mood begins to rise. Raymond's downright grinning, and it's hard to resist grinning back. The minute I do, he can't keep quiet anymore.

"Come on, Ada, you know this is going to be great," he says.

I shove my shoulder into his.

"It is, isn't it?" I say. "Pearl would love this!"

Raymond looks away.

"Yeah," he says, then focuses his attention on Cayden, who's looking stressed.

"Come on, Cayden. Show some school spirit," says Raymond.

I nod, trying to act like Raymond's nonsense isn't getting to me. I guess I understand why the grown-ups are all weird about a kid winning the Sweepstakes for the first time in the history of ever. Parents expect to keep their kids until they grow up. Now everybody's wondering if their kid's next. But I don't see why Raymond gets to be uncomfortable. I'm the one who lost my sister.

He's still pep-talking Cayden.

"You seriously showed up at the perfect time. We've been waiting years for this."

"You've been waiting years to chase adults around town for their signatures," Cayden says.

I sigh. At this point, he's just being dense. We've talked his ear off about canvassing for the Sweepstakes.

"Think of it as the biggest game of capture the flag ever," Raymond says.

"Right," I say. "And the adults are the flags."

"You don't think it's a little weird that the grown-ups run away to avoid signing up for the Sweepstakes?" he asks.

"Ugh!" I groan, looking up at the sky for assistance. Alien ships are really hard to see without their running lights, though. "I told you, it's not like that. Think of it as a safety drill where the whole town participates. We've been watching for years, and it's hilarious. It's the best thing about becoming a fifth grader!"

On the way into school, we walk past the flagpole, which has acquired some new swag. A smallish purple alien, mostly neck with four short legs, has clamped on to the pole with its teeth. Its whole body sticks rigidly sideways.

"Is it waiting for the flagpole to surrender, or does it think it's a flag?" Cayden asks, glad for a change of subject. Nice to see he has a sense of humor about aliens now. Apparently it's possible to live your whole life not knowing Earth is an interplanetary commuter hub. I'm not saying he screamed the first time he saw an alien, but I'm not saying he didn't, either.

Inside, bold blue-and-white posters plaster the walls, all emblazoned with a design as familiar as the smell of

Thanksgiving Meat-Substitute Gratitude Loaf: the outline of a boldly striped tent, arcing above the words WHEN YOU LOOK IN THE MIRROR, DO YOU SEE A WINNER?

It's Sweepstakes time.

I guess Ms. Winters had a post-morgue setback, because the principal comes in to introduce her replacement, Mr. Bishop. After roll call, Mr. Bishop drops a stack of glossy foldouts and a stack of ink pads on each desk to be passed back. The words on the foldouts blare:

SWEEPSTAKES!

You wait all year, and now it's here!

All stamp books and customer loyalty cards honored.

The greater your loyalty, the better your odds.

Eat, drink, be merry, and buy it all at
GREELEY's state-of-the-art grocery.

WATCH FOR THE BLUE TENT.

Mr. Bishop starts working his way through a prepared statement from the city council.

"As you all remember, the Greeley's Sweepstakes fundraiser accounts for a substantial amount of the school's operating funds for the year. Ammunition, window replacement, the fees we pay for school assemblies and paramilitary training all come from the Greeley's drive . . . as does the end-of-year party.

"Now, if you're new, you'll want to make sure you pair up with someone who has grown up here, for safety."

Someone does that thing where he pretends to sneeze, to cover what he actually says: "Fresh meat!"

Cayden turns pink, and some of the kids snicker. I flush. It's one thing for *me* to pick on Cayden. I'm his friend.

"Each of you must canvass an assigned section of Oddity," Mr. Bishop continues, "knocking on every door or . . . well, anything that's serving as a front door for someone. Tent flaps, corrugated metal roofing, garbage can lids, rope-ladder rungs . . . you get the idea. Each individual in your canvassing zone must place a blue thumbprint on the chart by his or her name. What's the rule for thumbprints?"

"Press the pad, lick the thumb, stamp the chart," chants the class.

"That's right. Make sure you wear your latex gloves, so you don't contaminate the samples." (We have them in our PKs, preparedness kits, in case of bodily fluid or ectoplasm exposure.) "It is vitally important that you canvass everyone in your assigned area.

"Make sure they see you. Regularly. Be visible in the corners of their eyes whenever possible, whether you have their thumbprint or not. Discover their habits and make a practice of standing silently on people's porches or lawns when they exit their homes in the morning. . . ."

The longer he talks, the more impatient I am to get out there and try it for myself. This is going to be like a live-action MMORPG. I can't wait.

The classroom door snicks open, and I turn in my seat, along with everyone else. One more perk of being old enough to canvass: we get celebrity visitors. The Protection Committee is here.

Mr. Whanslaw steps into the room, clicking as he comes. His puppeteer walks behind him, stone-faced, working the controls. Same one, different one. Can't tell, don't care. They're a little blurry if you stare straight at them, anyway, so I generally don't. We all turn back around in our seats and try to look capable, like troops being inspected.

Puppet and puppeteer stroll down the row beside my desk. Whanslaw's head is level with mine, even though I'm sitting down, and if he turns his head toward me now on that creaking neck, I'll be looking straight into his black, shining eyes. I don't look. He makes his way to the front of the room, puppeteer obediently attending him, and sure enough, just past me he begins turning his head left and right, staring at anyone reckless enough to look back. Though all I can see is his fuzzy, white, fleecy hair, I am sure he catches Cayden's eye. Cayden's hand trembles on his desk.

Mr. Whanslaw turns to face the class. His eyes shine with intelligence, and his head and limbs bob, the tiniest bit, as he comes to a halt. He folds his fingers in a way that ought to be impossible without getting the strings tangled, and looks at us. Then he speaks, in his deep, bullfrog voice.

"How are we this morning, children?"

There are some muttered "goods" and "fines." Behind the puppeteer, Mr. Bishop is giving us the hairy eyeball—like we'd ever act up in front of the Protection Committee. New teachers, I swear.

"I look forward to a wholehearted effort on the part of the fifth grade this year," Whanslaw continues. "In this way, you will set an example for younger children when they follow in your footsteps. There is also great satisfaction to be found in the pursuit of signers. To hunt down the reluctant, to track them when they go to ground, is . . . invigorating. It *gets* the *blood pumping.*"

At this last, he homes in on Eunice in the front row, and I think for a minute that her braids are going to stand on end. After a moment, he breaks his stare to gaze once more around the room, like a hawk who changed his mind midstoop and is circling, looking for new prey.

"I trust," he says slowly, pacing the front of the room, brocaded coat swaying, blue head bobbing, "that I will see you all circulating your assigned territories, doing your civic duty. I am quite certain that no activity, however novel, could possibly be more important."

His head cranks around, wood squealing on wood, and this time, those shiny, black, merciless eyes are fixed on me.

He moves on so quickly that by the time my stomach stops turning surprised flips, he's already looking at Bea. Then Charles. Then Raymond. Ralph, hulking in the back row. His crony, Delmar. Cayden. All of us are Nopesers. Uh-oh. Are our afternoon activities some kind of problem?

I guess we have been poking into things grown-ups might

prefer we stay out of. Something's not right here, though. I appreciate an intimidating puppet as much as the next person, but I thought the PC's visit to our classroom would be fun, like we'd enter this secret circle of heroism. It isn't turning out like that at all. It's almost like Whanslaw's trying to scare us—and enjoying it.

The door rattles open, and Myrtle, who sits right beside it, actually shrieks as a tall puppet with a rag-doll face pops her head in through the gap. She takes in our startled expressions with her shoe-polish eyes and lets out a high giggle. Once we get over our surprise, we grin back, but I can feel that mine lacks some wattage.

Maggie may be the strangest of all the puppets, even more so than fish-faced Lanchester. It's hard to decide, moment to moment, because let's face it, living puppets, but Maggie's blank good humor and wide Raggedy Ann smile just freak some people out. Not me, but some people.

Whanslaw treats her like a daughter. "Well, my dear, are you finished . . . encouraging the sixth graders?"

She pushes her way into the room, her long, old-fashioned white dress sweeping the floor, puppeteer dressed in black behind her. Maggie is all angular limbs and thrusting energy. Just for fun, she slams her wooden hands down on Myrtle's desk and gets all nose to triangle with her.

My feelings are all over the place. On the one hand, I'm a little bit scornful of Myrtle for leaning away. Show some backbone, kid! Then again, heroes should know better than to bully people. Maggie cocks her head right in Myrtle's red, freckled face, and Myrtle's already-fading smile vanishes completely.

I push my books off my desk and let them fall with a slap to the floor.

Maggie and Whanslaw both jerk around to look at me, and they don't look like heroes at all at the moment. They're like sharks in puppet form, and I'm their chum. As they're heading my way, the end-of-period bell rings, and the door opens a third time.

Three Protection Committee members in the room at once. Kiyo, as elegant as Maggie is primitive, is a Japanese puppet with a white face, red lips, and black hair, and wears a long, traditional silk costume. It's not a kimono—there are too many layers—but maybe there's one under there somewhere. In every picture I've seen, women like Kiyo are serene, but not Kiyo. She always seems a twitch away from sneering. Usually I like that, when she's sneering in the face of danger. Today, it's one thing too many.

"Stop playing with the little *dears* so we can leave!" she demands, motioning impatiently to Maggie, who giggles and goes to join her. Whanslaw keeps coming, right up to my desk. Bending down, he does something no puppet should be able to do. He picks up each of my books, returning them to my desk one at a time with his blue jointed fingers, keeping his black glass eyes fixed on me the whole time. When all the books have been replaced, he bends down once more, and I remember that my canvassing form was under the stack. He puts it on top, instead, and caresses it with a jerky motion.

"Make sure this comes first," he says to me. Then he makes his bobbing way out of the room.

We don't leave the room when the bell rings, even though we're allowed. We sit in uneasy silence, and no one dares to go out in the hall until we're sure the puppets are gone.

I stare out the window at the Protection Committee's headquarters, the big mansion up on top of Havasu Hill. I've always liked how school is halfway down the hill from it. Today, it's a reminder that the puppets aren't just watching over us, they're also watching US, and we'd better toe the line.

When someone is on your side, you forget that being scary means they can scare YOU.

I guess the Protection Committee showed us.

Chapter 8

Pole Sitting

I'm in a funk the rest of the day. Come dismissal time, I trail the others out the door, but I'm barely even listening as Raymond and Cayden check Nopes on Cayden's phone.

"It's not the greatest picture," Cayden says.

"Hey, nobody else has one," says Raymond.

"Yeah, why is that, freak?" asks Ralph, elbowing Cayden as he goes by.

"It's *Freaked*," says Cayden. We should maybe change his Nopes handle. That joke has outlived its usefulness.

Ralph swings around to face us. "That's the part that don't make any sense," he says. "No way somebody who's always freaked went all the way out to Sunset Ridge and snapped that pic."

"Oh, he got it," says Raymond. "And he had to go toward the Blurmonster to do it."

Ralph scoffs. "You never saw the Blurmonster."

Delmar barges right through us like he's a bowling ball and we're pins. "Of course they didn't. It's invisible."

"Transparent, not invisible," I say, as I notice a crowd beginning to gather around the flagpole.

"Say what you want," says Raymond. "That photo's time-stamped, and we're the ones who took it. That's a win."

I agree in theory, but it still feels wrong to "win" a competition that's about finding six missing kids. This kind of story . . . we kids tell it, generation after generation, but we don't really think about certain things. I have no idea where the Sunset Six's parents might be now, or if they're still looking for their loved ones. Now that we've found them, maybe some of the Six's relatives will notice the posts on Nopes.

Will city officials admit that Mike Hannagan didn't have anything to do with it? Probably not, that's what I think. But *we'll* know. That knowledge is surprisingly heavy.

I walk past Ralph and Delmar toward the crowd of kids. They're in a ring around that little alien, who's still doggedly hanging on to the flagpole by its teeth. I'm inclined to keep walking. Things are tough all over.

Then Ralph and Delmar come up behind me, which is bad news for the alien. Pearl called Ralph and Delmar the trolls. They're the biggest kids in our class—short on brains and long on fist reach. I'm usually all right with Ralph and Delmar. They let me lead, and they love a good fight.

They're bad news for the little alien, though. The trolls love free entertainment. From where I'm standing, the situation is actually kind of adorable—they're trying to heckle.

"Lookit it running its face up the flagpole!" says Ralph. He elbows Delmar, who hyucks and shoves him back. They mostly communicate through moshing.

"It's so . . . purple. I'm gonna call him Purple Nerple."

"That's dumb. It don't even have nerples." Delmar pokes at the alien. I find this pretty ill-advised. Dangling from a flagpole may not be the smartest hobby, but that thing's got choppers for miles. I bet it could take somebody's hand right off.

Ralph rubs his chin in an "I've got an idea" kind of way.

"You know," he says, obviously enjoying the circle of onlookers. "Nerple here doesn't look like a flag to me at all."

Delmar's surprise is probably genuine. "It doesn't?"

"Nah. I think it looks more like . . . a tetherball."

Uh-oh. I back up quick so I don't end up with a face full of baby alien. What happens instead is, despite everything that has gone on so far, the most interesting event of the day.

"Stop!" Cayden shoves between the trolls, turning to face them. In the process, he puts his back to the flagpole alien, proving once and for all that he does not listen to a single word I say. It would serve him right if the darn thing peeled off there and attached itself to his neck like a tick.

The trolls are puzzled.

"You wanna . . . serve?" rumbles Delmar, drawing his head back to show his confusion.

"What? No! Leave that thing alone. It's little."

Even the trolls know that for flawed reasoning.

"I know you're new," says Ralph slowly, "but you should maybe have figured out by now that there's a lot of nasty stuff around here that's little."

"It didn't do anything to you."

"It's been on the flagpole all day. It's going to do something—it just hasn't done it YET. I don't like it—"

"Hanging out?" I venture.

Cayden scowls at me through the hair that has flopped over his eye. The devil made me do it. Or, you know, genetics. Whatever.

"Leave it alone," Cayden insists. "Find something else to do."

They glance at each other, and for once in my life I'm pretty sure the trolls and I are thinking the same thing. There's no real reason why they should listen to Cayden. They could squish him like a radioactive slug, with less contamination. Then Delmar shrugs.

"Forget it, Ralph," he says. "If we're going to get back before dark, we'd better leave now."

"Watch out for the Blurmonster," says Raymond with a grin.

Ralph rolls his eyes. "We had this discussion already. You can't see it."

He and Delmar amble away from the flagpole.

Cayden looks surprised that things didn't end in a fight—though Delmar does throw his shoulder into Cayden as he passes, to make a point. I'm not sure saving the alien was a great idea, but it is really little. And cute in an ugly way, I guess.

Those big flat choppers are a little unnerving, though— even more so when the thing lets go of the flagpole and drops to stand on four stubby little feet. I know its mouth was open really wide to bite the flagpole, but even with it shut, I can't see eyes. Its whole round head is almost completely composed of those huge flat teeth, and his lips don't completely close. At least, I think it's a *him*. It's not always easy to tell with aliens.

He stands, swiveling his head slightly this way and that, and though I can't say he's looking, exactly, he certainly does seem to be seeing us. He homes in on Cayden and patters a few steps closer, then cocks his head.

Raymond shifts uneasily. "That thing's trying to figure out how we taste," he says.

"Maybe," I allow. He does have the expression of a baby dinosaur trying to decide if we're worth any trouble.

Cayden's starting to get nervous again. "It's too small to eat anyone."

Raymond shrugs. "Shows what you know. You weren't here for the carnivorous squirrel explosion."

"Listen, I have an idea that should not go to waste," I say. "We don't have time for this. Walk away, and he'll probably go home."

Raymond and I turn. Behind me, Cayden says, "Okay, well, uh. No big deal. Glad you're all right." He follows us.

Feet patter behind us.

"Um," says Cayden, "we're going home. You go home, too."

I glance over my shoulder. The creature is nodding enthusiastically.

"Okay," says Cayden, confused. "Good. You go home. Great."

He starts walking again.

Pattering.

I shoot Raymond my most annoyed and long-suffering look, the one Pearl used to call "Our Lady of Perpetual Impatience."

"Cayden," I say. "Can we please GO?"

We start walking again, and this time, I fall back. When the pattering starts again, I grab Cayden's arm and keep him from stopping.

"Like a stray cat," Raymond advises. "If we don't feed it, it will go away."

Cayden pales a little at the mention of feeding.

The alien follows us all the way home, then stands, confused, in our front yard.

"Can't you make him leave?" I hiss. "I'm in enough trouble as it is."

"I don't think you need to worry about that," says Raymond.

I look around. From every corner of our overgrown yard, zombie rabbits are eyeing the alien balefully.

Chapter 9
Punkball

To understand why the situation in our front yard matters, it's important to know more about two sorts of creatures here in Oddity: little aliens, and zombie rabbits.

Little aliens are not at all like the big ones, who are pretty responsible. (I should point out here that it's possible to be responsible and still be evil.) There are the tall, glowing ones who do things like save random people from life-threatening injuries, or reverse natural disasters at the last possible moment in a dramatic, peaceful show of power, like when that volcano erupted on the south side of town when I was four. There are the green-and-beige ones with the big, black almond-shaped eyes, who disobey traffic laws and know all the best Chinese restaurants. There are the guys with the tentacle chins who like to wear pinstriped suits and fedoras even when it's a hundred and ten degrees outside.

You know. All the standard aliens.

The little ones are something else again. There's always one kid in every group, right? The biter. The one who tells kids every gross or private thing their parents never wanted them to know. The one who breaks all the toys . . . over someone else's head.

That's what the little aliens are like. Like every alien from every culture on every far-flung planet packed up all their brattiest offspring and left them at the Oddity fire station.

Like the Pied Piper does parents a favor, and Oddity's his dumping ground.

Like the first bully guffawed for the first time, and the guffaw broke into a thousand pieces, and they all started trying to swagger. . . .

You get it.

Could be they're the interstellar version of pigeons (though most of them don't look a thing alike). Maybe Oddity is some sort of free-range alien day care. Either way, it seems the little aliens are here to stay. The only good thing to say about them is that they're entertaining. But the truth is, it's perilous to laugh too hard, because the tiny mob that ties your neighbor to his clothesline today will come for you tomorrow. Daddy thinks they're funny, which I guess makes sense when he spends his days dealing with coyote gang violence and sludge monsters at the waste treatment plant, but they're getting to be a problem. There's a huge posse of them in our alley. They hide in storm drains and pop out at people. There've been a bunch of WUT meetings about how to get them to stop moving manhole covers. Fortunately, they do have one main focus for their delinquency.

Zombie rabbits.

Like I said, zombie rabbits aren't really rabbits and they're not really zombies, either. But whatever they are, they've got rabbit ears, and they aren't strictly alive. They're short, walk on two little stumpy legs, and have stubby arms. They wear footie pajamas that go all the way up over their heads and become long pockets for their ears. They make the jammies out of basically whatever they find, and zombie rabbits must live a long time, because some have things like FLOUR and SUGAR printed on them. They don't have rabbit teeth, either. More like baby teeth. I can see them even when their mouths are closed, like they all have tiny overbites.

They're the perfect nemesis for the little aliens.

And *that* is why the situation in our yard is such a problem.

From the bushes and gutters and basement stairwell come shrill cries, like birdcalls. "Punk! Punk! Say that to my face, you little punk!"

I grab Cayden by the elbow.

"Oh no. They're going to play punkball."

It's a sport. And it's a war. Every game of punkball is different. We're going to be lucky if the house is still standing tomorrow. Piping shrieks begin in the alley, and then a rock with a panic-stricken bird plastered to the front of it goes whizzing past my head so fast there's no time to duck.

There's maybe a very small chance I could get the rabbits to stage the war in the side yard instead. I'm their primary marshmallow distributor. I've still got one hand on the door-knob, so it's worth a try.

"Guys!" I say. "Rabbits, hey! GUYS!" There's a slight break in the din. Raspy little voices confer in the weeds.

"You like marshmallows?"

More whispering.

"Yes!" a voice calls back after a pause. "Bring some now."

I go inside, and return a minute later, the brightly colored bag clutched tightly in my hand. Sure enough, the second I'm out, I see a blur to one side, and a zombie rabbit tries to skunk me and grab the bag. I hang on tight, glaring. The little punk (all players of punkball are, by definition, punks) dangles grimly from the stretching plastic.

"Gimme!" he yells, widening his beady little eyes at me.

"Not gonna happen," I say. I've found I have to be firm with them, treat them like Mason all hyped up on cold medicine.

"Yes! Marshmallows! You will provision the troops!"

"That's fine," I say, "as long as you move the game over there." I lift my bag hand with the rabbit still dangling at the other end, and motion to the common area between our yard and Cayden's.

"No way."

"Why not?"

"No cover! Tactical disadvantage!"

Indignant cries of "Offsides!" drift over from the alley. The aliens have wandered out from behind the trash cans to watch, snickering. Our purple refugee sidles over to them right away. A zombie rabbit lingers too close to the newcomers, and is kicked across the yard with a squeak as if he's a blow-up toy losing air. A nasty chorus of jeers rises from the alien . . . um, team.

"Cheeky monkeys!" screeches one of the rabbits, and there's a near rush as the aliens and zombie rabbits start to engage.

"No!" I say, brandishing the bulk bag of marshmallows with a shake that makes the zombie rabbit lose his hold and fall with a dull thud to the ground. He emits a sullen "Hey!"

"Move the game," I say. "More marshmallows in the morning." I eye them beadily. Bets has taught me well. "No move, no marshmallows."

The rabbits are muttering and nudging one another. Raymond and Cayden are on the front porch, eyeing the situation nervously. I gauge the distance to the front door. Then a lone rabbit breaks away from the pack and heads over to the side yard, like I asked. I recognize him immediately, with that derpy little gait and yellow and green flowers on the ears on his pajamas. He's actually listening to me? Well. No good deed goes unpunished. I tear open the bag far enough to pull out a fat marshmallow.

"Hey!" I yell. "Derp!"

He turns around when he hears my voice.

"RUDE!" he yells.

My cheeks heat up. Schooled by a zombie rabbit.

"Well, what's your name, then?"

"Snooks!"

Because of course.

"Catch!" I say. The marshmallow sails through the afternoon air.

"Ohhhhhhh," hums the morass of zombie rabbits.

Snooks catches it. With his ears.

I'm kind of impressed by that.

I keep my promises. I grab the bag front and center and shred it. Marshmallows soar across the side yard like shooting stars, and there's a stampede of zombie rabbits, their striped and flowered ears flapping as they run. They start fighting over the marshmallows before they've even reached them, ramming one another sideways, head-butting one another, and screaming. Always, always screaming. I'm pleased to see that Snooks has already stuffed his face. I can see his creepy mouth full of baby teeth chewing and chewing away.

Something moves in my peripheral vision, and I press my back against the house instinctively. It's the aliens from the alley, of course, ambushing the distracted rabbits. I don't really have a dog in this fight, but something impels me to yell, "HEADS UP!" Then I practically fall in the front door before slamming it behind me.

When we pull up recent posts on Nopes, every one is about our find in Sunset Ridge.

Brush fires everywhere. Can't get in.

Why bother? Freaked got the shot.

No way that's real.

Emblazoned on the screen is our photo of the Sunset Six, complete with Mason mugging for the camera.

"Nice photobomb, kid," says Raymond.

I don't love that Mason's in the picture. Still, his presence adds to our credibility, making it less likely to be a fake. Heck, I saw it in person and still don't quite believe it, so I'm glad to have some evidence, however slim.

Raymond went back in and geotagged the pic last night. I'm surprised. He never normally admits he's been anywhere. But there's his handle, *SomeoneElse.*

I smirk at him.

"Someone had to swagger," he says. "You were MIA."

"Chargerless phone upstairs, murderous aunt downstairs."

He nods.

"One thing about your aunt," he says. "Nothing else is quite as scary in comparison."

I grin at him, real big. "Oh, good, then our next mission should be no problem."

Cayden groans and flops back in his beanbag chair.

I wait.

Raymond breaks first.

"Are you going to tell us?"

"*We* are going out to Casa Grande."

"No way," says Raymond. "That's Blurmonster territory."

To be fair, Blurmonster territory basically rings Oddity all the way around. But after our freaky encounter, I can understand Raymond's caution.

"Look, we see the wreckage from Blurmonster attacks on the news. Smashed-up buildings, that kind of thing. But does anyone ever see one of these attacks happen?"

Cayden snorts. "*See* is maybe not the best word."

"You're not wrong. But can we all agree the Blurmonster is large?"

Raymond nods. Cayden thumps his head against the beanbag chair in despair.

"It's a little bit strange that the Blurmonster is doing all this damage without any witnesses, don't you think?" I ask.

I pull up the latest map of Oddity, and point.

"Casa Grande is overdue for an attack. The trolls wanna get all skeptical about our picture? Fine. This time let's score some video footage."

Chapter 10

Signal Boost

When Raymond goes home for dinner, Cayden leaves, too, but my head is churning with plans for this new sneak. I want company. Daddy's "working late" again. Aunt Bets is reading *Kids Who Didn't Hide* to Mason in the living room. I could go to Raymond's, where it's tamale Tuesday and I could stuff my face till my cheeks puff out like a prairie dog's, but I'm still on thin ice with Bets, and shouldn't go too far from the house this close to nightfall.

So I chase Cayden down, which turns out to be the easiest thing I've done all day. He's still crouched on our back stoop, looking for a way through the punkball melee.

"You had to move them to the side yard, huh?" He scowls at me.

"You'll be thanking me when you need to use your doors."

His scowl dies back to a frown but he's not convinced. "You say that, but I can't go through the alley."

"Why on earth not?"

"The cans! Do you want me to get eaten like your aunt?"

"Oh gosh, Cayden, the trash cans are harmless. It's the dumpsters you have to watch out for."

He stares. "You know normal dumpsters don't eat things, right?"

"Hey, we're a zero landfill town because of those dumpsters. Didn't they have wood chippers or anything in Chicago? You have to treat certain stuff with respect."

He shoots me this look, almost like he has a spine. "I don't find that very comforting."

"I will show you how to get home, mister. It's not that big a deal." I lead him around the far side of the house, through the xeriscaping in the front yard, to his door. I can tell he's been staying out of the tall grass out of fear, because he's looking around all nervously. I keep this little trail of ours pretty clean, though. There are a couple of zombie rabbits and an alien dangling from my snares, which aren't as good as Raymond's, but do the job. The rabbits cuss as we go by, taking little swings at us, but nothing connects. Their friends will let them down later.

At Cayden's front door, he hesitates with his hand on the knob. I don't say I want to come in, but I don't leave, either.

Finally, he sighs. "Just . . . could you try to act normal, please?"

I bug my eyes at him. "Excuse me, now?"

He hunches his shoulders. "Look, it's just different here from anyplace else we've lived. I don't think my parents really get it yet. If you say anything about the stuff we've been doing, I won't be allowed to go anywhere, so maybe try not to talk too much?"

Before I can open my mouth and reduce him to a pile of smoking ash, he opens the door and calls, "I'm home!"

I walk in slow, just in case.

"Cayden!" his mother says. She sounds delighted to see him. "How was school, sweetie? Did you give your report on President Washington?"

"Yep."

Cayden tries to walk us through the room quickly, but his mom is really enthused. "Did you tell them the part about how he didn't even want to be president?" she asks, with the tone of someone who helped him write his report the night before.

"Sure."

"And the part about how his mother wrote to the Continental Congress demanding butter and totally embarrassed him?" She beams, obviously loving that little tidbit.

I'm so surprised by these things, none of which I've ever heard before, that I blurt without thinking, "You didn't say any of that. You told about how he was a Freemason, and how he secretly tried to stop the American Revolution to maintain a state of transoceanic Masonic brotherhood, and how he left secret instructions for the design of his memorial—"

Cayden's mother frowns, and I shut up. I've put my foot in it by letting on that he rewrote his report. . . . Good thing he did because he got a passing grade. He's gonna get an earful later, I bet, though his parents aren't the sort to slap a bald cap on him, so there's that.

"Well, have a snack," his mom says. "I've got lots of Signal Boost and Full Bars!"

This does not mean what you might think it means.

I grimace. I've been wondering what the deal is with those. Greeley told the Coateses that Signal Boost (a drink) and Full Bars (an energy bar) are custom made, artisanal snacks just for Splint employees.

Lucky them.

While I may find Greeley's creepy, there's no denying they have the best sodas in town. They make and bottle sarsaparilla and chocolate egg cream and prickly pear (my favorite) right on site.

Signal Boost, however, is just plain lousy. Cayden's mom poured me some the first time I came over. LIFT YOUR MOOD WITH SIGNAL BOOST! reads the old-timey writing on the bottle. I spring into action when I see it, but only to leave the area.

Cayden's parents love it, though. His mom opens the pantry, and my jaw drops. That thing is wall-to-wall full of bottles of Signal Boost (which comes in three flavors: orange, green, and red) and Full Bars (which come in one flavor: cardboard).

"Help yourselves!" trills Cayden's mom.

"Don't you ever want spaghetti or something?" I ask, but Cayden overrides me.

"Thanks, Mom!" he says. "We'll eat upstairs!"

He grabs a few of each, waving off his mom when she

tries to load us with extra bars, then leads the way to his room.

I slam his door, with feeling.

"What the heck was that?" I ask. "If she's trying to get rid of them . . ." I consider. "Well, that would actually be pretty funny. But she could be less obvious about it."

"I guess Oddity has trouble keeping cell phone providers?" he says. "I dunno. Greeley sends them over to the Splint office as incentives, and now she's serving them for every meal."

"Yeah," I say, flopping down on his bungee chair. "Cell service here stinks."

He throws the bars in the general direction of his desk, where they slide off the enormous pile that's already there. "Last week, Dad told me we were ordering pizza, but when he opened the box, it was crammed with Full Bars."

"That's a mean joke."

"That's the problem. I don't think he WAS joking. They both kept talking about how the pepperoni wasn't as good as in Chicago."

"They're not eating those cacti in the front landscaping, are they? They look good, but those things will mess you UP."

"No, I don't think so." He pulls out his bottom dresser drawer. . . . I mean all the way out, and sets it on the floor. He reaches into the empty space beneath it and pulls out bottled water, a jar of peanuts, and a chocolate bar, and hands me a share.

"That's okay," I say. "It sounds like you need it more." I only take the chocolate bar.

As I sit down on his bed to eat, I look out the window. The little alien is down in the grass at the corner of the house, taking a break from punkball. He kicks a rock into the front bushes. Something throws it back. It whacks him in the head, and I see him snarl.

Cayden looks nervously over my shoulder. "It's still there?" he asks.

"Just don't feed it," I say. I reconsider. "Or you could offer it a Signal Boost."

Planning the Casa Grande mission may have kept me busy yesterday afternoon, but Aunt Bets would've had my head if she'd realized how late I was up last night, mapping my canvassing route and plotting. Stella was not thrilled about sharing the closet, but it kept the light from showing under my door. Goal number one: pick up more signatures than Raymond before school this morning.

Aha. Here comes Mr. Metzger, right on schedule. I'm about to get my third Sweepstakes signature and thumbprint.

For Mr. Metzger, right on schedule means just this side of late. He works at Oddity Bodkins, and everyone knows first shift starts at eight. But here it is, 7:53, and he's dashing out the door with a dribbling travel cup in one hand.

I sit perfectly still in his backseat and wait.

He scoops his newspaper off the driveway, with its jaunty blue Sweepstakes flyer sticking out of the top, and shoves it under his chin. He opens the door one-handed, retrieves the paper, and throws it into the back without looking, along with his jacket and his lunch. He drops into the seat, sloshing more coffee from his cup, and jams it into the cup holder. He backs up without even checking the rearview mirror, which is his second mistake. The first was leaving his car unlocked . . . again. Then there's the third—no seat belt. I've got mine on, of course. I've seen him drive.

Away we go, down the street toward downtown. He rolls right through the stop sign where Roswell Street spills into ours, proving I'm right to make Mase look both ways. Then he finally looks in the rearview mirror, to see if any cops saw what he did, I guess.

Aw, how cute. He's screaming.

I'm piling out of Mr. Metzger's car in front of Bodega Bodega, having successfully gotten his Sweepstakes signature, when Betty Fischer, that lady who likes to bowl in the middle of the street even when there's traffic, runs out of the alley, also screaming. Raymond's right behind her, form and pen in hand.

He stops when he sees me, and grins.

"How's that working for you?" I ask.

"So far, so good!" He holds up his canvassing foldout. Four signatures already? Shoot!

"How did you manage that?"

"I've been jumping out at them."

I can't help laughing as I watch Mrs. Fischer disappear over the next hill. "How do they sign and run away at the same time?"

He shakes his head in self-disgust. "I cornered the rest of them. Forgot about her bowling ball, and she freaked out and threw it at me."

I don't think he's scary, but then he does every fool thing in front of me that Mason would do. Also, over the summer his feet developed stench. That makes it hard for me to take him seriously.

"Four signatures." I shake my head.

"They're not always conscious when they do it but they sign."

"Oh, come on," I scoff. "Fake fainting? Nobody would ham it up that much, even for Sweepstakes canvassing."

"Why?" he asks. "What'd yours do?"

I shrug. "Scream. Hide. Hop fences. Nothing I couldn't handle."

I pause.

"They are really convincing," I say. "Even without fake fainting."

Raymond shrugs. "They only get to do it once a year."

"Yeah, but—"

"Hey, Ada, wave!" says Raymond, raising a hand. I turn to see Daddy driving by in the animal control van. He worked late again last night, and he's back on the job already? I narrow my eyes against the glare from the van's windows, and wonder.

Chapter 11

Hunting

It's one thing for a neighborhood to show up unannounced. It's another for it to be empty of people when it gets here. My daddy says when Casa Grande appeared on the outskirts of town in 1982, there was bare tar paper where some of the pastel, one-story houses hadn't even been finished yet. It's all been downhill from there. Casa Grande's a ghost town too poor to afford ghosts, full of staring windows—some with no shades, others with rotting ones that peel apart like paper. The streets are so full of sand it'd take months to clean up all the drifts. It's being swallowed, like the kingdom in that Ozymandias poem Mr. Bishop likes. But the desert swallows things slowly, so there's plenty of time for us to lurk around like crows and see what's shiny.

Hunting down the Sunset Six was a quest, something

you could go and do. Finding an invisible-ish monster some-where in a fairly big ring of territory, that's recon work, and recon takes time. The only good news is that if it's smashing things up, we should be able to hear it before we . . . don't see it.

I like the people who lived in the house we're prowling through, whoever they were. Their stuff is nice, not costumey. Stored well, so the heat hasn't crisped and ruined it. I find a velvet jacket, faded blue. A sailor blouse, yellowing but still good, ready to be mine. There's a plaid wool skirt that would be too granny on the wrong girl, but if I use a belt or pin the sides or something, it'll hit right on my calves and be perfect. There's an armload of stuff left for Song even if I take the things I like, so I can maybe trade for saddle shoes, if she's got them.

Raymond comes in from the garage. His backpack sags on his shoulder, so I'm guessing he found tools. I've already grabbed things from the kitchen and bathroom, my favorite sources for weaponry. Pearl used to go for jewelry boxes.

"What did you get?" I ask, dropping my backpack on the dusty kitchen table.

"I did okay," he says mildly, showing me.

He's got a short-handled pruning scythe in there, and heavy-duty clippers, and a couple of saws.

I can't resist. I pull out my best find.

Finally, he looks interested. He whistles.

It's an absolute beauty of a pocketknife, a genuine Oddity Bodkin. I've gone through two cheap knives in the last few months, but from the weight of this one in my hand, and the sharpness of the blade when I tested it, I should be good for a long time.

We join Cayden at the front door, and step outside. As we walk, Cayden falls behind. He's not as used to wandering around the desert as most of us, though with two parents working for Splint, his family is practically a UHF-signal-tracking dynasty, so I guess he'd better get used to it.

"Do we even know where we are right now?" he asks.

"Sure," Raymond says. "We used to come out this way for field trips, but we haven't done the Cursed Campout in two years."

"My old school quit doing field trips, too. They said it was budget cuts."

"Ours said the fatality rate got too high," I say. "Somebody always has to look right at the specters' eyes and ruin it for everyone."

Cayden doesn't talk much after that, just plods along, kicking at tumblegeeks with his janky, Chicago-boy sneakers.

I love tumblegeeks. They do their best, but their frantically paddling little feet are a dead giveaway that they're just tiny dudes using tumbleweeds as camouflage. I don't see them as much in town, so I consider them a treat—a special discovery Pearl and I made when Daddy took us on hikes.

The landscaping in this neighborhood died out years ago. Some front yards are just fields of chia bushes. Mr. Bishop says that chia was one of the primary food staples for indigenous people who lived in this area. It's hard not to take the word *staple* literally when I end up with scratches and punctures all up my doggone arms.

When I bring this up, Cayden laughs.

"He also says that the indigenous people in Oddity were made immortal by aliens and were treated by the Anasazi as gods, but whatever."

"Cayden, honestly. Look, I'm sorry your last school was underprivileged—"

"We lived in Oak Park—"

"—but you have to stop acting like everything you learn here is wrong. You already have a hard enough time fitting in without arguing about how many dimensions of existence there are, or telling Mr. Bishop that cubits aren't an up-to-date unit of measurement."

"But they're NOT."

We're puffing our way up a hill. I use that as an excuse to stop talking for a minute then change the subject.

"Song's going to love what I found. I'm going to use the cash to restock my skulduggery kit," I say. "I'll need it if we're going to keep—"

I am interrupted by a tremendous crash.

All three of us drop to a crouch, getting stabbed by more chia in the process.

Cayden pulls his phone out and glances at it, and I'm impressed for a second because I figure he's getting his camera ready. Nope. He's checking his signal.

"No bars," he mutters.

"No one would get here in time anyway, Cayden," says Raymond. "Whatever happens is ours to handle."

"Terrific," he mutters.

"Come on," I say. I set my phone's camera to video, then head in the direction of the noise.

We creep the rest of the way up the hill, dropping down on our bellies when we get to the top, and I aim my phone down at the scene below us. When I see what's making the noise, I almost drop it.

Greeley is out there with a couple of blue-shirts, directing a third, who is currently driving a bulldozer into the side of an abandoned house. Now that the sounds aren't bouncing off things on their way to us, I can hear the diesel engine I missed before.

"That's not a full patrol," I say. "Why risk making so much noise?"

"Are they cleaning up an old attack?" asks Cayden.

"Maybe they're doing salvage, like Badri," I say.

But they're totally not, because one of the blue-shirts is playing mailbox baseball with a big aluminum bat, and when the mailbox is trashed, he demolishes the post, too. Greeley is grinning like he's watching little kids chase butterflies.

The bulldozer backs out of the hole it's made in the side of the house with a stuttering roar. Greeley hollers something I can't make out to the driver. I guess the blue-shirt can't hear, either, because he drops the engine down to an idle. This time, Greeley's voice rings out loud and clear.

"Hit that next one at an angle!"

The bulldozer lurches over to the house next door, dragging its blade across the front of the pink stucco like I trail my fingers along the cinder-block walls at school. It leaves a nasty, gashing hole.

I continue to lie there not believing what I see until they're using those push brooms that look like giant mustaches with handles to recreate the Blurmonster's signature scuff marks in the sand.

"Good job, kids," says Greeley, clapping a blue-shirt on the back with his big old ham hand and just about sending her flying. "That ought to keep the Protection Committee happy for a while."

Then they all pile onto the bulldozer and pull it onto the road, driving it deeper into the neighborhood, to stash it in some empty garage, I assume.

I stop recording.

We all sit back against the low, brushy ridge over which we've been peeking.

"What . . . was . . . that?" says Raymond.

No one has an answer.

Chapter 12

Flamed

"They call me Greeley. I am but a poor traveling salesman who hasn't had shelter or a decent meal since Santa Fe," says Delmar, who is wearing an enormous cardboard mustache (beards must have come later) and a straw porkpie hat that's too small for his troll-like head. "Your town is strange, but I find it suits me well."

Someone's throwing stuff at him from offstage. Spiders. Caps. Every time the caps pop, spiders jump off into the audience, which at this point is just long-suffering Mr. Bishop in a folding chair. His twitching is getting worse.

"It's nice to know some things are painful everywhere," Cayden mutters.

I'm not consoled.

What I am is coated. In glue, glitter, and sap. The sap is

figurative, but it's what's annoying me most. Mr. Bishop can call this a historical reenactment all he wants, but I know a pageant when I see one.

I should've remembered—the fifth graders always do the "Battle of the Blur" on Sweepstakes Day, but once you've seen it a couple of times, you're over it. I've skipped it for years in favor of stuffing my face and causing trouble.

If Pearl was here, play practice might actually be fun. Right now, she'd be making glitter bombs, and I'd be snickering in a corner with Raymond.

Instead, I spent half the afternoon reglittering the scrolling words across the side of a cardboard caravan. It's a reproduction of the one in the museum, which the original Greeley drove into town at the tail end of New Mexico's gold rush. Painted on the side are a big jar full of wavy liquid and the words:

C. W. GREELEY'S MEDICINE SHOW & PUPPET THEATRE! ELIXIRS! ENTERTAINMENT! INSTANTANEOUS RELIEF FROM ALL YOUR WOES!

It turns out you can get paper cuts from glitter.

Under your fingernails.

Worse, Raymond noticed me being bad at glittering, and he didn't do a very good job of hiding his smirk. He's sitting out of arm's reach, I notice.

"What beast approaches to defool this town?" demands Delmar from behind his mustache.

"Defile," calls Mr. Bishop from the rows of folding chairs in front of the stage.

"Huh?"

95

"There's no such word as defool. Say defile."

"Defile."

Mr. Bishop sighs gustily. "No, I mean say your line, but this time, say it correctly instead of defiling it."

"Oh. Okay, yeah. What beast approaches to defile this town? Be not afeared, but behold these miraculous puppets!"

Cayden's the new kid so he gets to be the mule that pulls the caravan. He's so disgusted he doesn't even need a costume. He looks plenty stubborn as it is. He's unhitched right now, though, and he's breathing in my ear, which is driving me up the wall.

"Cayden, stop it!"

He gets louder.

"Chicago boy. If you do not back. The heck. Up. I will—"

That's when I look at him, and I scoot sideways with a yell, before I realize the big blue face coming at me isn't Whanslaw, it's Cayden in a mask. I fall over, past the curtain to where I'm visible onstage, which is not where I'm supposed to be. Class play practice is mostly about staying out of the way and being awake for your lines.

"Ada," warns Mr. Bishop, "I'm not sure what kind of shenanigans are going on up there, but if you're not skilled enough to fly under my radar, you're not qualified to be doing them."

I scoot back behind the curtain, pursued by the snickers of my classmates. I am the opposite of gruntled. I give Cayden a shove.

"What were you thinking?" I hiss.

"Mr. Bishop told me to bring you the puppet masks to

repaint. He said you should finish them at home and I should help"—he grins—"because you're finding it challenging."

He shoves the Whanslaw mask into a plastic shopping bag, out of which peeps Kiyo's scowling visage.

"Shut UP," I hiss, and Mr. Bishop rattles his chair and clears his throat in warning. "Just because I'm not a glitter fiend like Pearl . . ."

I trail off, because over Cayden's shoulder I can see Raymond, who has a look on his face like he swallowed a parasitic worm. Because I said MY sister's name.

Cayden looks back and forth between the two of us, his smile disappearing. For a minute, I think he's going to actually try to talk to us about our feelings or something, and I'll have to glitter him to death. Instead, he reaches into the pocket of his hoodie and pulls out a travel can of BASH!, of all things.

"Lean forward," he says.

I do, but only to argue. "Cayden, do NOT get that stuff on me," I say, but instead, he uses the cover my body provides to begin spraying the cinder-block wall I was leaning against.

"What are you doing?" asks Raymond.

"You," says Cayden, very softly, "are not the only people around here who know how to pull a stunt. I am going to get us out of play practice."

"And BASH! is helpful how?" asks Raymond.

"Stench is his superpower," I say. Cayden elbows me in the back.

"You know what's really great about all these art supplies you like so much?" he asks.

"Um . . . no?" I say.

"They're incredibly flammable," he says. "Mr. Bishop will never know this was BASH! and not paint thinner."

He pulls a lighter from his pocket and flips it on, leaning the gleaming flame toward the shiny BASH! slick he's made.

"Simple," he says. "It'll burn just long enough to set off the fire alarms, we'll have a fire drill instead of play practice, and—"

Raymond lunges to stop him just as I hiss "NO!" but it's too late. The flame is already greedily licking the BASH! and racing up the cinder blocks. Raymond and Cayden overbalance, and Raymond falls against the wall. I hear the hissing of the BASH! can. Cayden must have landed on the button. The flames climb the spray emitting from the can and light the heavy velvet stage curtain on fire. Cayden's mouth drops open.

Right about then, Raymond untangles himself from Cayden and sits up, which is when I realize the sleeve of his olive T-shirt is on fire. We all start beating at the flames, hissing commands at one another like a bunch of serpents.

Out on stage, Ralph, who's playing the town's original mayor (it literally says ORIGINAL MAYOR in the script) declaims, "I have never been so amazed in MY. ENTIRE. LIFE. These here puppets have saved our town from sure destruction, whereas I have engaged in arson and collusion. I will now upset myself—"

"ABSENT," yells Mr. Bishop, losing patience. I look up and see that the curtain valance that frames the stage is now also on fire, and the rafters are full of black smoke.

"Aw, come on, Mr. Bishop," says Ralph. "Teachers mark you absent; you don't do it yourself."

"When he says he's going to absent himself," says Mr. Bishop, twitching more than ever, "he only means he's going to leave."

Ralph makes a gusty, frustrated sound, throwing his arms up. "Well, obviously! If he's absent, he shouldn't be there in the first place!" He rolls his eyes, and catches sight of the BASH!ferno blazing overhead.

"Whoa!" he yells. Caps popping under his sneakers, he flees the stage, along with several spiders disturbed by the ruckus.

Mr. Bishop stands so fast he tips his folding chair, which hits the floor with a clank. He storms up the stairs onto the stage.

"Ralph!" he shouts toward the wings. "Get back here!"

At that exact moment, the flaming curtain collapses, right on top of him.

The fire alarms finally go off.

So does the suppression system, which dumps an inch of chemical powder on everything. It's in my hair. It's in my mouth. It's all over the props. And the one thing it resembles more than anything else is . . . glitter.

There are screams, laughs, and roars of consternation from the stage. Mr. Bishop is gibbering under the flaming curtain, not about fire, but about angry spiders attacking him.

"Hey, Cayden," says Raymond. "You know who's going to have to clean this up?"

From the way his head is hanging, yeah. He knows.

Chapter 13

Butterfly Wings

When we get to my place after school the next day, Aunt Bets is already there, and she's got company. I thought pirates were supposed to loot things, and pillage. Or something. But Badri Hassan Khalid is at our house again, and I'm starting to get suspicious about what kind of booty he's interested in. Namely, my aunt's.

"You want to tell me how she got up on the counter?" I mutter to Mason as I come in.

"He put her up there!" says Mason admiringly. I don't know what's gotten into him. He saw Daddy lift her when she first got hurt. I guess those pirate muscles of Badri's make it impressive. He's a lot scrappier than Daddy, though. Daddy's built like a tank. Makes me a little bit proud.

Speaking of Daddy, either he's taking a well-deserved

day off or he's home early. He's definitely here to stay, because his feet are bare, and he's discarded his tan work shirt. His white tee glows against his brown skin. I rush over to him. On top of whatever sneaky thing he's up to, he's been working a lot of extra hours because of all the work Mama missed right after Pearl left. I miss him! He lifts me up in a big smiling hug, then goes back to peeling sweet potatoes into the sink. He could pulp one with his bare hand if he wanted to, but hopefully he'll make sweet potato fries instead. I kiss his cheek.

Aunt Bets is leaning back on her hands and smiling at Badri, who's busy talking. Like, really talking, and sketching things out in the air with his hands for her. Something he wants to build, probably with the stolen scrap from Sunset Ridge.

Then I remember how he bailed us out that night, and feel sort of guilty for being all suspicious.

"Hi, Badri," I say.

He actually smiles. Who knew he could do that?

"Hey, Ada," he says, and his accent sounds even better coming out of a smiling mouth.

I want to be a smart aleck and ask if he's volunteering with the fire department because Aunt Bets got stuck up a counter or something, but I can't really be my usual charming self because while Badri might be distracting Aunt Bets with his air drawings, if I say too much she'll remember how she met him in the first place, and she and I have had a sort of truce since bald morning.

I get out the fixings and start making sandwiches, putting them on napkins since the plate cupboard is behind Aunt Bets.

"All those sandwiches, Ada?" says my aunt, proving that no matter how cute the pirate in her kitchen is, she's still paying attention.

"Two are for Cayden. Trust me, he needs them both."

This meets with no comment from either of our responsible adults, so I'm in the clear. One thing I appreciate about Daddy and Aunt Bets: they do not gush like Cayden's mom. I guess Mama used to do that, a little, back when both her daughters were around. But Aunt Bets's way suits me down to the ground.

I take the sandwiches downstairs and Cayden about yanks his out of my hands, like some kind of magician's trick where he can take the top one and the bottom one and I will miraculously not drop the ones in the middle. I may possibly kick one of his shins in ~~retaliation~~ the process of maintaining my grip.

"Whoa," says Cayden as we hunch over the laptop.

I scroll through a sea of new comments on our video. Some Nopesers think our footage is a hoax, of course. But others think the Blurmonster is an insurance scam Greeley created to make money on abandoned real estate.

"Ada, stop scrolling so fast," says Cayden, mouth full of sandwich.

"Keep up, neighbor boy."

Raymond is shaking his head at the ghost preservationist who claims Greeley is destroying crucial spook habitat. Right under that, a chia farmer demands that *more* empty houses be knocked down to make way for his xerifarming.

The comments that get to me, though, are the ones explaining that it's all a big misunderstanding, and Greeley is definitely probably doing this for totally aboveboard reasons—like maybe he's trying to knock down things the Blurmonster could hide behind.

For some reason, those hurt.

"So we go back out," says Raymond. "Get real Blurmonster footage this time, and show these fools."

"I don't think so," I say. "I've got a better idea."

"I didn't want to say anything," says Cayden, "but I don't actually like a lot of your ideas."

Aw, he made a joke.

"*I* don't like it when the Protection Committee sends Greeley to invent disasters. All this time, we were so sure the puppets were protecting us from things like the big, bad Blurmonster. Well, they fooled us, didn't they? You know what my daddy likes to say? *Trust, but verify.*"

Raymond laughs. "He says that when he's checking up on you!"

"The POINT is, no matter how much you admire a person, what they say isn't a fact until you've checked it out yourself. That's what we're going to do from now on."

"I'm not sure the Blurmonster takes interviews," says Cayden.

"I'm not talking about the Blurmonster anymore. I'm talking about Greeley."

I watch their eyes get wide. I've got my work cut out for me if I'm going to get them to agree to this.

Fortunately, I'm very convincing.

A tiny, masa-smeared hand smacks against my cheek.

"Let me get that, sweetie." Raymond's round, brown mom comes at me with a spoon, skimming the cornmeal mush from my skin and popping it into the mouth of the neighbor baby on my lap.

Weekends are always like this at Raymond's. Home-cooked chaos with a side of rice. Raymond's family works just as hard as mine, but since his mom has a little sculpting studio out back, and his jefa runs a hair salon out of their converted garage, they're around all the time—which is pretty funny, because they spend a lot less time managing Raymond than Bets spends managing me.

"What have you three been up to, wandering around by yourselves?" asks Jefa as we eat our empanadas. A lifetime as the most sought-after stylist in town has honed her approach and her short black rock-star hair to razor sharpness.

The good news is that the best approach with Jefa is the same as with Aunt Bets. Lie with confidence and loads of eye contact. The bad news is that Raymond rarely bothers, which means that word of my more dangerous exploits often makes its way home from Raymond's house. Drives me up the wall.

Cayden's no help. He can't focus on anything but food. He stuffs his mouth with empanadas and washes them down with a swig of kombucha. Raymond's mom is big into the health benefits of kombucha, almost like she's been brain-washed by Scoby. Personally, I'll drink soda made by a weird little spongy alien when they pry my rigor-mortis-locked jaw open and pour it down my throat. If it revives me, then we can talk about making it a regular thing.

Baby neighbor shoves more masa in my face, which makes it hard to answer Jefa but easy to mask *tells*.

"Just treasure hunting," I say. "Song's looking for some new stock for the store."

"That's funny," says Raymond's mom, spooning more masa off my face to feed to the baby. They don't worry much about germs around here. "I was in there looking for something, and she said she hadn't seen you."

"Yeah, she's gonna come drag me from my house if I don't find something good soon. I've been doing it for a while now. My usual spots are getting pretty picked over."

It's a point in the Mendezes' favor that they know I sneak into abandoned houses, and never make a big deal about it. They see knowing all the abandoned houses in town as good disaster preparedness.

"Treasure hunting, huh? That what you were doing out at Sunset Ridge?" asks Jefa, her eyes glinting dangerously.

"Yeah, that was a bust. I guess the houses are too new. I've been looking around on the other end of town. There might be some places tucked away that no one has gotten to yet."

"Watch yourself," says Raymond's mom. "Dangerous crea-tures can seek shelter in abandoned houses."

What does she think I am, a rookie?

"She's a smart kid, Dee," says Jefa, giving me a wink.

"I know, but it's got to be said." Neighbor baby is getting fractious, and Raymond's mom is trying desperately to wipe her down before she gets free, but mostly, everything's getting on my clothes. I'm not wearing any good finds today, at least.

"Forget it," says Raymond's mom, surrendering. "I'm gonna strip her down and give her a frozen juice bar. Go grab them out of the garage freezer, would you, Ada?"

I close the door behind me, looking around in the dim light that comes in through the windows. Across the room, there's a clank as Raymond sets a wrench on the floor. He's on his back under one of the rinse sinks, fiddling with something. For the moment, I ignore him. I haven't been out here in a long time. I've been avoiding it. I'm old enough to do my own hair now, I guess. But it's not the same.

We used to make such a party out of it. Sunday afternoons, the only time Bets could get free. I run my hand along the back of one of the shiny red salon chairs and give it a spin, closing my eyes. For one minute, we're all back in our right places. Pearl and me in the chairs, Bets behind Pearl on her own two legs, Mama behind me. Jefa sitting backward on a regular, non-spinny chair, with no one's hair to cut, for once. Everyone gossiping, everyone laughing.

"You must be growing," Bets says, like she always does,

"because I do not have to pump this chair up as high as I used to!"

Pearl and I sit side by side, our freshly washed and conditioned hair curling up tight, as the grown-up sisters we want to be like someday start making parts along our scalps.

"Work toward the left ear, Bets," Mama says. "I'll work toward the right, and these girls will match like a pair of butterfly wings."

I remember Mama braiding my hair, left under, right under, picking up new strands as she works her way down, until my whole head is tingling from her undivided attention.

I can't remember the last time she looked me in the eye.

When I open my eyes, I'm staring at myself in the mirror that faces the chair. I'm annoyed for a second because what do I think I'm doing, daydreaming out here? Then I close my eyes again quick, as details of grown-up gossip emerge from the haze of my memory. I feel my way around the chair and sit in it, listening to my memory of a conversation I only half heard at the time.

". . . but anything she does has to be a good thing," Mama says. "Last time I was there, it sounded like there were things alive in the back."

Jefa speaks up from where she's leaning on her chair back. "He used to say it was the mannequins in the basement. I guess it could be."

"I was more worried about bugs." Mama uses her comb to separate out the next section of my hair.

"Well, she's cleaning so hard I can see the dust flying all the way from the bakery door. She had soft hands the first time she came in for a snack, but she's all-over blisters now."

"She's got a story," says Mama with a sigh. "They always do, when they wander into town like that. What's her name again?"

"Song, I think," says Bets.

Jefa shakes her head, though her sharp black haircut doesn't move. "That's what I thought she said, too, but I think Song's a last name in Korea, not a first name."

"It's the only name she's answering to." Bets shrugs. "Better not to ask too many questions. Whatever she was running from, she's here now."

Raymond thumps a piece of sink pipe down on the checkered linoleum, interrupting my memory. He mutters something under his breath.

"It's broken?" I ask.

"Yup." He winces, rolling to the side as guck drips out of the pipe end hanging down from the drain. "And clogged."

He heads for the kitchen with the busted part in his hand, and I go to get the frozen fruit bars. I open one for myself right away, because I can trust them to be made of real fruit juice at Raymond's house, as opposed to the straight-up beet juice I got the last time I asked Bets to buy a box from Scoby. I bathe my face in the cold air from the freezer to help me calm down and think.

Between Cayden's complaints and the PC's fishy behavior, I've been feeling all off center. I'm an Oddity girl, born and bred. I don't owe anybody an apology if my town's not their cup of kombucha. Still, might be nice to talk to someone who came here on purpose.

I'll drop in on Song soon. I'm overdue to take her the arm-load of swag I found, and the more I think about sneaking into Greeley's, the more I know just what I'm planning to do with my pay.

Chapter 14

The Queen of Shenanigans

I don't get to For a Song as soon as I'd hoped. Raymond, Cayden, and I spend the rest of the weekend canvassing. We're hoping to kill three chupacabras with one stone, or something. But things are starting to get weird, and by weird, I mean weirder than usual.

I expected the people we canvassed to bail out of windows, hide in closets, take evasive maneuvers. That's the fun of it.

But.

Mr. Shen ran face-first into a utility pole trying to get away from us.

We had to drag Mrs. McCutcheon out from under her front porch, feetfirst. She was wearing a skirt and some kind of bloomers. We may all be scarred for life.

Mr. Eflin tried to eat Raymond's canvassing foldout.

"You guys realize how weird this is, right?" asks Cayden, venturing a cautious look at me from under his curtain of hair. "I mean, this goes way beyond making canvassing tough for us."

My usual urge to defend my hometown comes boiling up, but when I open my mouth, nothing comes out.

Ralph and Delmar go lumbering by, chortling as they chase a postal worker who's shedding letters from her bag as she flees.

"It's like we're the only ones who notice," I say.

Raymond rubs the back of his neck. "The Sweepstakes has been going on for years. We're all used to it."

"Yeah," I say, "but the trolls are Nopesers. They know the PC has been lying to us about stuff."

Cayden shrugs. "From what my folks say, lying is what most politicians do."

He's probably right, but I'm uneasy, as if something's lurking nearby. I mean, something's always lurking nearby, but this is different. It's like I'm forgetting something, something big, and I'm going to remember one crucial second too late.

"Well," I say, "maybe the Greeley's sneak will help us make sense of things."

The total silence that greets this statement makes me turn around to look at my friends. Raymond's scowl is so big I bet it could be used as a power source, and Cayden's hiding behind the sweep of his hair.

I squeeze the straps of my backpack. "What?"

If you can believe this, Cayden talks first.

"We're not sure we should do it, is all."

For a second I'm so flummoxed I can't answer.

"Cayden is speaking for both of you now?"

Raymond won't look at me.

"And are you going to tell me why?"

Raymond frowns and doesn't answer right away, which means I am not going to like this.

"Ada, the other sneaks were great. But this?"

"Hey, if this is getting too difficult for you—"

"I didn't say that. I'm not sure it's a good idea, is all. The things we've done so far, they're like training exercises. We get smarter and tougher and stay out of the grown-ups' hair. Everyone wins."

I close my eyes so I won't kill him. "But?"

"Breaking into Greeley's is more like climbing into the grown-ups' hair and lighting it on fire."

"So? What's the problem, Raymond?"

"You already got into trouble with your aunt once this month. Are you ready to bring Greeley and the Protection Committee down on us just to get more hits on Nopes?"

"Since when are you worried about getting in trouble?"

"I'm not. I'm worried about *you* getting in trouble."

My eyes roll so hard, they might get permanently stuck up in my head. "First of all, we'll only bring the Protection Committee down on us if we get caught, which I have no intention of doing. Second, I think it's pretty interesting that the guy whose moms let him do a-ny-thing he wants—"

He huffs aloud. "That's easy for you to say. I'm their only child, Ada. I can't—"

"WHOA."

My scalp prickles until it feels like my braids are sticking straight out all over my head. There's a rushing noise in my ears, and my vision swims with darkness and light.

"I hope that sentence had an amazing ending, Mendez," I say. "Because it sounded an awful lot like you were saying that Pearl and I played fast and loose because our parents had a spare."

"There's no such thing as a spare! You get that, right?"

My eyes sting. "Of course I get that! If there was, my mama wouldn't—" I can't finish.

Oh, I am not going to cry in front of these boys.

When I can look at Raymond again, his face is all scrunched up, like he's as upset as I am. I think back to that moment during play practice when things got awkward. He looked the same way then.

"You never talk about Pearl," I say. "Do you know how much that bothers me?"

His cheeks go red, and he mumbles something.

I storm off toward home, almost ramming into Oddity's local Sasquatch as he comes out of Fair Weather Bakery with a paper coffee cup in one hairy brown hand. Aunt Bets would kill me if she knew. He's super shy and a really good customer.

"Sorry!" I mutter, but I keep going.

"Ada, wait!" yells one of the boys behind me.

My braids are practically glued to my head with sweat. It's undignified, and I know it, but I don't look back. Without Pearl, those two boys are the only backup I've got, and now they're quitting on me? I'm starting to feel the full weight of sneaking into Greeley's with no help at all.

Raymond catches up, trying to block my way, then walking backward in front of me when that doesn't work. I can feel Cayden approaching behind me, but before he gets here, Raymond mutters, "I'm scared to talk about Pearl."

I was not expecting that.

"You're not scared of anything."

"I am now. Ada, they never took a kid before. You, me, and Pearl, it was supposed to be us forever. Now Pearl's gone, and I know she's probably happy, but I'm not. I miss her. What if they take you next?"

"They don't usually take too many people from one family—"

"Right, like they don't take kids." He rubs a hand over his buzz-cut hair. I've never seen him lose his cool this way. "I'm just saying ... think twice before jumping into this sneak with both feet. I ... would feel better if you stay off the radar."

Stop watering, eyes. I can't swallow back tears and yell at the same time.

"I'm tired of doing what I'm supposed to! I make good grades, I kick butt, and I canvass for the Sweepstakes, and look how it is! I know it worked out great for Pearl, but it's a little bit different for me, Raymond!"

He looks like he's frantic to shush me but also positive I'll pound him if he tries. He's right.

We stand there staring at each other. Cayden waits just outside our bubble of silence.

Finally, Raymond takes a deep breath and says, "You're going to do this no matter what I say, aren't you?"

"Yes!" I don't tell him that our sneaks are the only things that seem to be worth doing lately. I didn't realize how special being a twin was until I was nothing special anymore. I will settle for being Oddity's reigning queen of shenanigans.

Raymond and Cayden look at each other and reach a decision.

"Just . . . promise after this we'll stick to stuff that won't end up on our permanent records if we get caught," says Cayden.

Conviction, and loads of eye contact.

"I promise," I lie. Cayden nods in relief, but Raymond looks skeptical. I need to distract him, quick.

Like a wish granted, Cayden's little alien comes blazing out of the park, chasing a tumblegeek. He's snapping his choppers, and man, it is LOUD. Of course, as soon as he sees us, he trips over his stubby feet and suddenly he's jerking himself upright. If he had identifiable hands he'd be stuffing them in his pockets in an attempt to act casual, and for a second I think he's going to start whistling.

Cayden's mouth opens in alarm. I think he keeps hoping

the alien will forget he exists and find another flagpole to fixate on, but the little guy seems pretty attached.

Cayden starts walking again, shooting us a look that plainly says to watch his back. As he passes the alien, the little guy falls in behind him, like he's one of us, or a particularly unfortunate-looking dog. How many times can he bail on the other aliens who hang out in our alley before they won't take him back anymore?

"Cay-den."

Whoa.

"CAY-den."

Our tiny, toothy shadow has officially distracted Raymond, bless him. Poor Cayden is frozen on the sidewalk, like he's hoping maybe he didn't hear what he thought he heard.

"Cayden?"

Cayden slowly turns around.

"Yeah?" His voice is a bit hoarse. I actually think that this once, mine would be, too. The little aliens, they're all over the place, but they've never talked to us.

"Xerple."

"Zur . . . zurple?"

The little guy's bobbing his head. He's really, really excited that Cayden's talking back. "Yes! Xerple!"

"Xerple."

"Hi, Cayden."

"Um . . . hi."

"Hi."

They stand there looking at each other, Xerple so excited

he's just about vibrating, Cayden all awkward like . . . well, like someone who has an alien following him around for reasons unknown.

I bet they could both stand here all day. I break the stalemate. "Hey, uh, Xerple? Walk with us, okay?"

Which is probably a reckless thing to say, because I never really know how these things translate when I'm dealing with someone with a totally different culture. For all I know, I told him we're bonded for life. But whatever. I want to swing by the house, grab my swag, and get to For a Song before it closes. And it's fun to see Cayden so nervous when he's frankly driving me up the wall.

Xerple hisses a bit when I say his name, but by the time I finish, he's into it. He looks back at Cayden, for permission, I guess. "Cayden?"

"Yeah, uh—" He shoots me a dirty look. "We're headed home. You can come if you want."

"O-KAY!" he says, with tremendous enthusiasm, and though I still have no clue how he can see where he's going when he has no discernible eyes, he practically skips over to Cayden's side and begins to march alongside him.

Chapter 15
Unwanted Guest

The bell jangles as I shove my way into For a Song, my arms loaded down with swag. "Bee-Bop-A-Lula" is playing on the stereo.

"Finally!" says Song, rounding the counter in a swirl of pink and black. "I was starting to think you had abandoned me!"

How does whoever Song left behind feel about her? Do they miss her? I would. She lives over the store, but I've never seen any mail in the mailbox at the bottom of her steps.

She reaches over and pulls the top half of the pile out of my arms with pale pink fingernails. "Did you bring me anything blue?"

I look down at her black peep-toe heels in an effort to seem modest. "Some."

"Ooh, you did good!" She dumps her armload on the counter and extracts the blue-velvet jacket, examining it closely. "Even the lining is okay. Ada, you are a pro."

I don't answer. I'm thinking about how glamorous she is, always done up and perfect, head to toe. She must be from a big city, right? Somewhere glamorous. Aunt Bets said Korea, so . . . Seoul?

"Song?" I ask.

"Hmmm?" She's buried in my finds, checking seams, snapping things straight so she can get a good look at them.

"Do you like it here?"

That gets her attention. She looks me over. "Here, give me those," she says belatedly, taking the rest of my stack. She sets them on the counter, her back to me, quiet, fussing. Then she turns. "You okay?"

I frown. "What? Me? Yeah. Why?"

She reaches over and tugs on the collar of my Peter Pan blouse, straightening it and smoothing it down. "You are brave. Smart. I forget sometimes that you are just a kid."

Uh-oh. She's got the "leftover sister" look. Now I'm cranky.

"Are you feeling sorry for me?"

"What? No!" She puts her hands on my shoulders, takes them off, puts them back. "I am being supportive. That is what friends do, right?"

Oh. I . . .

. . . I'm a huge jerk. Because I know that it would be totally wrong to take advantage of Song right now, and I'm going to do it anyway.

I turn around, twisting out from under her lacquered nails to go to the window and look out, like I'm sad. The mannequins turn their heads curiously as I come up behind them. One of them is wearing a fedora with a way-too-long-for-fashion feather in the band. I put a bracing hand on each of their shoulders.

"It's just . . . ," I say, deliberately trailing off.

I wait, and after a long moment, Song's heels clack two times as she steps closer.

The mannequins return to looking out the window. I wait again. I listen to the electric clock buzzing on the wall. Finally, I say, "Sometimes I wonder what it would be like to live somewhere else."

"Oddity is better than a lot of places, Ada."

It would be rotten of her to say otherwise when us kids are basically stapled to our parents until we grow up. On the other hand—

"It's easy for you to say stuff like that, Song. You chose to come here."

She laughs aloud. I'm so shocked I turn around. "What?" I ask.

"Technically, yes, I guess I chose, but I was not so much running toward Oddity as running away from everything else."

She reaches out a hand to me, and I take it. We swing our arms gently back and forth between us, like a bridge, while I wonder what Song was running from.

Song chose Oddity. I bet Cayden would literally ride a rocket without a seat belt if he thought it would get him out of here.

"Why do you stay?" I ask.

This time she giggles, like a kid. "Sometimes I still don't know. The night I moved into the apartment, I heard rats running around down here and called an exterminator. Only it was not rats I heard, it was the mannequins. At first I was scared of them, but mostly they do what I say. I've gotten used to the strangeness of this place."

She side-eyes me. "Besides, Oddity has its upsides for us new people. Badri Khalid has been spending a lot of time at the bakery, hasn't he?"

Shoot, does the whole town know?

Song sighs. "The truth is, Oddity is the kind of place that makes you think anything is possible, and I need to believe that's true.

"Now," she says, taking her hand back so she can circle the counter. "I can give you—" She names an insultingly low price.

"Riiiiight," I say. "Give me the inspirational talk, then lowball me." I'm going to get my price, and the brown clothes I've been scoping, too.

Song rests her hands on the counter and leans forward, eyes gleaming. This is my favorite part.

I don't realize until I shut the door behind me, with most of the money I wanted in my pocket and all the brown clothes I wanted in my arms, that I still didn't find out where Song's from.

Rotten pirate. Who does he think he is?

I lift my head from my pillow long enough to scowl at the

door I just slammed. As I thump my head back down, to the side this time, because I'm done screaming, I see Stella-in-the-closet. She's got her arms folded, and I'm a bit surprised to find she's frowning at the door, not me. Even she gets it, and nobody's made her dinner in who knows how long. Maybe that's why. I squeeze the locket in my hand.

It has been eleven months since our mama has packed my lunch, made me dinner, or stocked our pantry with Malicious Pixies breakfast cereal (*We Don't Know What They Put In There!*). Here I come upstairs after a horrible day, and what do I see? Badri Hassan Khalid, large as life, bringing my mama a plate like he's a member of the family. Mashed potatoes, buttered roll, and everything. My stomach is growling like Mr. Phillipi's ice cream truck when it broke the sound barrier, but I'm not going down to dinner now. No way.

He was talking nice to her and everything. Called her Mrs. Roundtree, like he's a Kiva Scout instead of a raider of the high seas.

I wipe my eyes on my pillowcase and turn my head to the other side, so Stella-in-the-closet can't see me crying.

Rotten pirate.

Chapter 16
Zombie Rabbits

I've got my team, my gear, and a solid plan. It's time.

My feet crunch in the dry grass as I approach one of the sleepy piles of zombie rabbits scattered across the side yard between my house and Cayden's.

"What are you all doing lying around? Aren't you going to get stomped by the aliens?"

Snooks, dusty and bedraggled, looks over without raising his head. "Halftime" is all he says.

Perfect.

"Snooks, I think it's time to refuel. You need to keep your blood sugar up," I say, though there's absolutely zero evidence that zombie rabbits have blood.

He eyes me with interest. Good old Ada, provider of snacks.

"You know where I would go if I were you?" I ask.

He sits up. I hear rustling as the rabbit piles around me begin to stir.

"Tell me now."

Oh, I can do better than that.

Dinnertime at Greeley's is a nightmare. For one thing, most people are done with school and work for the day, so the store's already busy. Greeley's has cornered the market on basically everyone's favorite convenience food. There's fried chicken, fish fry, a taco bar, take-and-bake pizza, and a sushi chef. The whole place is crammed with parents who are short on patience and kids who are using up the rest. It's also cocktail hour for every resident of Oddity who drinks dinner, and the ones who live out in the desert pay their tab by scavenging cans and bottles and bringing them in for the deposit fees. The front of the store is jammed with shopping carts and wagons filled with trash bags full of sour-smelling recyclables. It's chaos.

And we're about to upgrade that to bedlam.

I watch from around the corner, where I'm drinking a soda I bought at Bodega Bodega. The parking lot isn't any calmer than the store. Not a minute goes by without a near fender bender. Customers already tired from the store are close to snapping as they jockey for position in the pickup line by the conveyor belt. They're so busy that they fail to notice small flashes of movement under the sea of parked cars. Likely no one inside has time to glance at the security camera. Either way, if they don't know exactly where to look, like me, there's nothing to see.

I hope they remember what I told them. Then again, what difference does it make? Some people have an inherent ability to create chaos. Besides, whether I can count on them to pay attention to my directions or not, they're fixed on Greeley's like it's a giant electromagnet, and nothing is going to turn them away.

When the attack finally begins, it's almost unimpressive. I can't see anything much from here, except for the automatic doors staying open for a really long time, and some startled people flailing, then falling down. A white plastic grocery bag gets shot-putted up into the air, shedding frozen burritos as it goes.

Then comes the stampede.

Customers come running out of the store, still pushing their carts and hauling their bags. A clerk chases after a woman in a snug maxi dress, demanding she pay for her purchases. She rounds on him, jabbing his chest with her finger. I can hear her clear across the road.

"I'm not going back in there. That place is infested! I'm going to call the health inspector!"

Inside, there are shouts and crashes.

"It's about that time," I say, setting my soda on the ground against the bodega wall and wiping my wet hand on my brown pants.

Cayden and Raymond flank me, also wearing brown. Xerple's bobbing around behind them. He refused to stay home.

"If the bunny comes, I come!" he said, and honestly, I didn't have time to argue.

"Ready?" I say, and Cayden grins nervously. Raymond nods, his eyes never wavering from the front of Greeley's.

We head across the lot, casually dodging fleeing patrons as we go. I feel anything but calm, but we've got to act like we belong here. We weave our way between the cars and squeeze through the crush of freaked-out customers.

It's a zoo in here. A very specialized zoo, full of zombie rabbits. It was ridiculously simple, getting them to come. All I had to do was tell them one thing:

Here there be marshmallows.

They're everywhere. Log rolling through the produce section on watermelons. Standing atop a pile of potato sacks, hurling portobello mushrooms like Frisbees. A cart sails past full of rabbits using brooms as oars, like some kind of rowing team. "Stroke!" yells one of them, standing up in the child seat in total violation of the diagrams. "Stroke! Stroke! Stroke!"

I go straight to the customer service desk. A beleaguered blue-shirt whose name tag reads DEWEY is flipping through a tattered old phone book, muttering, "Animal control, animal control" under his breath. I recognize him right away as Greeley's nephew, though he probably won't know me.

"Why didn't you look us up on the Internet?" I ask.

He doesn't even glance my way. "I have a Splint plan," he says, distracted. "My phone never gets a decent signal in here. And they chewed through the router cables."

Does he think I'm here to make a return, or what?

"Someone down the street was saying you've got a zombie rabbit problem?" I ask, as if it's not self-evident from the gleeful cackles and toppling displays of cans.

Finally, he looks up. "Kid, if you don't have Dale Roundtree in your back pocket, get out of here."

I shove my braids out of my face with one hand. "You don't see the family resemblance?"

"Your uniforms look the same," he says. He's going to go far in the family business, I can tell.

"Yeah, that's on purpose. I'm interning." It sounds more official than volunteering.

He looks over at Cayden and Raymond. I barely talked Cayden out of wearing shades. "And are your associates here interning, too?"

I roll my eyes. "Obviously."

Dewey looks pointedly down at Xerple.

"That's our . . . trained herding animal."

"Look, kid," says Dewey, then ducks as a stream of spray cheez flies at him from the direction of the checkout lanes. The cheez coils and loops on the counter, rising in an unsteady pyramid of fluorescent orange. "I don't have time for you to get cute with me." He rakes a hand through his thinning hair. "Oh no, they found the baking aisle."

I glance over my shoulder. About halfway between the

front and back of the store, a mushroom cloud of flour is rising. I gotta feel a little bit proud of the zombie rabbits' sheer destructive creativity. I return my attention to the pathetic, droopy clerk.

"Look, mister big man, I guarantee you I have way more experience wrangling these critters than you. Unless you want to explain to the boss why you let a herd of zombie rabbits have free rein in this town's finest grocery store, I suggest you let us handle things."

Greeley, of course, is in his weekly meeting with the PC. Nobody, but nobody, is going to interrupt that meeting unless Greeley's is actually on fire. I get exactly the reaction I was looking for.

"You're gonna handle this? Kiddo, I'll believe that when I see it."

I turn to the nearest zombie rabbit, who's jumping frantically up and down on a grocery scanner like he's playing Cayden's Dance Dance Revolution game. The machine's beeping out desperate Morse code. "Please remove the item and wait for an associate," says the computer.

"Hey!" I holler, with all the authority I can manage when I feel like laughing. "Get down from there."

He turns toward me, and I see that it's the rabbit who wears the sugar sack. He grins.

"Make me!"

I reach behind my back and slide one of the nets I pilfered from Daddy's supply closet out of its holder. These are older ones he got tired of fixing, and lack some of the curses and wards on his newer models. The red thread that binds the best ones is old and faded. But to the layperson, I figure they still look pretty good. I give this one a shake to make sure the net is loose and moving freely, and advance on good old Sugar. He faces me fully, thumping his hind foot threateningly on the scanner. The computer, totally confused, tries to argue with him in English, then Spanish, then surrenders and just buzzes instead. A low growl rises and falls in Sugar's throat. He crooks his creepy little hands and crouches.

"Maybe you should step back, kid. Kid? Shouldn't you wait for your father?" calls Dewey from where he's hiding behind the customer service counter.

I crouch, too, glaring at Sugar just as tough as I can. "Bring it."

"WAAAAAHHHHHHH!" he screams, and leaps at me.

"RAAAAAHHHHHHHH!" I scream, holding my ground.

"AAAAAHHHHHHH!!!!" shrieks the clerk from behind the counter.

I step sideways, whip my net around, and bag Sugar, neat as neat. If Daddy could see, he'd about bust with pride.

Sugar puts up a truly excellent struggle, snarling and chewing on the net and basically making himself so disagreeable that I wonder if zombie rabbits can get rabies.

I swing the net around and present it for the clerk's edification, dangling it over the edge of the counter. He whimpers and scrabbles back across the floor. How this guy got through school here in Oddity is beyond me.

"You want me to let him go?" I ask in my most helpful voice.

"Outside!" Dewey squeaks.

I shrug. "Fine."

He pulls himself back upright, clinging to the counter for dear life, and tries to look like he's had a spine this whole time. "I'll lock the automatic doors. You put them out the side fire entrance, one at a time, and I'll start getting the remaining customers out of the store."

Good. That'll take him hours, especially if some of the customers are pinned down by rabbits, which is highly likely, since that's how I planned it.

"Okay. Hats." Me, Raymond, and Cayden pull ball caps out of our pockets and jam them on our heads.

"Hats?" asks Dewey, confused.

"Keeps the vermin from grabbing our hair. We never go anywhere without them." Which is nonsense, of course, but he's obviously buying every word.

Xerple takes off to add to the chaos. Cayden, Raymond, and I march away down separate aisles, impossible for the overhead security cameras to tell us apart in our identical brown uniforms and ball caps, leaving Dewey to do . . . whatever completely useless thing he's about to do.

I take Sugar over to the side entrance like I was told, and dump him outside the door. Of course, I hold it open long enough for him to sneak straight back in, but it's all about the letter of the law, right? Which I dutifully followed. He races off, grabbing a pool noodle from an end display as he goes. A store employee appears from around the corner, and Sugar charges her, holding the noodle like a lance and screaming.

As I pass through the frozen food aisle, I see rabbits playing hockey with burritos. They're also taking turns shutting one another in the freezer cases. Two of them are eating ice cream with their faces in the containers, and one of them is slo-mo miming at me as I go by.

When I get to the back, I duck behind the meat counter. "Hey, careful with that!" I hiss at a zombie rabbit who's using the industrial slicer to make an enormous mountain of shaved salami. He looks at me, and two of the butchers rush him, trying to retake the deli area. He jumps down from the metal table and whips their aprons up over their faces before they know what's happening. One of them trips and goes down in a pile of bologna slices. The other goes face-first into the nearby lobster tank. The rabbit lands on top of his head, reaching in with a paring knife to slice the bands on as many lobster claws as he can. "Ha HA!" he cries in triumph, as unleashed crustaceans go after the butcher's face and his hands where they're gripping the side of the tank. His feet pedal frantically on the wet floor as he tries to pull himself out. The aquarium teeters, then goes over sideways, smashing beneath him. He wheezes and sucks in a huge breath before screaming as the lobsters swarm over him.

The invertebrate invasion is excellent cover as I crab-walk through the swinging doors into the dim interior of the stockroom.

Chapter 17

Schnoz

I think of Greeley's as a really big store but I never expected the back room to be this cavernous. Away in the distance on all sides of me stretch tall steel shelves filled with pallets of food, and other, less identifiable things. I can't make out the actual back of the store. It's like it's bigger on the inside.

I'm slow, low, and as silent as the grave, but thankfully I don't see any employees back here. The rabbits have strict instructions to stay out unless there's an emergency that needs my attention, in which case they're supposed to send Snooks. I made him a lieutenant. He's already lording it over everybody.

As I continue to edge my way in and nothing moves, I cautiously rise to my feet. I'm waiting for some alarm to go off, but unless it's silent, there's not one. I guess they couldn't leave it on all day, or every time someone came after a flat of disposable diapers they'd set it off.

This place looks like your basic warehouse. It's downright boring. I bet Pearl thought she was getting majorly cheated when they brought her and the other Sweepstakes winners back here.

I thought I'd find some answers, but nothing looks like I expected. It's well lit, too, which makes no sense. If I can see everything, so can the blue-shirts. They can't all be in on the Sweepstakes, can they? That Dewey kid couldn't keep a secret in a safe.

I slide my way down long rows of tall steel shelves, scanning for anything that could be helpful, but all I see are groceries. Then I spot something interesting. . . . The floor slopes back here, until it's practically a hill. On the back wall is a row of shiny steel doors. I've seen doors like that before, when we went on a field trip to Cryogenesis (*Freeze This Moment Forever!*). Those are cooling units.

On one hand, it's not a surprise that a grocery store needs cold storage in the back. On the other hand, it's pretty inconvenient to put it so far away. On the surgically grafted third hand, maybe they're not keeping groceries in there at all.

I sidle down the sloping aisle as fast as I can go, keeping my eye out for blue-shirts, but they're all too busy dealing with marauding rabbits. I swear, if I'd realized how useful those little boogers could be, I'd have been using them for months.

Daddy has a jacket that goes with his uniform, with DALE

embroidered on the pocket. The fake uniforms I cobbled together from the trades I made at Song's all have short sleeves, which made perfect sense on a New Mexico afternoon, but I'm freezing by the time I pull the latch handle on the fourth unit. This one is a freezer, I discover. The air whooshes around the seal, and I haul the heavy silver door open.

I can't see the back of the freezer from the entryway, not because it's deeper than the others, but because there are . . . things hanging from hooks in the ceiling. Huge, frozen things, wrapped in some kind of plastic casing. My nightmare brain kicks in, and for one panicky second I believe in my bones that I've found a bunch of Sweepstakes winners, frozen for safekeeping. I take a step inside, straining to read the packaging in the dim light that spills in through the open door.

Beef. Ham. More beef.

I relax. This must be the stuff the butchers cut up, before they cut it up.

Then it occurs to me that there's a zombie rabbit out there with SUGAR written across his pajamas. There's such a thing as taking labeling too seriously.

I pull my Oddity Bodkin from my pocket. Acting braver than I feel, I slice open the plastic wrapping on the biggest frozen hunk of meat I see. Even in the low light I detect the marbled red and white of frozen meat. I don't know if I was expecting someone in blue jeans and a jacket, or what. Frozen meat is not actually reassuring, of course, except for the fact that no one could ever get a single piece this big from a human.

Suddenly I realize that it's getting darker in here. With a soft sound like a rubbery kiss, the freezer door seals behind me, and I'm alone in the dark in a maze of meat.

I fumble toward the door, and in the blackness I run straight into the frozen cow I just opened, which turns out to be as hard as a brick wall. The fireworks that explode behind my eyes are gone too fast to be of any use. When it stops hurting a little, I reach a hand out in front of me, only to feel something cold and hard brush past.

"Whoa!" I say aloud, then mentally slap myself for making noise when I'm sneaking around.

It's just the cow, swinging on its hook because I ran into it. I hear it sklonk into something else in the dark. A ham, I guess. Great. This is like being in a room full of desk toys.

My collision with the beef has got me as turned around as any of these things swinging on hooks. I can't find the door, or any telltale strip of light that might tell me where it is.

It is so, so cold in here.

I stand still for a minute. No point ramming into everything. When I can't hear the squeak of the hooks anymore, I strain my ears to see if I hear anything else. I hear an exhaust fan blowing softly. Where do they usually put exhaust fans in these things? At the back, I bet. I turn and head in the opposite direction. I feel in front of me as carefully as I can, but my fingers are going numb.

I picked the wrong way. It's taking much longer than it should to reach the door. At least, I think it is. Maybe I was already halfway in when the door shut. When I get to the wall, I'll know, and I can go back the other way if I need to.

And I do find the wall. Wow, I might actually have done this right. My fingers trail left, and graze the seam of what's definitely a door. I can't find a handle, though. It must be on the other side. I feel my way across the door, then stop, my hands just above shoulder height.

Doors don't usually have big, rounded bumps in them.

Some of these are the size of my hand, some are smaller. I circle that area of the door with my hands, figuring out how many of them there are, framing them. Then I work my way back in, trying to understand what I'm feeling. There's a long shape at the "top," like an oval on its side. Then two indents below that, with round bulges inside them. Between those, there's a sort of ridge, curving down into a bump, and below that—

I jump backward, slamming into a frozen slab of meat, which swings on its hook and smacks me a second time for good measure. My back stings with impact and cold, but worse is the panic clawing around inside me like it got lost in there. I touched a mouth, complete with teeth. Which means the rest of the bumps make up a face. And now that I've realized *what* it is, I also know *who* it is.

I was just nose-to-nose with a sculpture of Mr. Whanslaw.

My skin crawls like I'm covered with spiders.

I'm 100 percent positive I'd have noticed if the head . . . of the head of the PC was on the inside of the freezer door when I opened it. Which means this is a different door.

I spin around, too freaked out to be careful, and flounder back across the freezer, running into things willy-nilly and setting them swinging. Reaching the right door, I claw for the release latch, desperate to at least get some light in here. I find and pull it.

It doesn't work.

I fumble for a light switch all around the door. I can't find one. I'm shivering all over, and being all alone and scared out of my wits is making it really hard to gauge my cold exposure. Raymond would be so disappointed in me.

Just when I'm about to really lose it, I hear the outside handle clunk as someone pulls on it. The door swings open.

There's no one there.

I stick my foot in the gap just in case as I cautiously peer around the edge of the door to see if my rescuer is friend or foe.

It's Snooks. As I spot him, he lets go of the handle, drops to the ground with a squish, and comes around to join me.

"Why are you standing in there with all the beeves?" he asks me.

"I'm sorry, the what?"

"The beeves. The many hanging cows."

Where the heck are the zombie rabbits from? I shake my head. Then it occurs to me that the ruckus sounds a lot closer than it did before.

"Snooks, why are you back here?"

He blinks. "Oh. Yes. EMERGENCY!"

Chapter 18
Shiny

I shut the freezer door as softly as I can and crouch next to Snooks, scanning the parts of the storage room I can see.

"What is it?" I ask.

"I don't know, but it's wearing a name tag and very unpleasant!" says Snooks, which both does and doesn't answer my question. "Is wearing a straw hat. We have all the marshmallows. Come now!"

My heart clenches like a fist over the straw hat part. The loud noises in the distance sound like they're being made by full-size people, so there's no time to hide here being scared. There are emergency exits back in store land, so as much as I'd like to grab Raymond and Cayden, head into that freezer, and pry open the door to the secret tunnel I'm now sure exists,

I'm going to have to run right at my pursuers. Maybe I'm in luck and they don't actually know I'm back here.

Snooks is amazingly fast for a pajama sack of rabbit parts. I was afraid I'd have to carry him, and instead I have to run to keep up. As we begin flashing past shelves full of groceries, zombie rabbits cackle and store employees curse. Stock comes crashing down from the big steel shelves.

Snooks looks back at me, worried. "Emergency, right? I told them to make lots of trouble, make people with name tags cry. Good?"

"Good," I pant. "Snooks, do you know a good way to get out?"

"Away from the crying," he counsels. I wish he would be a bit more specific.

Sugar appears in front of us, ears vibrating and teeth biting his chin in nervousness. He waves his stubby arms at us frantically, and dashes away between shelves. I hope he's beckoning and not waving us off, because I'm following him.

There's a huge commotion going on in the center of the stockroom. Forget marshmallows. I am making these weirdos some S'MORES, because I have a totally clean shot toward wherever Sugar is taking me, which, as far as I can tell, is . . . uh-oh.

Seriously?

Into the dark, gaping mouth of the conveyor belt.

He's right to do it, I know that. But I can't shake the idea that things are alive in there, and given the big rubbery hand that lives in the freezer case, I don't think that's completely out of the realm of possibility. Imagine every time you ever thought someone was going to reach out from under your bed and grab you. Now imagine a tunnel full of those hands, because that's what I'm picturing.

Behind me, I hear a sound so horrible that at first I don't understand who's making it. Then I turn to look, and Greeley, roaring, is coming at me across the stockroom like a silverback gorilla in full charge. His big white teeth are bared. As he comes, he rips a metal support from the wreckage of a toppled shelf.

That's all the encouragement I need. I leap up onto the conveyor belt.

"WAH!" yells Snooks, looking back over my shoulder, and I lunge forward just in time. The shelf leg crashes down on the belt behind me. I scramble after the rabbits into the conveyor tunnel's lightless maw, and a moment later the leg whispers through the dank air, grazing the top of my head as it goes by. I cry out. When I check my head, it's wet with blood.

Behind me, Greeley howls with laughter.

"Have fun in there, kid!" Then he yells something in a language I don't understand, and laughs some more. It frightens me more than anything else that has happened so far. If he thinks my exit strategy is good news, that's very very bad news for me.

Even so, at first I think I'm in luck, because the belt is turned on, so we're practically flying, like we're running on the moving walkways at the airport, only with crawling and desperation.

Then snickers and gibbers begin to echo off the walls, and worse, there are places where there is no echo, and that means those are openings.

Something grabs my leg. I lose my balance and land on my stomach, spread-eagled on the conveyor belt. Whatever's got me yanks me backward, and I scream, grabbing for the edges of the belt, which scrape my fingers. I hang on for dear life, but the hand is so strong. Its nails cut into my leg through my pants, and I feel a hot trickling of blood down my leg. I can't let go to fight, or it will drag me down, down underneath to where the conveyor machinery churns, Morlock-style. I don't understand how it's keeping its hold on me, because the belt is still moving.

Another rough yank drags me backward, and the friction where my hands are gripping the edges of the belt cuts my fingers. I scream again, and a deep, feminine voice chuckles below me.

"Snooks! Help!" I yell, not knowing what exactly I expect him to do, only that it has to be him, because there's no one else.

Pattering feet are coming my way, and I call again, desperate now, because the hand has switched from yanking to a slow, playful drag, increasing in intensity until I'm being stretched like a rubber band. It goes slack suddenly, and I hold my breath, but it doesn't let go, and starts making sharp, rhythmic pulls accompanied by giggles. *It's playing with its food*, I think, feeling sick.

There's a shrill war cry, and Sugar leaps over my arm and rushes toward my feet. From the noises he's making, he's biting whatever's got me, but I'm having a hard time believing those baby teeth of his are going to do any good. Snooks is crouched by my face, and whatever he's saying, it sounds urgent.

". . . find something sharp, be right back, you stay put. Okay?"

Finally, my mind makes sense of his words, and I struggle to answer before he bounces off and vanishes.

"Snooks. Snooks! I have something sharp. I have a knife in my pocket. Get it!"

There's another yank that just about takes my leg off. I scream again, but the light at the end of this nightmare carnival ride is getting brighter. I can see the plastic strips that hang down across the entrance. I squeeze the belt despite the pain blossoming in my hands.

"Which pocket? This one?"

"No. Other side. Snooks, please hurry!"

The Oddity Bodkin slides from my pocket. "Ooh, shiny," says Snooks admiringly, then he's gone. A moment later, there's a bloodcurdling, gurgling scream, and the hand slides abruptly from my leg. I drag myself forward and turn to look over my shoulder. In the growing light, I see a big blue arm slide down the conveyor belt and off. Snooks leaps lightly from its wrist back up onto the belt, and stabs the hand once before it vanishes, for good measure. Sugar kicks it as it goes.

"Good! You go away and you like it! Your person is foul!" he shrieks.

Snooks cheers approval, brandishing the knife. The blood on it might be smoking a little bit. I take it back, wiping it on the conveyor belt, but keeping it out and ready. I pull my legs in to keep them as far from the edge as possible.

"You guys . . ." I wheeze a little as the plastic strips slide across my face and we roll out into the slanting evening sun. "You guys, thanks. Thank you."

Snooks shrugs. "I get the bathroom first," he says, and hops down onto the asphalt.

Figures.

Did Greeley see my face? I don't think so. First I was facing away from him. When I looked back, I had my hat pulled down. Then I remember a little wrinkle. A wrinkly little wrinkle.

"Hey, Sugar, remember that Dewey kid that was working up front? He knows who I am."

Sugar snickers. "You sure?"

I remember shoving my hair back out of my face and telling that little worm I'm my daddy's girl.

"Yeah, I'm really sure."

"Heeee's not," says Snooks in a cheery little singsong.

I frown, slithering down off the belt to crouch against the side of the building. I look Snooks in his wide, creepy little eyes.

"What did you do?"

"We asked if he remembered you, and he said yes. We

told him the answer was no, but he kept forgetting. So we jogged his memory."

"On the head! With a can of pineapple juice!" says Sugar, puffing up with pride.

Snooks nods. "We had to jog it a couple of times. But he remembers not to remember you now."

I have got to install a second lock on my bedroom door.

Snooks and Sugar head straight back into the store through the conveyor belt. I limp through the parking lot, car to car, and make my way across the street and behind Bodega Bodega. Cayden's there, but Xerple isn't. He must still be wreaking havoc with the zombie rabbits. I've never been so glad to see Cayden, but—

"Where's Raymond?" I ask.

"Here," he growls, ducking down behind me. He's got a cut on his forehead, and his hair's all wild. He takes a good look at me, pulls a tiny first aid kit from his backpack, and starts roughly doctoring my cut-up leg. I roll up my bloody, shredded pants as well as I can, and wince at the nasty cuts in my calf from the blue arm's fingernails.

"Did the cameras get us?" I ask, sweating from the deep sting of the disinfectant.

He scowls. "Not when I was done with them, they didn't. It'll be days until they find the mess I made so they can fix it." Woe to anyone who ever thinks Raymond is hired muscle and nothing more. He's the Swiss Army knife of friends. He's smart and he's tough.

And he's furious.

Chapter 19

Who's Fooling Who?

It's late in the day for visible heat waves, but I'm pretty sure I see them rising off Raymond. He watched the cameras before he sabotaged them, so he knows perfectly well what happened to me in the store.

We snuck to the outskirts of town as fast as we could go with me limping, but I'm seriously worried that we should have gone our separate ways and done everything in our power to look like we'd been home all afternoon. Instead, we skulk our way over a ridge and into the nearest sagebrush.

"Bets is going to kill me if I don't come home," I say.

Raymond scowls, and I can practically hear him saying *Greeley almost killed you.* If he says it out loud, I'm going to grab an ocotillo branch and beat him within an inch of his life. But all he says is, "Maybe she won't find out."

I bulge my eyes at him. "What are you talking about? In a few minutes, it's going to be pretty obvious."

"You can pull the sleepover trick," he says.

"Oh my gosh, Raymond, that's the oldest trick in the book! You know she'll check up on me, and your mom and Jefa won't lie to her."

Cayden looks scared to death to be out here, which goes to show he can get smarter if he tries, but he also looks like he has a plan. It's an interesting combination.

"I know Bets won't believe you're at Raymond's," he says, "but I bet she'd believe you were at my house. We haven't known each other long enough to get in much trouble together yet."

"You lit me on fire," says Raymond.

There's a brief silence.

"Cayden, my aunt is diabolically smart. She is going to call your parents."

Cayden pulls out his cell and checks the display. "Huh. Full bars." I assume he means real ones, not heinous snacks. He frowns for a second then shakes his head a little and dials. I can hear his mother's ridiculously happy greeting from here.

"Hey, Mom. No, we're out for a walk. I won't get dehydrated. Yes, I brought Signal Boost. Red. Hey, I wanted to tell you that Raymond and Ada and I are going to be down in the basement until really late. We downloaded a new Minecraft modpack, and we're going to have a marathon. Yeah, hopefully . . . the Wi-Fi was working yesterday, but not this morning. That's okay, Mom. I know you guys are trying. Listen, I promise we'll be quiet. Is it okay if they stay over? Okay. Cool. But don't come down or anything, please? It's embarrassing. Okay. Okay." He looks at us, cups his hand, and mutters, "I love you, too. Bye."

"Cayden, this doesn't solve our problem at all. She's never going to keep that promise. She'll be down there every five minutes, offering us Full Bars."

He shifts around, opening and closing his mouth several times. Finally, he says, "Look, I don't know what's in Signal Boost, but my mom and dad have started literally collapsing in the middle of whatever they're doing at eight thirty every night. I had to lie and tell them they've always gone to bed at eight, because one night my dad was walking around when he passed out, and he fell down the stairs. I'm seriously ready to buy them crash helmets. Get your aunt to call them before eight, and we're in the clear until morning. That leaves plenty of time to figure out how to handle this."

My aunt is no fool. This is going to take some doing. I pull out my own phone. Figures I'd have less bars than Cayden. Freaking Splint.

"Hey, Aunt Bets?"

"Where are you, young lady?" Uh-oh. I think fast.

"I'm over at, um, Eunice's place."

"Oh." Aunt Bets sounds surprised. Jackpot. "That's nice. You and Eunice used to be such good friends. Is her mother home?"

"No, just her invisible dad." Parents never want to come right out and call Eunice a liar about that.

"Well . . . that's nice of you, to spend some time with her."
I can tell Aunt Bets is picturing me carefully pretending
Eunice's dad exists all afternoon.

"Yeah, well. She really likes Cayden." I figure I'm skating
a fine line here. If I sound too nice and helpful, it will make
Aunt Bets suspicious. Cayden's raising his eyebrows at me,
but I just shrug. Aunt Bets is snickering, which is an amazingly good sign.

"Well, he's a nice boy. Nice-looking, too."

"Bets! Stop that!" I mean it.

"Hey, you can't say you haven't noticed. That boy's got
style like this town hasn't seen before."

"RaymondandIarestayingovertheretonightifthat'sokaybe-
causeit'sokaywithhisparents."

"I'm sorry, what? You find Cayden adorable?"

"NO I DO NOT. We. Are staying. Over. There. Tonight."

"With Eunice?"

"No, not with Eunice. Her invisible dad said no."

"All right. I'll check in with Cayden's folks. . . ." She pauses
threateningly, to see if I'll cave, but getting around her has
helped me make guile an art form.

"Okay, cool," I say. "Don't bother bringing snacks over.
They're really into these Full Bars they get from Greeley's,
and they're all excited to share them."

Aunt Bets gnars into the phone, just a bit. I grumble back
at her, because I really do share her contempt for people who
don't know the difference between factory food and fresh
baked.

"Well, I guess it'll just be your daddy and Mason tonight."

I'm surprised. "Why? Where will you be?"

"Oh, Badri had some ideas about increasing efficiency at the bakery. I figured I'd hear him out."

As I hang up, I wonder, *Who is fooling who, here?*

We reach the area where we planned to meet if we got separated. It's far enough away from town that we won't be easily found, and scrubby enough to give us plenty of places to hide if we need to. I whip off my trashed-out baggy brown shirt and pants, revealing the light blue tee and black bike shorts I had on underneath. Thankfully, my locket's still safely around my neck.

I hide my dad's gear under a tan canvas tarp I stashed out here ahead of time. I kick up sand around the edges to make it blend in, and weigh it down with a few rocks. I'll be back for it later. Hopefully.

I pick a different spot to cache our brown clothes and ball caps. My Nopes post about Greeley's is going to explode some heads, and if any of the Nopesers want verification, I can send them here.

Raymond gets his uniform caught on a chia bush as he's bringing it to me. He yanks it free with a growl, and I hear something rip. He pitches the bundle to me, hard. I chalk it up to stress and hide his stuff, but when we circle half the town and he's still growling like an aggravated honey badger, I get fed up.

"If you need to talk about your *feelings*, Raymond, you should just ask me," I say.

"And you'll what? LISTEN?" he says, so loudly his voice squeaks on the last word. That shocks me. I've been cackling madly every time the boys' voices crack, and it makes them cranky. They control their voices around me as much as possible.

I say, "I know things didn't go quite like we expected—"

"Do you even hear yourself right now?" he says. "Like we expected? Ada, we're both bloody. We could have been caught and taken home by the cops—and Greeley attacked you!"

"You're making it sound worse than it was," I say. "It was a great sneak. We planned it just right."

Cayden actually grins a bit when I say that, until he catches Raymond shooting him a dirty look. Cayden's feeling the adrenaline this time, I can tell. He's finally starting to get why we pull shenanigans.

Raymond doesn't even slow down.

"If we'd planned it just right, no one would have gotten hurt. What were we thinking, doing something so dangerous?"

That seems unfair. "We couldn't have known it would be like that."

"Then we stink at intel."

When he says we, I hear you. We all remember whose idea this was, right? I can feel my nostrils flaring, and I know it probably looks ridiculous. "If that's how you really feel, Ray-mun-do, then maybe you should take another way home."

He scowls at me in total disbelief. "You know what? Fine." Then, even though he's got the whole darn desert to walk in, he pushes past me on his way back toward town.

"I can't believe him!" I say loudly, in the direction of his departing back. "This ought to be our biggest moment. The best sneak ever."

"Yeah," begins Cayden slowly, like maybe he only partly agrees, and I shoot him a glare to make sure he understands that I don't actually need him to participate in this conversation. He clamps his mouth shut like a smart neighbor boy.

A tumblegeek rolls out of the brush. I glare, and it rolls the other way. I feel like I'm getting some excellent training in being scary today.

Except I'm not so tough, am I? The truth is, there's a creepy Whanslaw-headed door in Greeley's freezer, and I was too chicken to try and open it.

Instead, I found out that prying into the Sweepstakes might actually get a person killed. And now Raymond is being totally holier than cow. You know how cows are sacred in India? Yeah, he thinks he's better than them. Logic dictates that I should do the opposite of what he would do. So I'm in the right, right?

Right.

Except that I'm also freaked out. I don't understand why anyone would hurt me for trying to find out more about something that's happy and great. And now I'm on the PC's radar, even if by radar I mean Dewey, who is likely having technical problems right now. I picture a rainbow spinny wheel over his head.

Cayden's not beside me anymore. I turn to find he's climbed a boulder to look around, making a perfect target of himself. I'm trying to decide whether to tell him to get down from there when he stiffens, and squints into the distance.

"Hey, Ada?" he says.

"What?" I ask, dragging the word out.

He points.

I can't see a thing from down here. I climb up next to him, staying quite a bit lower than he is, leading by example. When I spot what he's talking about, I'm impressed he saw it. The sun's almost down. Not a good time to spot anything, especially . . . I groan.

The Blurmonster. That thing is like a bad penny lately: turning up everywhere. Then I notice the sweaty boy smell to my left.

"Doggone it, Cayden!" I hiss. "Are you wearing BASH!?"

He winces. "I forgot."

The Blurmonster emits a purring growl.

Chapter 20

Hide-and-Shack

Cayden's BASH! addiction is an increasing problem, but at the moment I'm more worried about where to hide until the Blurmonster moves on. Which is why I'm hunting for the base the older kids used to use when they played hide-and-shack, back when the Blurmonster wasn't coming this close to town.

"Hide-and-shack? Why do they call it that?" asks Cayden.

I'm prowling around a clearing trying not to look directly at anything. Between that and trying to hide from an invisible monster, my peripheral vision is really messed up right now, so his question makes me trip, which makes my leg holler at me (figuratively speaking) to let me know it's about done for the day, thanks.

"They call it that because base is super hard to find," I say.

He peers over his shoulder into the gloaming, which is the word I prefer to use when the gloom is looming.

"It just figures that in Oddity you'd have to go looking for base, instead of whoever's 'it' looking for you," he says.

"Being base is a dull job. Our base got bored, and innovated."

Cayden looks distinctly nervous.

"So . . . your base is alive?"

I'm not actually sure how to answer that.

"Um . . . alive is relative, I guess."

I still don't see the darn thing. I try not to look like I'm looking, which fails miserably.

"You can't find it, can you? We're going to get eaten." Even in the shadows, I can tell his face is red. I hope the BASH! makes him taste horrible.

"It has to be around here somewhere!" I say. The brush crackles maybe thirty cubits behind us, and I feel an unpleasant new emotion. I think it might be desperation.

Cayden fists his hands like he's going to freak out at me, but instead he does something I should have thought of first. He yells, "Olly olly oxen free!"

The twilight shadows seem to shake themselves, like a wet dog in slo-mo on TV. And then there's a shack in the clearing, where a minute ago there wasn't. Behind us, the crackling heads our way.

We leap for the door. I remember just in time to shut it

quietly. With luck, the Blurmonster wasn't close enough to see where we went.

"How long do you think we've been in here?" Cayden asks, after what feels like forever.

"I don't know. It's pretty dark." I didn't think to check the time when I called Bets, and now that it's all the way dark outside I don't want the light from the phone to show through the windows. If the shack's still visible, that is. Possibly a passerby would see only an empty clearing.

"Maybe one of us should look out the window," he begins, but trails off as he realizes how hard it will be to spot the Blurmonster in the dark.

I should tell him not to talk, but the quiet is weighing on me. My hurt leg starts to cramp, and I shift, my sneakers scraping on the gritty wooden floor.

"Ada?" he asks, and why are all these boys having feelings today? I start to tell him that this is not called the Sharing Shack, but the next thing he says totally throws me.

"Tell me about what happened to Pearl."

I stare through the dark in his general direction.

"You know what happened to her. She won the Sweepstakes."

He's quiet for a second, in a way I don't totally understand. Not like I successfully shut him down, but like he's handling me. I don't like it.

Finally, he says, "I know about winning the Sweepstakes,

but I've never actually been there for Sweepstakes Day. What's that like?"

Maybe he's just embarrassed that he has to ask. He's literally the only person in town who doesn't know.

"It's the best day of the year. My daddy saves up for months so we can eat at as many food trucks as we want."

"I love carnival food," he says. "Funnel cakes and lemon shake-ups."

What the actual frack?

"No, Cayden. *Good* stuff. Cactus candy, and Elvis-on-a-stick. And the squid-chinned aliens make epic barbecue."

He doesn't answer me. I notice he does that sometimes, when he decides he's had it with whatever I'm saying.

We sit in silence for a minute, and I'm surprised by what I say next. It's not something I want to admit.

"You were right, you know. It doesn't make any sense."

"What doesn't?"

"The way the adults have been running from us."

"What do they do the day of the Sweepstakes? Show up and look happy?"

I consider. "Basically, yeah." I say, "I always assumed they really meant it, because the puppets are very insistent about that."

"They insist that you mean it."

"Naturally."

There's a pause. I take comfort in the nothing I hear outside.

"That was what I noticed most, when Pearl won. All the

grown-ups, all MY grown-ups, kept saying how happy they were for her. Over and over. You ever notice how if you repeat something enough times, it stops meaning anything? But they wouldn't stop. They kept on saying it, with smiles so stiff that *everyone* looked like puppets, until I wanted to smash things, until I was lying in bed with 'I'm happy for her' running through my head like some kind of ritual chant. So I climbed out my window to get away from it, and ran off, and—" I'm not about to tell him I was crying. "It was really dark, and before I knew what I was doing, I was in the park."

Cayden hisses. I look at him, already nodding. "Yep. Spiders."

"You're lucky you didn't get eaten." The very first time we had to school Cayden, the day he moved in, he was headed for the park with a soccer ball. I know he's picturing the same thing I am: dark, malicious orblike forms slowly lowering themselves from the branches above, the moonlight glittering on their outspread legs. . . .

"I felt something sticky on my cheek, and then it started to burn. By the time I finally clued in, spiders were suspended around me everywhere I looked. I tried to follow standard spider attack rules—"

"Shut up and grab a stick," murmurs Cayden.

"—but by that point, I was so scared and confused that I snapped. Oh, I grabbed a stick all right, a big one, and I was swinging away and hitting spiders like they were piñatas, but I was screaming cuss words at the top of my lungs the whole time. It should have gotten me killed, but it saved my life instead. My dad came charging through the darkness, swinging a bat, and the next thing I knew, he had me stuffed under his arm like a football and was running the other way."

Cayden says, "I bet Bets grounded you for a month."

I shake my head.

"That's the whole problem, isn't it? My family acts like things are all business as usual. But no one ever said another word to me about that little stunt, when they should have put me on restriction for life. And my mama's a mess. And—"

I sit there as my worst fears come bubbling up like the aftereffects of Anti-Ven-Om Nom Noms, even though Old Joe's been sold out for months.

I glance at my quiet neighbor boy. "You always thought it was strange, but I didn't listen. I mean, you think everything here is strange, so sometimes I don't take you seriously. But the grown-ups, they aren't just playing around with us. They're really scared of winning. I never knew that before. Now it turns out the puppets are liars, and kind of bullies, too, and kids never used to win, but Pearl won. Greeley . . . he was trying to *kill* me, and—Cayden, if the Sweepstakes is bad, then *what happened to my sister?*"

"We'll find out."

I know he's pretending to feel brave when he says it.

It still helps.

Chapter 21

Night, Gunnar

It's pitch-black outside when we finally decide the coast is clear. By the time we get home, I'm limping pretty bad. We circle our block, in case Dewey forgot not to remember me after all, but nothing seems out of the ordinary at either of our houses. We should probably talk, but I'm so tired I can barely think. All I want is to cry myself to sleep in my own bed.

"I'm going to tell them we decided not to sleep over after all," I say, and Cayden nods wearily. I wave good-bye, but he's already disappearing through his front door.

I can just make out a little cluster of screaming aliens over on one side of the field, the field being our side yard. I shake my head over them as I head inside in search of a snack. I'm not about to get involved. They've been known to riot like soccer fans. Once they even set the Hollowells' car on fire. As I put my hand on the front doorknob, though, someone squalls piteously, and I recognize the voice.

It's Xerple.

"But I did not know it was a rule infraction!" he pleads, and I draw closer to listen in spite of myself, grabbing a rake that Mason should not have left outside because it could very easily get used on one of us. I've armed myself without having to go to the garage, though, so I guess he gets a pass this time.

"You did not KNOW? The ugly bunnies are our mortal enemies!" This comes from an alien who is almost entirely head. It's round, and orange, and its arms and legs appear to be wearing a suit and fancy shoes. When it shouts, its whole mouth blows open like when we flap a parachute in gym class after using it to practice emergency skydiving.

"I was not helping the bunnies, I was helping Cayden!" wails Xerple.

"Ahhhh," burbles a squishy pink alien, who has a permanent frown and some kind of brain coral growing out of its head. "But the Cayden helps the bunnies, doesn't he? He and the landlady have been resupplying the bunnies since the punkball game began."

I'm a landlady, huh? I guess I am the human they see most often. If I'm the voice of authority, maybe I can help Xerple out.

"Uh, fellas? The marshmallows are part of a previous agreement. They don't have anything to do with punkball."

Three little faces look up at me, two glaring, one cringing.

"We live here, too," gargles the squishy alien. "You do not give us marshmallows."

I frown. "Do you eat them?"

Its mouth opens and closes several times in outrage. "No!" it says at last. "But it's rude not to offer."

Long on mouth, short on logic.

"Look, Xerple helped because he owed us one. We helped him out when he was, um, up a flagpole." Xerple is bobbing agitatedly behind the other two aliens, shaking his head frantically. Too late.

"Whaaat?" shrieks Bigmouth, its lips and cheeks billowing out to expose its choppers. "The flagpole is a solitary ritual! No one is supposed to have help!"

It turns to Xerple, who rushes around to hide behind my legs.

The orange and pink aliens look at one another and nod grimly. Then they turn to Xerple. As one, they begin to chant.

"Your person is foul. Your person is foul. Your PERSON is FOUL!"

Other aliens race over, taking up the cry. "Your person is foul! Your person is foul!"

Before I know it, there's a ring of gleefully furious aliens around me and Xerple, who is sobbing, "Not a person foul! Please!"

The light dawns. "A . . . do you mean a *personal foul*? Like in basketball?" I almost laugh. It's just like them to get something like that wrong. Then my smile vanishes in a hurry.

Their punishments are really awful. Xerple's more likely to get killed than benched. And we're surrounded.

A door clacks from across the yard. "Cayden!" I holler. "Cayden!" I brandish my rake at the tiny, vicious mob. "Respect your landlady!" I holler.

A gray alien with teeth like tusks and ears like jump rope handles attacks Xerple, who puts his back to my leg and fights him off, enormous choppers clacking.

"Cayden!" I yell again. I smack the gray alien with the back of the rake, and it leaps into the surrounding mob.

Finally, that neighbor boy of mine gets here. He sweeps through the crowd, literally. Like, with a broom. I rush through the gap, heading for Cayden's house. A despairing bleat behind me alerts me that the aliens have already closed the gap. They're not concerned with me. They only want Xerple. I turn to go back, but Cayden's already there, wading right into the middle of the mess. He uses the broom to shove back the aliens, then reaches down to grab Xerple around the neck. Xerple's snapping at anything that moves their way, but a couple of the aliens jump to hang from Cayden's legs. Bigmouth even bites him, like Xerple was doing to the flagpole when we met him. Cayden hollers with pain, and I whack that nasty little orange booger into next week with my rake. From the bushes, the zombie rabbits cheer.

"Some help you are!" I mutter, but I can't really blame them. They already did me one big favor this week.

We back away from the advancing horde, brandishing our weapons, until I about trip over Cayden's back porch steps.

Before we can get inside, Bigmouth pushes its way through the crowd, returning from wherever I knocked it to.

"You can't take him!" it roars at me, mouth flapping.

"Why? What were you going to do with him?"

It squares its nonexistent shoulders. "We were going to send him away. FOREVER!"

All the little aliens cheer.

O . . . kay.

"You," I say, "have done an amazing job. You have sent him all the way over here, to Cayden's house. He is hereby banished from that property." I point at our yard.

"Says who?" asks Jump-Rope Ears.

"Says me! THE LANDLADY!" The crowd goes wild. Vengeance. Even sweeter than marshmallows.

We lock the kitchen door behind us, just the same.

Xerple won't eat the Full Bars. He won't drink Signal Boost, either. He takes one sniff and snarls.

"Nasty medicine. I not need." He shoves it away with one foot. Cayden and I frown at each other over his head. Medicine?

"Suit yourself." Cayden takes it with a shrug and raises the bottle to his lips, pretending to drink.

"No!" Xerple jumps at him, Chuck Norris–kicking the Signal Boost from Cayden's hands and sending it spinning across the kitchen, spraying red Signal Boost everywhere. "You don't need medicine, either. Is nasty!"

"It's not medicine, Xerple," Cayden says. "I mean, I'm not saying it's real food. But it's really okay. It won't hurt me."

"Won't help, either," says Xerple. "You forget."

"I forget what?"

"Things. Worries. You drink that, you have very good day because you forget there is any such thing as a bad day, until BAM! Bad day to the face! Then you go down like a Floost ship in the Gammar Wars."

"Um." Floost ships are the Samsung Galaxies of alien invasion ships, but they were decommissioned way before the Gammar Wars according to Mr. Mitchell, who replaced Mr. Bishop. But I am so not getting into that with Xerple.

"Bottom line, you no drink it. Just no. Take it for me. Is nasty."

"Xerple, you're exaggerating. My parents drink this all the time."

There's a thump as Cayden's mom runs into the door frame on her way into the kitchen. "How long has that been there?" she asks in confusion. She rubs her forehead. "Just came down for more Signal Boost. Daddy and I are stocking a mini fridge by our bed, in case we get thirsty between our bedtime Boost and our wake-up Boost." She has to mess with the fridge for a minute before she figures out how to open it. Xerple makes a fake surprised face at Cayden, which mostly involves opening his mouth very wide while craning his whole head to one side in fake shock.

Cayden's mom pats him on the head as she comes back by. "Hey, get the dog off the table, okay? And take him out before you turn your light off. Give him some Signal Boost in his bowl. Good night, Gunnar."

"Mom, Uncle Gunnar's in Latvia."

"Right. Night, Gunnar." She turns off the light on her way out, plunging us all into darkness. I whack my hip on a chair going to turn it back on.

"Okay, that was kind of weird," I say.

Xerple is bobbing on all four legs like he's about to do a polka. "So, now you see," he says, in rhythm with his bobbing. "The drink is bad. It is nasty. It make you sad."

"She's not sad," says Cayden. "She doesn't seem to feel much of anything."

He stops bobbing. "Sad like pathetic, not sad like crying," he explains. "You see how sad she was? I not dog. I not even a mammal. Her nomenclature all irrational."

"My parents *have* been acting really strange lately." He hefts a bottle of Signal Boost in one hand. "Do you think someone's drugging these things?"

"I guess it's possible," I say. "Maybe they just really like it, though."

"Okay," says Cayden, "but DOG? D-O-G? When we first got here, they thought the local news was an elaborate hoax. When there were aliens in the alley, they said some of the armadillos looked kind of inbred. Now they don't think anything is unusual, ever."

I shrug. "It's like that for all the newbies. First they freak out, then they adapt."

Cayden rolls his eyes. "You do not get it, okay? My parents

used to make a big deal about living in a good school district. They bought charity coupon books. They shopped Black Friday sales after Thanksgiving."

"They went out on Black Friday? Everyone is supposed to huddle in their basements contemplating their own mortality and being quiet so the crawling chaos won't hear them."

"No. They are supposed to buy flat-screen TVs and polar fleece pullovers. I'm supposed to learn about Lewis and Clark, not the body snatchers who returned to Washington in their stead to spread misinformation. We are supposed to have our pizza delivered in thirty minutes, not have thirty minutes to find it before it self-destructs—"

"I thought you enjoyed that—"

"When we talk about politicians being dummies, that's supposed to be a METAPHOR. It is very suspicious that my parents don't think anything is wrong."

"Maybe they just like Oddity."

"Right. And our new dog."

Xerple is yawning, and his top lip wraps all the way backward over his head. When his mouth finally shuts, he glances around, spots a bag of coffee beans on the counter, jumps over there, and enthusiastically tips the contents of the bag into his gaping maw. "Mmmmm," he says, crunching away.

Cayden rubs his forehead. "I have to memorize twenty spelling words of ancient Sumerian origin by Monday morning," he says with a groan. "Why am I even talking about this?"

As he drifts away muttering, our conversation in the shack

replays in my head. He promised me we'd find out what happened to Pearl, but neither of us agreed on how, or how soon. I've wasted so much time already. I have to figure this out now.

If only I could make sense of the door in the freezer. Part of me has been worrying away at the problem for hours. I was all the way at the back of Greeley's, so I don't see how there could be any more store behind the creepy puppet door. I also can't imagine how I'm going to get back in there to find out. My eyes start to water.

Cayden returns with a broom and dustpan to clean up the coffee-bean bits Xerple left all over the floor. I wipe my cheeks in a hurry while he's occupied, and look up at the ceiling to coax the rest of the tears back into my eyes where they belong.

That's when it finally clicks. It's like Cayden's house vanishes, and all I can see is Greeley's. More important, I can see what's behind Greeley's. Havasu Hill.

I turn to Cayden.

"Study over the weekend. Right now, you need to come with me."

"I already hate this idea," says Cayden. "Where are we hypothetically going?"

"To spy on Mr. Whanslaw."

"I'm sorry, did you say you were planning to go get murdered by Mr. Whanslaw?"

He follows me out the back door anyway, locking it behind him while Xerple runs in circles around his feet. The aliens have dispersed, but as we start across the yard toward the street, a rectangle of light appears ahead of us, on my front walk.

"Shhhh!" I whisper, and pull Cayden against the side of his house. An enormous shadow swallows the patch of light, then I hear the front door click shut. A minute later, the dome light in Daddy's truck comes on as he gets in. His taillights kick on. I watch their red glow travel down our street. He turns, and they vanish as he pulls through the middle of town, then reappear as the truck begins to climb up Havasu Hill.

"Well," I huff, stepping out onto the grass, "that does not look like working late to me." I think of all the hemming and hawing Daddy and Aunt Bets have been doing, and shake my head. This stops now.

They ought to know better than to think they can keep secrets from a Roundtree girl.

Chapter 22

Spang in the Middle of It

Daddy doesn't go all the way up Havasu Hill. And when you're only halfway up, you're neither up nor down—you're at Oddity Middle School.

There are a lot of cars in the lot for this time of night, but it looks like whatever's going on has already started, because everyone's inside by the time we get there, and the front doors are locked.

Not a big deal. We all know how to break in, in case we're ever outflanked and ousted from our own school—which will never happen, obviously, but it's good knowledge to have all the same. There are rotating security systems inside to keep us from sneaking in to pull pranks on the weekends, or so we're told. I don't believe it, any more than I believed Mama and Daddy when they claimed they armed a laser security grid in the stairwell on Christmas Eve to keep us from capturing Santa.

Anyway, any countermeasures would be turned off right now.

We find the right exterior vent cover, the one that's solid and fake, instead of a complicated double-baffle meant to let air in and keep small invaders out. We still have to crawl through air vents, though.

By the time we let ourselves down on a science lab table, we're cobwebby and cross, but to my surprise, Cayden's only puffing a little bit.

"Those safety drills are paying off, Chicago boy!" I say.

He smiles behind that swingy hair.

Voices, amplified by microphones, echo down the empty hallways with their well-buffed floors. They lead us to the cafeteria. We hug the doorway, peering in.

The scorched curtains have all been removed from the stage, though I still detect the twinkle of fire-suppressing powder here and there when I look closely. There are rows of chairs set up on the cafeteria floor with an aisle down the middle. On the stage, at a row of folding tables, sit the members of the WUT, and at their center, presiding over the meeting, is Greeley.

You'd never know he'd been bellowing at me mere hours earlier. He's as groomed as ever in his turned-up white shirtsleeves. His iron-gray hair gleams under the stage lights. His voice is grandpa-kind as he addresses the big man standing at a microphone in the aisle—my daddy.

"Sir," Daddy says, "I don't question my need to serve

this community, and show my gratitude to the Protection Committee. But adults make an informed choice to participate in the Sweepstakes. My Pearl—"

I gasp to hear Daddy say her name out loud.

"—is a child. Even if she signed her name like you say, her mother and I did not give her permission, and she couldn't give informed consent to something like this."

Greeley holds up a calming hand. "I assure you, the young lady was quite excited to be chosen."

My daddy rubs a hand over his shaved head, a sure sign he's trying to keep his temper. "But there's just no way a child can be as useful. . . ."

Useful for what?

"The puppets know their needs. Their reasons are not for you to fathom."

"They are for me to fathom when they involve my child!"

Greeley leans forward, smiling that big, toothy smile of his.

"I suggest you think carefully about that statement. Why, every last person in this town exists at the whim of the Protection Committee. You are alive because of their careful stewardship. So you see, in a larger sense, your daughter is not yours at all. She is part of the Protection Committee's flock."

A week ago, when he said *flock* I'd have thought of the puppets as shepherds.

Now I'm thinking wolves.

Cayden is pulling on my arm. I start to shake him off, and he points. An elderly couple is working their way up the side of the gym toward us, casting worried looks over their shoulders at my daddy. Other people are rustling in their seats as well. No one is used to anyone questioning the Protection Committee. If we don't get out of here, we're going to be seen. We ghost our way back down the hall and around the corner; then I have an idea, and freeze.

Cayden looks back at me. "What?"

"Wait here. I need to get something." I reach for the handle of the door to my left, which leads backstage.

To his credit, he doesn't look surprised, only resigned. When I ease open the door, he takes the handle and motions me to go. Clever boy. Since I don't have to baby the door shut and keep the latch from clicking, I'm up the short flight of steps and back in a twinkling.

All I saw of Greeley was the brim of his hat, but my hands are shaking. I press the brown grocery bag full of masks close to me to keep it from rattling, while Cayden shuts the door and slowly lets the latch button rise.

In no time, we're back in the lab. I boost Cayden into the vent and hand the bag up. Then Cayden pulls me up after him. As I army crawl through the ducts, pushing the bag ahead of me, I think about Daddy. I sold him short. He's trying. It's not his fault the grown-up way's not working.

My turn.

What's on top of Havasu Hill? A mansion. What's in the mansion? A bunch of puppets I used to think were heroes. Really, there are only four of them, but four is enough, when they're so creepy.

"But everything here is creepy," whispers Cayden, as we prowl closer to our destination.

"What on earth do kids *do* where you're from?" I whisper back. "I still just . . . I don't even. If you're not foiling evil plots, what do you do all day?"

"I don't know. Watch TV. Play video games. Play a little ball outside. Go to the mall."

"Do the mannequins ever try to take over the mall?"

He sighs, the way I used to when he couldn't fend off leopards by himself. "No. We buy hot pretzels with cheese sauce instead of curdish substance for Humans Class B. And we shop at Hot Topic, not Sanctioned Slogans."

"I'm sure it's great," I say. I can't wait to level up to Human Class A. They don't give those curdish substance. They think Class B violence is partly caused by lactose intolerance.

"What are you expecting to find at Whanslaw's, anyway?"

I look up at the big Gothic wooden house that overlooks Greeley's. The one we're moving toward, when people with sense would be moving away. "I don't know. But if there's a tunnel behind that door, and it goes somewhere important, doesn't it make sense that it would lead here?"

Cayden frowns. "Why, because it has Whanslaw's face on it? Are you even sure that's what it was? You said it was dark in the freezer."

"Believe me, if it happened to you, you'd know," I say.

"Besides, it makes sense. Whanslaw's the puppet in charge."
Somehow, calling him the head puppet sounds confusing.

"Is he?" Cayden asks. "It always seemed to me like they're all equal. He doesn't have any special title or anything."

"I know. But they all listen to him. The way I've always heard it, the first two to take up with the original Greeley were him and Lanchester. And Lanchester definitely does what Whanslaw says. I've heard stories that Maggie and Kiyo weren't even puppets, not at first—Whanslaw made them."

"Made them . . . like he made people into puppets?"

"Or put their souls in puppet bodies. I guess it doesn't make much difference, does it?"

Cayden stops walking.

"Cayden. He's not going to put you in a puppet body. He only does that for his friends. You, he'll kill."

"You need to work on your social interactions, Ada. You are the opposite of reassuring."

We're close to his fence now, and should really be quiet. "I'm not trying to be reassuring. I'm trying to keep you on your toes."

The puppets have the weirdest yard in Oddity. Spang in the middle of a square patch of sandy desert is a picket fence, and inside that is a manicured garden, complete with those bushes pruned into animal shapes, and a lush, emerald-green lawn. They even have IVY. Not the plastic kind old ladies put in pots so it looks like they garden. The real stuff. Sitting in the middle of the Garden of Eden like that, the dark gray house is even more stark. Of course, even the parts where the paint still sticks are gray. Gray house, gray wood, gray everything. But the lights are on. I see Whanslaw's creepy puppet head bob past one of the lit windows at a slow, measured pace. A blink later, his puppeteer moves past, working the strings.

This house has always loomed in my imagination. After Pearl won the Sweepstakes, I even had a dream in which the front door was a mouth, opening and closing, saying something, though I didn't know what. Then the door started getting closer, and closer. . . .

Now I have to think about how to get *inside*, and my stomach is shaking like it's trying to jump right out of me. Stalling for time, I work my way around the side of the yard. I figure there won't be another gate, and we'll have to get creative about hopping the fence, or else go back around front. But there is a gate, leading away from town, out into nowhere. There are visible drag marks from Whanslaw's robes, heading off into the desert, and that creeps me out more than anything I've seen so far.

The grass begins right at the gate in an abrupt, perfect line. There's no wear from feet passing back and forth, no withering along the edge. It's as richly green as sod someone laid yesterday. It has to be fake. Cayden reaches down to touch it, and for a second I reach to stop him, almost believing that alarms will sound and spotlights will glare the second his fingers make contact. But he picks a few blades and brings them up to eye level, and I smell their sharp tang at once. They are unmistakably the real thing.

This makes me not one bit less nervous when I step onto the puppets' lawn. Explosive mines. Angry and embittered moles. Attack dogs. These are just some of the things potentially awaiting us in the fabulous world of Evil Puppet Garden.

"That should really be a band name," Cayden mutters. I must have said it out loud.

It's more like walking across a carpet than a lawn. . . . An impossibly thick, plushy carpet. It's beautiful, but also unnatural, like a museum exhibit of a house and yard. I get the feeling that in daylight, I wouldn't see any living things within this fence. No birds, no armaduinos. No anything.

In the center of the yard, there's a gazebo, which is almost the strangest thing of all. Nothing stays that white in the New Mexico sun. It's surrounded by little arrangements of weeping trees and fountains of roses, so we're seriously, dangerously close before we have a clue there's someone in the gazebo. Several someones. We drop to the ground behind a bush shaped like a horse as a harsh, familiar female voice begins to speak.

"I don't know why we're giving him time to foment rebellion, when we could arrest him now. For all we know, he could be one of these Nopes people." It's Kiyo. Now that I know to look, I see her painted face wagging, and her puppeteer standing behind her in a dark suit, like a Secret Service agent. The more suspicious I get of the puppets, the more curious I get about the puppeteers. I look hard at this one, and she doesn't seem as blurry as usual. Then again, it's dark out here.

The voice that answers Kiyo has a sort of glub to it, so it must be Lanchester, the fish-headed puppet. "Not time to plot. Time to think. He still has one child left, you know. What will happen to her if he makes a nuisance of himself?" Lanchester's latest puppeteer has a pinched little mouth. It surprises me. You know how they say people look like their dogs? Lanchester's puppeteer should have a mouth that bisects his face. I stare at that one, too. It almost looks familiar. . . .

"Likely his little speech tonight was the end of the matter," says Lanchester. "Either way, scared is good."

"It's never the end of the matter with these people," says Kiyo. "They're like devious children."

Lanchester makes a glubbing noise that causes the braids on my head to prickle up like a chia blossom. He's laughing. "As if all the town's children aren't devious. Whanslaw said one of them was openly insolent during that last school visit."

Kiyo makes a rude noise. "Well, that's certainly not my fault! If you recall, I wanted to change the schools to manufacturing facilities running twelve-hour shifts. But no, you and Whanslaw wanted to take advantage of their potential as paramilitary training and indoctrination centers."

"The children were quite useful during the last armed invasion," says Lanchester.

"As if children strong enough to run an industrial loom wouldn't be able to wield weapons effectively," she snorts. "As it is, you've taught them skills they can use against us as well as anybody. Soon they'll be revolting. More than usual,

I mean. I already found them revolting." She snickers, her wooden chin wagging up and down.

Beside me, Cayden shudders.

"Ah, well, it's not our way to waste a resource," says Lanchester. "Today's rebels may be tomorrow's lackeys. At any rate, if we're not going to have anyone yanked from their beds tonight, we might as well get some rest ourselves."

Puppets sleep?

They sway down the steps of the gazebo, puppeteers behind them, and make for the house. We hide in the shadows until the back door closes.

"Who on earth were they talking about?" I ask.

Cayden shifts beside me. "I've got a guess, and you're not going to like it," he says.

I look at him.

"I think they were talking about your dad."

He's right. I don't like it.

The whole point of being a Nopeser in the first place was to be one step ahead of everyone else, and instead I'm running to keep up. All my dad accomplished tonight was to antagonize the puppets, and they're monitoring Nopes, too? The rude kid at school must be me. At this rate, our family's going to be on some kind of most-wanted list. So do I go for it, and rebel like Kiyo expects? Or do I shut down our sneaks and try to distract my daddy until this all blows over?

I stare up at the house and think of all kinds of creepy things that probably aren't true. Security systems made of puppet strings, all connected back to Whanslaw. The odds of being turned into a puppet myself. I need a look inside before I commit to one path or the other.

"Stay here," I say.

Cayden groans a little. "What are you going to do?"

"I'm going to get up on the porch roof and see what I can see."

"Ada, wait a second—"

I grab a mask from the bag, pull it down over my face, and sprint for the house before I can talk myself out of it, ignoring the stinging, stretching pain in my leg. The last bit of lawn I have to cross is totally exposed, and I hold my breath, waiting for floodlights to switch on and an alarm to blatt, but nothing happens. I make for a trellis, and scale it as quickly as I can without shaking it like a leaf.

The porch roof is steep, but not too steep for me to manage. I stay low, and creep up the roof to the nearest window. I keep as close to the corner of the window as possible, and slowly ease my masked face up until I can see inside, though my heart is stuttering.

The first thing I see is glassy puppet eyes.

I duck just as Whanslaw turns his head fully toward me. I press myself against the wall beneath the sill, trying to make myself tiny, trying to stop shaking. I can hear the clack and sway as Whanslaw approaches the window.

The noise stops. He's looking out. I'm sure of it. First I'm terrified he'll open the window, reach down, and grab me with hard wooden hands. Then I remember my friend waiting down in the garden. Please let Cayden be well hidden.

I wait for so long that my legs fall asleep. So long that I wonder if that's where Whanslaw stays all night, at the window, looking out. Maybe they station themselves like that, one puppet at each window. It would explain how they always seem to know everything.

If it's true, we're sunk.

Finally, finally, I hear the clack and thump of Whanslaw moving away. I should leave, right now. Instead, I slowly, slowly raise my head and peek over the sill.

I watch as Whanslaw and his puppeteer amble over to an enormous wardrobe on the far side of the room. Whanslaw opens it and, turning, the puppeteer backs inside, and hangs Whanslaw up in front of him like a suit. I stay as low as I can, to avoid Whanslaw's gaze. The puppeteer reaches out with both hands, grasps the edges of the wardrobe doors, and pulls them shut.

I almost fall.

I recognize Whanslaw's puppeteer.

It's Sparky, our old mailman. He was our nemesis for years. Every time I saw him he was either smoking like a chimney or had smoke coming out of his ears. Then again, we did keep putting explosives in the mailbox.

He was a Sweepstakes winner last year, like Pearl.

Like Pearl.

I slide on my belly back down the roof, and slither over the edge onto the trellis without ever glancing up.

"Did you see him?" I gasp to Cayden. I barely resist hugging him, I'm so glad he didn't bail.

"I saw him," says Cayden. "You're gonna be surprised to hear that I don't want to go in there."

For once, I totally agree with Cayden, but there's no question now. I have to.

Chapter 23

The Pits

It's a scary, whispery while before we find our way inside the house. I guess even evil puppets lock their doors most of the time. Finally, we find a high little rectangular window. . . . Too high for puppets to reach, which I find reassuring. It folds inward when I push on it. If we stand on one of the wicker chairs on the porch, we can just reach to pull ourselves up and in. I'm even more relieved when I get my head and shoulders through and can see that I'm in a bathroom. After all, what use could puppets have for toilets? Once I'm sitting on the sill, I pull my legs in and drop to the floor as quietly as I can, wincing. Cayden follows, and I make a cradle of my hands so he can step down, making even less noise than me.

An ear to the door tells me the hall is quiet. We ease our way out. What do I think I'm doing? I know nothing about the layout of this place. Usually I scout this stuff out ahead of time. It's amazing what you can find if you try. Floor plans, all kinds of things.

Just because it's quiet doesn't mean nothing is lurking, but I don't see what else we can do but prowl the house looking for clues. If the Greeley's tunnel does connect to the mansion, I bet it's *down*, somewhere. Especially if they use it to sneak people and things back and forth. On the main floors, it's too easy to make noise or be seen through a window. So I need a door that leads to some kind of basement.

That worries me more than I like to admit. Cayden and I didn't see any outdoor exits. We could get cut off and trapped. But I'm beginning to wonder who we might find. So I mouth-breathe my way through the house, trying to get air through my cardboard mask, looking for clues.

The house seems to be laid out in a circular plan. The hallway leads us to the kitchen, which is empty, and also full of those full-length glass doors facing the yard that we already tried and found locked. It creeps me out that my masked reflection looks like Whanslaw. Beside me, Cayden's disguised as Kiyo.

We keep going, and find ourselves in a creepy, old-fashioned parlor, with high-backed chairs and big tasseled lamps. It's hard to make things out in the faint light, so maybe it's just my eyes playing tricks on me, but the scale of everything is a little bit off, like it's slightly too small. Puppet-size. I eye each chair, afraid I'll find a member of the PC sitting in it, watching us.

"Where are they all?" Cayden murmurs in my ear. I want to shush him, but *S* sounds are surprisingly loud, so I just put my finger to my lips and keep going, into a front hallway with a wood floor and a long tapestry runner. The next door leads to a dining room, and that leads back into the kitchen. Hm. I quickly check what little hallway is on the other side of the bathroom. There are three doors. I check them all. One leads to a broom closet. The next, the one at the very end of the hall, opens on the garage. Again, I can't see much, but I can smell oil, and new-car smell, and hear the faint ticking of a cooling engine. If I'm remembering correctly, it's at least a three-car garage. The PC likes to do things in style.

One door left. I try it, and find . . . a washer and dryer. What on earth? There has to be some door leading down, and now I'm getting annoyed. I head back through the dining room into the front hallway, trusting Cayden to trail along behind me, and cautiously, with a nervous glance up the stairs, ease open the lone door I find there, hoping it won't creak. I swing the door open wide enough to see inside, sick with dread that there will be a puppeteer in there, reaching out for me with both arms, the light from the upstairs hallway glinting on its sunglasses, pulling me inside to—but there's nothing inside but coats. Then Cayden touches me on the shoulder, and I have to stifle a scream.

I punch him.

"Ow!" he whisper-breathes. "Cut it out!"

I glare, but I'm secretly impressed he stayed quiet. I punch pretty hard.

"In here," he mouths, motioning, and I follow him back into creepy puppet parlor.

Cayden has pulled the big Oriental rug back. He pulls my hand down and runs it across the wood floor, and I feel seams. One corner, down to a second, a third, and my heart leaps at the fourth.

"A trapdoor!" I breathe. I feel around some more. "Where's the latch?"

"I couldn't find one, either."

"Who puts in a trapdoor they can't open?"

"It must open from underneath," says Cayden. "But it doesn't look like anyone's used it in forever. There's wax in all the seams. Who waxes their floors nowadays?"

I shake my head. "Okay, so there has to be another way down. But we've checked all the doors, so—"

"So it must be a door we can't see."

We search the edges of the room. I move knickknacks to see if they open doors, which makes me feel like I'm in a cartoon mystery. I hate this part, the desperately-silent-searching-in-the-dark part, because we're just begging to knock over something fragile and get caught. Cayden comes in handy, though. I'm still goofing with the stuff on the fireplace mantel (and seriously, why do they have a fireplace and a big old-fashioned-looking parlor-type room in New Mexico?) when I hear a soft pop on the other side of the room, and Cayden pulls open a section of wainscoted wall. He peers into the resulting gap, then motions me over.

It's a stairwell, and even though I figure it was added after the trapdoor, the steps are broad and shallow, with a dip in the center of each one, as though feet have been passing this way for a long time. I feel for a handrail and don't find one, but the walls are definitely adobe. I smell it, and it doesn't have the artificial straight smoothness of poured concrete. Instead, it has that familiar, faintly uneven texture under my hands, like the walls at Raymond's house. Why would a big old Victorian house like this be sitting on an adobe basement?

As we descend, the air around us cools, so fast that the skin on my arms prickles. Going down into the dark not knowing what's there is unnerving.

"Let me get my flashlight," I mutter, digging into my pocket for the tiny LED light I carry.

"Don't," says Cayden. "I've never seen a movie where the flashlights didn't give the heroes away. You might as well shout, 'Here I am!' "

He has a point.

As we fumble our way down the shallow steps, though, another smell pushes its way to the head of the line. Sawdust. It's usually comforting, the smell of new things being made by someone special who knows how, but right now all I can think about is that puppets are made of wood and I Smell Wood and it's dark down here. I don't care what Cayden says, I still wish I could use my flashlight.

Instead, I fumble my way along the wall. There must be a switch, right?

Something long and thin snakes its way over my head,

like a puppet string. I stifle a shriek and reach up to yank it away from me.

A bare bulb in the ceiling lights up.

"Shut that off!" hisses Cayden. I pull the cord a second time, and we're plunged into darkness again.

The good news is that the afterimage glaring on my eyeballs is of a hallway, with no one in it.

The bad news is that there are two dark wood doors on the left-hand side, and another on the right, and we're going to have to open them, because there's no place else to go.

I reach out with one arm, stretching out as far as I can, hoping to touch the new wall before I let go of the old one. I don't quite make it, but I only have to free-fall in darkness for a second. On the new wall, I quickly find the first door. I press my ear to it, but again hear nothing. No light shines from beneath it.

I tap Cayden. "My LED light is smaller than the overhead bulb," I point out. "We have to see."

"Yeahhhh." He sighs. "I guess we do. Just be careful."

Easing the door open, I point my light inside. The smell of sawdust is overwhelming. Cayden's face pokes in beside mine, and we both flinch. We're in a room full of spare puppet parts. There are arms, legs, even half-finished heads hanging in rows on every wall. In the middle of the room is a large worktable, as clean as an operating table, with a neat row of saws, chisels, and a stack of sandpaper waiting for use. And string. Spools and spools of string. I smell something sharp and oily.

Some sort of sealant or finish, I guess. We back out in a hurry, and I pull the door shut.

My hands are shaking, which means the light is shaking, so of course Cayden can tell. I press the hand with the flashlight against my leg to hold it still. He's looking down, which means his hair's in the way, and I can't see his face.

After a second, he says, "Ready for the other door?"

My voice sounds hoarse when I answer. "Yeah."

We move down the hallway, and open the last door on the left-hand side.

It's dark inside, and quiet, but I could swear I hear breathing. I lift my light.

The room is instantly familiar in a way that I can't quite place. It's round, which I did not expect, and big enough that I can't make out the far side. The ceiling is made of thick logs, and all around the walls, about halfway up, are arched recesses with barred doors. . . .

I've got it!

"It's a pit house!" I say, forgetting to be quiet. The Pueblo built them, but not around here. . . . At least, I didn't think so. After everything I've learned about them, it figures the puppets would build a house right on top of one. It's like spitting in the eye of indigenous people. The barred doors aren't right, though, and the fire pit in the middle of the floor is way too big and deep. It's like the puppets paid somebody for a creepiness upgrade. Then I detect motion out of the corner of my eye. I spin. A hand extends from one of the recesses, between the bars. A hand about the same size as mine.

I'm there so fast I don't remember going. I reach out to hold the offered hand, and it matches mine perfectly.

This is the reason why I've never looked twice at a Curtis Clone. I'm the only person in Oddity who never needed one. For the first time since she left, I say the word that is on the tip of my tongue every second of every day, the word my family won't say.

"Pearl."

And she smiles.

Chapter 24

Pearl

Pearl is filthy, and her braids grew out long ago. From the neck up, she looks like the head of a dandelion, only brown. Raymond's jefa would have a fit if she saw her. But she's alive. When I get her hands in mine my brain shuts down. Then the flashlight, forgotten between our fingers, shines in my eyes and blinds me. I squint, and she must think I'm about to start in on her, because she says,

"If you say one word about my hair when you're wearing that janky mask—"

Relief floods me. Yes. Let's argue. That's where we shine. I never realized until she was gone how miserably lonely it is to argue with yourself when you're used to arguing with another person.

"Why didn't you use your hair to saw through the bars?" I ask. The withering look she gives me makes my heart sing.

Light flares behind me as Cayden finds another string. I pull my knife, and slide it into the old-fashioned lock on this cage they've got my sister in.

"That's not Raymond," Pearl says, looking at Cayden's long hair.

I focus on my lock-picking. "Nope. New neighbor."

She doesn't ask why our best friend isn't there helping us, but for the first time I feel a wash of shame for not offering him the option.

"How did they get you here from Greeley's?" I ask, even though I already know.

"There's a tunnel in one of the freezers."

"I don't understand the point of keeping you locked up like this!" I say. "Their puppeteers are all upstairs. What are you, the spare?"

"One of them. All these cells are full of Sweepstakes winners. Turns out the Protection Committee is into renewable energy. Evil's gone green."

She gestures at the pit and then at the other cells, which I now realize are occupied.

"You're saying the puppets, like . . . run on people?"

"On souls. One of us gets used up, they plug in another one."

I don't like the sound of that. "Used up?"

"A lady named Mrs. Markham wore out yesterday. Died.

Maggie came down here to swap her out. She looked like a corn-husk doll."

I shudder.

"I saw Sparky," I say.

Pearl looks at me sharply. "You can see them? The puppeteers?"

"I can now. I look harder now that I'm suspicious of the puppets."

She sighs.

"I never could, or I wouldn't have been so excited about the Sweepstakes. It's some kind of magic, I think. But once you realize, you see through it."

We didn't know any better. But the adults, some of them must've learned to see through it. That's why they run from us when we canvass. *They* know.

Do our parents?

"Why doesn't anyone DO something?" I ask.

"The PC is protecting them from worse things," Pearl says. It's a hard idea to let go of, even when I've seen the truth with my own eyes.

"Pearl, they're not. They've been faking the Blurmonster attacks. We need to go. Someone needs to tell this town the truth."

The lock still won't give, but I keep trying. I'm not leaving Pearl.

"How can we take her?" asks Cayden. "The minute anyone sees her, they'll tell the PC."

"We're twins," I say. "We'll take turns going out."

Cayden looks over his shoulder. "Hurry, Ada. They've got to have an alarm system or something. No one knows we're here. If we get caught—"

If we get caught, there's no cavalry coming.

My sister reaches for me through the bars of her cell.

"Get me out of here, Ada."

I've never heard my sister's voice tremble like that before, and it hits me. We're the cavalry.

"I'm hurrying," I say to both of them.

I jam my knife into the lock on Pearl's cell hard enough to practically snap the tip, but it still won't pop open. People in the other cells are starting to mutter demands for help.

Cayden and I exchange a glance. We can't really get all these people out of here by ourselves, can we? On the other hand, they'll make a heck of a lot of noise if we try to leave without them.

I hesitate, trying to figure out what to do.

Pearl reaches through the bars to hug me around the neck. I lean against the bars.

"Give me the knife and I'll take a turn," she says. "Maybe I can get it."

I start to slide back so I can hand it to her. Her fingers catch in the chain of my locket.

"How did you get past the puppet on guard?" she asks.

"Um, what?" asks Cayden.

At that moment, Maggie, giggling through her shoe-polish mouth, rushes at us from the pit house door, brandishing a butcher knife.

There's no time to think, only react. I feel a sharp tug at my neck as we hurl ourselves in opposite directions, Cayden one way, me the other. The knife flashes down through the space where we were. Even now, as Maggie's attacking us, I'm startled to realize I know the puppeteer holding the controls. She used to work at Crash Diner. She doesn't even look at me as I run by, though she pivots so that Maggie can chase me with her button eyes twinkling like the blade of the knife.

Maggie giggles again. It's a horrible sound, at once friendly and mindless. I need to put something between me and her, or sooner or later she won't miss. The pit is my only option. I race along the edge.

The hands that the other prisoners were waving through the bars of their cells are speedily withdrawn. I look over my shoulder to see how close Maggie is, only to find she's going after easier prey. Cayden likes sports, but he's short on running-for-our-lives practice, and it shows. I need to refocus Maggie's attention.

"Hey!" I yell. "Pinocchio!"

The puppet ignores me, closing the gap between her and my neighbor boy, puppeteer jogging behind her. I run after them. What else can I do? I'm tougher and more experienced. If I can distract Maggie, maybe he can get away.

What would insult a puppet? "Look at me, you Muppet!" I yell, but that doesn't work, either.

Maggie slashes with her knife, and it slices through Cayden's T-shirt. From her cage, Pearl shouts, "Jump, NOW!"

Cayden hears her. He takes a running leap, and disappears into the pit.

I give a wordless shout of disbelief, and rush to the edge to look in.

Cayden is already getting to his feet. The pit's too deep for Maggie to reach him, but not nearly as deep as I thought. I don't understand, though. How am I going to get him out of there?

I turn to scan the pit house, and Maggie's blade whisks past my cheek. One of my braids falls to the floor, beads clicking, but I still have my knife in my hand. Before she pulls back for another strike, I lunge into her and stab her in the middle of her canvas face, jerking my bodkin left and right to make as big a mess as I can. The fabric rends, and sawdust explodes in a puff all over the place. Maggie flails wildly with her butcher knife, but I duck behind her. The ripped edges of her empty head flap open when she moves, making it hard for her button eyes to see me.

There's only one way to stop her for sure. While she's still seeking in front of her with her knife, I step up between her and her puppeteer, and with one sweep slash all her strings.

Maggie falls to the ground with a clatter, facedown, backside in the air, and lies unmoving.

I wait, knife held ready, to see what the puppeteer will do. Her hands, still holding the wooden controls, fall limply in front of her, and she stands mutely, as if her battery has died.

When I'm sure the pair of them are out of commission, I finish my survey of the pit house. There, propped against the wall, is a ladder. The old-fashioned kind, made of two long poles with lengths of wood lashed between them to form steps. I drag it to the pit, pushing it across the opening until enough of it's hanging in the air to make it pivot down into the pit. The end that seesaws up hits the log ceiling with a clunk, and I wince. Why the heck is it that tall?

"Quick!" I hiss.

Cayden's working his way up when I hear a voice behind me.

"I think we've had enough nonsense for one night, don't you?"

Whanslaw is standing right behind me. In his blue hand is a small silver pistol. It is pointed at my head.

Chapter 25

Flight

"I like the mask," says Whanslaw, "but we'll have company shortly, and they'll be far less accommodating than I." He glances at Maggie, still sprawled akimbo on the floor. I look past him at Pearl, who's gripping the bars of her cell, watching. How am I going to get her out now that the puppets know we're here?

"There was no point to this, you know," he says, breaking into my thoughts.

"No point to what?" I hope he doesn't recognize my voice. I calculate how fast I can get to him, but don't know how I'm supposed to knock him down with Sparky behind him holding the controls.

"Releasing the winners, for a start. The town has already accepted the necessity of their sacrifice."

Tonight I can see that for the lie it is. "Nobody's accepted anything. They're just scared. The grown-ups in this town need to step up!" I exclaim, but it's like I'm betraying every grown-up I know by saying it. Aunt Bets, Daddy, Song, Badri . . . I think of them all in one guilty flash.

"They understand what side their bread is buttered on, that's all."

"You had no right to start taking children away from their families!"

He clicks his wooden tongue.

"I had every right. I make your world go round."

"No, you don't! You orphan children, and leave parents with dead hearts!"

"No thanks to you children and your little stunts. Greeley is checking behind every door for zombie rabbits, can't focus on anything. He's usually such a dependable sort of fellow. Were you involved? Would you and some of your little friends like to join Miss Roundtree in here? Because that can certainly be arranged."

I glare, though of course all he can see is his cardboard clone. I'm not going to say another word.

He isn't done, though.

"Truly, dear, why do you care? Is the other Miss Roundtree a classmate of yours, perhaps? I imagine things are rather looking up for her. A bigger share of sweeties, more parental attention . . ."

Of course, I have neither of those things. I have less than

I had before because Mama has one foot out the door and Daddy is barely holding things together. The truth is I'd be thrilled to have attention and sweeties right now, and I hate him for being right for all the wrong reasons.

There's a disturbance at the door. I shiver with dread.

The other puppets have arrived.

Lanchester has seen Maggie lying shredded on the floor and begins glubbing. He hurries across the pit house to her, and Whanslaw says nothing to stop him as he picks her up. Lanchester's fish mouth opens and closes in distress. I could almost feel sorry for him if I didn't remember Maggie's wild giggles and the flash of her knife.

Kiyo takes in the scene, then speaks with a rage that makes me tremble.

"Whanslaw, what are you waiting for? Shoot the little animal."

His answer is calm.

"I don't really see the point. Why waste resources? After all, that one's good for nothing but the compost heap now." He waves the pistol at Maggie's puppeteer, and I realize for the first time that she still isn't moving. I would have guessed that disconnecting her from Maggie would free her, but I've doomed her instead.

I'm so sorry.

Lanchester is still burbling on the floor. Kiyo begins to advance on me. . . . Just me, because I've just realized Cayden isn't up here yet. I might get past the two of them, but not without leaving Cayden in the pit. And how am I going to save Pearl? If only I'd left her the knife when I ran, so she could pick the lock.

"It's not a standoff, tsuu no!" says Kiyo impatiently. "It's just one bratty child!"

She flies forward, sleeves and hem rippling, and *SCREAMS*.

Then *I* scream because as she reaches me, her face transforms. Parts click, drop down, and reverse, making short, pointed horns rise up out of her hair. Her eyes have no whites and are ringed with red. Her sneering mouth is filled with sharp, predatory teeth.

I shove her, hard, connecting with something solid under her robes. Before she can hit me again, I have my bodkin back out. Her face is wood, not cloth like Maggie's, but I'll do as much damage as I can without slashing any more strings. She must be a little bit vain about those robes, because she hangs back, growling. My skin crawls, but I have a second of breathing room. I adjust my mask with one hand.

"Honestly, Kiyo, what did that accomplish?" asks Whanslaw, but he looks . . . oh, he looks like he liked it. Those glassy eyes just shine, and the almost-smile of his mouth seems larger.

We have to get out of here, and bless my BASH!-soaked neighbor boy, he understands what needs doing before I do.

"Help me!" he shouts, and suddenly the ladder, which is still sticking out of the pit, drops so fast it just about clocks me in the head. I end up trapped in a single rectangle between two rungs, and I'm dragged along as it starts sliding into the pit.

"What the heck are you doing?" I yell over my shoulder.

He jumps in the air to get a look at me, and I hear Kiyo hiss as she sees him wearing her visage.

"Push! Tilt it up! Hurry!"

Up? What good will that do? I waste a precious second staring wildly up at the ceiling. . . . At the trapdoor in the middle of the PC's parlor. Holy lipless cow!

I spin to face the pit, grab the nearest rung, and push up with all my might. The whole ladder starts moving toward me again, but this time, I get what Cayden is doing. Working with the momentum he creates, I shift my grip to the uprights and run the ladder up. When I get to the edge of the pit, and the ladder is standing straight up and down, I step onto it and shove off. I ride it in a freaky free fall until the top of it wedges itself against the roof just beneath the trapdoor, offering a perfect exit.

Cayden is already pulling himself up between the rungs below me, as if he's using monkey bars.

"Well, that's at least interesting," says Whanslaw. I hope he's serious about his conservation ethic. I don't want to get shot.

Then it hits me. What about Pearl? If I climb down, I'll get caught for sure, and my parents will lose both their daughters. If I call out to her, promise to come back, I might as well take my mask off, and Cayden's, too. The puppets will know exactly who we are.

Whanslaw looks up at Cayden and me.

"We really only need one of you," he says, and takes aim with his pistol. There's a bang, and I feel a breeze on my cheek.

I do the worst thing I've ever done in my life. I turn my back on my twin, my Pearl, and climb for my life.

There's a slide bolt holding the trapdoor shut on this side. It's old, and sticking a bit, but I'm banging on it with the hilt of my knife, and it's moving, when I hear Kiyo's hateful voice say,

"Let's play a game. Children like games, don't they?" She gives another shrill, garbled scream. I look down to see Kiyo's puppeteer fling her arms upward, sending Kiyo flying to the fullest extent of her strings, right at Cayden. Kiyo shrieks aloud with rageful joy. Cayden turns, bracing his back against the ladder and pushing her away with both hands, but the ladder shakes with the force of the impact, and I can't understand how any puppet could be so strong. Kiyo grabs for Cayden's mask, pulls his hair, pokes his stomach. Cayden guards his mask, arms extended against the attack. He tries to fend Kiyo off, but he can't make any sudden moves with his arms or he'll fall. If he turns to climb, she'll grab him from behind.

I have to get the trapdoor open. I bash the bolt again, as hard as I can, and it shoots back. The door lands on my head, hard. I see stars, but I start back down toward my friend to help. I have to get him out of Kiyo's reach.

Cayden's leaning back against the ladder, his arms hooked over a rung, kicking Kiyo with all his might every time she comes near. Lanchester's still glubbing over Maggie, and Whanslaw begins to laugh a deep, froglike laugh as he watches us fight for our lives.

Kiyo hits Cayden from the side one more time in a blur of

pink silk and black hair. Then I'm low enough to kick her in the head, higher than Cayden could reach. She reels backward, crashing into her puppeteer, and while they're getting untangled, we scramble up the ladder.

There's another shot, and chips fly from the log roof, so close they ping off my arms. I extend a hand to the hole of the trapdoor, to freedom—

I can't push through. Something's stopping my hand. *What is that?*

"I can't get out!" I scream at Cayden.

He's right below me. "It's the carpet! We rolled it back down to hide the trapdoor. Push!"

But I know pushing isn't going to work. That thing is huge. One last time, I pull my bodkin, and I thrust it through the rug as hard as I can. Another bullet smacks the logs somewhere nearby, and if Whanslaw kills me, Pearl will see it.

"Hurry!" says Cayden, as I pull the knife toward me through the fibers of the Oriental rug. Another bullet. I can't go any faster. It's a miracle the bodkin is this sharp. I make a second cut at a right angle to the first, hoping it will be enough.

To my shock, another knife blade plunges down through the rug. I almost fall off the ladder, but Cayden reaches up and steadies me just in time.

Instead of vanishing and plunging down again to stab at us, the knife makes a third long cut, connecting with my own. A familiar brown hand reaches down through the gap and rips the flap of carpet upward.

"Come on!" shouts Raymond, reaching a hand down to

me. I grab it and climb, letting him grab me under the arms and haul me up once my shoulders are through. Cayden's right behind me, and somewhere in the dark parlor Xerple babbles, "I bring the Raymond, just like you said."

"Good, Xerple. You did good," Cayden says.

"Pearl," I say to Raymond. "I lost her." I think I'm crying.

"We have to go, Ada," says Raymond. "We have to *run*."

And I'm so ashamed, but I do.

Chapter 26
Fist Bumps

So we escaped. I'm so guilty and scared, it's difficult to care. A while back, I said the trick to lying was to do it with conviction and loads of eye contact. I'm failing on both counts. I can hardly stand to be in the same room with my family. At breakfast, I keep my head down and shovel my food into my mouth as fast as I can, then ask to be excused.

I go rummaging in Pearl's room again. She has a thing for bow ties (the kind you tie yourself, not the clip-ons). She makes them into headbands and belts and stuff. She likes vintage watches, and those boyfriend sweaters with the patches on the elbows, too. I get through an hour by trying on her things, which is how I realize that, on top of everything else, I lost my locket.

If Daddy notices what I'm doing, he doesn't say anything

this time. No one does. As the miserable day drags on, though, something else nags for my attention.

My closet door isn't slamming as much as usual.

A bit of investigation yields strange results. It seems my closet is empty.

This should not be terribly surprising. After all, I'm dealing with a ghost. But ever since she first started showing herself, Stella has been easy to get a rise out of. Usually if I pick on her while she's invisible, the hangers come flying off the rod and the door flaps. She'll go from invisible to in my face in two seconds flat, but she's always in the closet. Now, when the closet looks empty, it is. She's not there.

Does she know I lost the locket? Maybe the locket was the only reason she was here, and now that it's gone, she's going to leave me. Like Pearl left me. Like I left Pearl.

I slam her door myself, just for company, while I listen for a fist pounding on the front door, for the idling motor of a black van, here to take me away. I spend some time patching up the masks, using Pearl's art supplies. My plan is to pretend I don't know where they are, that someone ripped them off from school. That way, in theory anyone could have used them. But if I do have to take them back into the building, I don't want them to show any evidence of our disastrous sneak.

Meanwhile, Cayden, Raymond, and I are in the strange situation of having to post to Nopes twice as much as we used to. You'd think we'd be keeping a low profile, but instead we have to be überobvious and keep our post count up—so that no one will suspect that the angry new anonymous posts are from us. And by *us*, I mean me.

There's some disagreement in the ranks about that decision.

Then again, there's no question I'm getting a reaction, and not just from that bunch of talking heads up on the hill. People believe us about the puppeteers.

At first there are only a few, each pair snapped in half.

Sunglasses.

Someone hits on the idea of taking a string and tying one end around each ear stem, so they can hang them from street signs and railings. Every one is gone the next morning, confiscated by the PC. But there are more the next day, and the next. Once we're sure that they are actually being confiscated, people start going to a lot of trouble to get them into the most inconvenient places possible. People sort out that they can sling the sunglasses-string combo at power lines, and it will wrap itself around several times, leaving the broken halves of the glasses to hang down. Those are harder to get, and there are a lot of power lines in Oddity. Street crews are visible during the day then, going up in the buckets of utility trucks, but they never get them all.

Cayden calls it throwing shades.

I don't participate.

"Maybe the masks worked," I whisper on Wednesday afternoon.

"Or the PC has bigger things to worry about," says Raymond.

He, Cayden, and I are sitting on my front porch, watching the zombie rabbits try to light things on fire with some sunglasses they stole from city workers.

"Like what?" I ask. "We could tell everybody they tried to murder us." In truth, I haven't for one second thought of telling. The only way to make things worse than they are now is to get my whole family in the puppets' bad graces.

I take it back. If I tell my dad and Aunt Bets and they don't believe me, that'll be worse.

Raymond says, "First the video of the Blurmonster 'attack,' now your post about the puppeteers. You got people all riled up."

"What should I do, Raymond? Hole up in the hide-and-shack?"

"It's not even here right now," says Cayden.

Raymond and I stare.

"How do you know that?" I ask.

"I thought I left my phone in it, so I hiked back out there."

"Alone?" Raymond asks. "You're lucky the Blurmonster didn't get you."

I disagree. "I don't think luck has anything to do with it. All this time, the PC's been telling us the Blurmonster's after everybody, but think a minute. It's been around forever, and the first time anyone remembers it bashing things up—"

"Was when the puppets came to town," Raymond says, turning to me in surprise.

I nod. "Exactly. I bet we never needed to be afraid of it in the first place. The puppets did."

"Those jerks," says Raymond. "We thought the PC was protecting us by teaching us to guard against it, and all this time, we've been protecting them."

That doesn't solve our bigger problem, though.

"Some of the grown-ups have obviously learned to see the puppeteers," says Cayden. "That's why they run from us when we come to sign them up for the Sweepstakes. Why haven't they rebelled?"

I snort.

"If they can't successfully rebel against ordering coffee in languages they don't speak, how are they going to handle this?"

Seriously, though. The town is so proud of those puppets. If some adults don't know about the puppeteers, and even the ones who do think the puppets are protecting us from something important. . . . I sigh. The grown-ups aren't going to get their poop in a group and solve this problem. It has to be us.

Mason comes hopping down the steps.

"Hey!" he says. "Look what I've got!"

He pulls a coin the size of a soup can lid out of his pocket.

"Whoa, Mase!" says Raymond. "How'd you get that?"

Mason flips it, trying to be all cool, then scrabbles for it when he drops it by mistake. Recovering, he says, "Got it from Uncle Dale for hosing out the armaduino cages. We just got back. Will you walk me down to the bakery? I'm buying."

Finally, something we all agree on. We meander down to the bakery. We also watch our backs.

Aunt Bets made bizcochitos, and I'm inhaling the licorice-cookie smell before I even open the door.

What I'm not expecting is the out-of-place noise that greets the four of us as we enter. It's a sort of metal-on-metal rushing sound.

I follow instincts born and bred in every kid in Oddity and drag Mason down in front of the counter. For once, he doesn't argue.

We listen. Whatever it is, it's fast, made by friction. It speeds up and slows down, but never completely stops. It reminds me of a metal boa constrictor, which is not outside the realm of possibility. I don't hear any screaming, though. Maybe it already swallowed Aunt Bets? Maybe some of the ductwork has come alive and uncoiled from the ceiling. Maybe I'd better go check, since she's family and all. Cranky, pain-in-the-butt, amazing family.

She can twist my ear all she wants if she just won't orphan Mason.

"You wait *here*," I say, grabbing him by the backpack straps and giving him a shake, proving once and for all that Cayden was right, and a one-strap shoulder bag you can slip out of is the best thing to carry to school. That's annoying.

After a careful glance past the edge of the counter, I duck-walk around it and toward the employee-only door that leads to the rear of the bakery. It's normally kept open so Aunt Bets hears customers come in when she's baking, but someone has moved the stopper. It's a swinging door, though. With a little luck I can ease it open far enough to see what's going on. . . .

Something whizzes past the crack I've made, and I'm so startled I fall back, and the door whooshes shut. Then comes a sound I'm not expecting at all. Laughter. Not maniacal, evil laughter, or the hysterical laughter of a lost soul surrendering to its fate, but genuine, helplessly happy laughter. It sounds like my aunt Bets, but how can it be? I can't remember the last time I heard her laugh that way. More than anything, it's my refusal to believe it's her that makes me brave enough to open the door again.

Something whooshes past my line of vision again, and this time I don't jump, because I'm too busy staring. Mason, who like younger relatives everywhere is biologically incapable of following the direction *"Wait here,"* crowds up at my elbow and gapes over my shoulder, Raymond and Cayden right behind him.

All around the kitchen, someone has installed some sort of bizarre gutter, like a marble run, or maybe a garage door track. It rises and falls in great, roller coaster–style hills and valleys. The shadow streaks past again.

It's Aunt Bets.

She's wearing a harness like a climber or a bungee jumper might use, and it's attached to a set of wheels that ride the track. The apparatus supports her all the way up past her waist, and straps wrap around her thighs but leave her stumps dangling free. She rolls right past her empty wheelchair, which sits forgotten in the corner. She goes sailing past the doors of the big industrial oven, drops down a slope in the track, and comes to rest with a shooshing sound in front of the slab table where she kneads the dough. Brakes. That's what I heard. I crane my neck to see the rest of this outrageous contraption in our bakery. It's been patched together from all different pieces of metal, but it stands steady and strong—and it will take her to every important place in the kitchen, faster than she could walk there if she still had her legs. The big mixer, the storage shelves, the coolers . . . everything. And she's giggling. Aunt Bets is giggling. I haven't seen her do that since Uncle Mike disappeared and she started doing everything herself.

"What on earth are you doing on the floor?" she asks, catching sight of us. A big black hand reaches down to grab mine before I know what's happening, and I'm hauled into the room by Badri. He has grease on his fingers, and I see a motley bucket of tools behind his beat-up boots. I forget to stop my forward momentum, and before I know what I'm doing, I'm hugging him. The whole room is very quiet suddenly, but I can't stop myself, even though all this squeezing is making my eyes water.

"Well, hello, Ada," Badri says, his voice soft as always. He sounds surprised, but not in a my-ribs-are-cracked kind of way.

I remember to let go after a minute. "Hi."

Mason is staring at me like I have two heads, and this is the new one.

I look over at Aunt Bets, figuring she's about to ask me if

I've lost my mind because she'll help me find it, but she's turned around in her harness, floury hands holding on to the rail, looking at me with that nice soft look she used to have when we were little, and I think she's glad I'm not going to scream you're-not-my-uncle at Badri. Like I'd even do that. But wow, this is a really great audition, if he wants the role.

"There's no food in the house," I say, realizing belatedly that I'm hitting Aunt Bets's don't-act-like-you-don't-have-family-that-feeds-you-and-clothes-you buzzer. I smile, even though I know it's wobbly, because I figure a smile for a smile is fair. And I want her to keep smiling. I want her to still be smiling when I come in every day after school, which I am going to do, because I want to see this new thing that lets her whiz around like she used to do on her legs. I want to stand and watch her like she's a piece of modern art and I'm pretentious.

"How will you carry the dough?" asks Mason, who's walking along the track examining it. He runs his fingers down inside the groove, and they come away faintly glistening with fresh oil.

Aunt Bets reaches around the edge of the kneading table and grabs a long metal gaff, like they use to drag school talent show acts offstage when the puppets start booing. We both jump back a bit as she reaches around with it, but she's only grabbing the handle on one of the carts, which has a big, clear kitchen bin of dough on it. She drags it across to her, and I see that someone, Badri I guess, has taken it apart and re-welded it so it will be the exact same height as the table.

She slides the bin onto her work surface. In the harness, she's tall enough to dump it herself, and she starts breaking it down into loaves like that hasn't been an act of torture for months.

"See?" she says as she works. "What do you think?"

"You're like a cyborg superhero!" says Mason.

My aunt grins, all white teeth and twinkling eyes. "Don't you forget it. Ada?"

I'm smiling, too, like my face is so amazed it can't help itself. "I think piracy builds important vocational skills." Okay, that didn't sound right. But when I look over at Badri, his knuckles are headed my way. We share a fist bump of swashbuckling solidarity.

"There are pecan pastries up front," says Aunt Bets, which is how she fist-bumps people.

Chapter 27

Faults

We're leaving the bakery when I see a flash of blue and red in the heat waves rising off the sidewalk. I grab Mason by the shoulder and press a wad of money into his hand.

"Mase," I say, "we're out of milk. Go over to the co-op and buy a gallon from Scoby."

As he starts to whine, I add, "Buy caramel apples with what's left. Say your mama sent you, not me, or he'll give you caramel onions again."

That does it. He's so pumped he forgets to look both ways when he crosses. Normally I'd holler at him, but right now I'm relieved he doesn't see who's coming.

I've been waiting for something like this to happen for almost a week. At least now I can stop dreading it.

There are moments, mostly when I'm really nervous, that

something strikes me funny when it really really shouldn't. This is one of those times. I'm imagining that Whanslaw, who has stopped being blue-and-red heat haze and is now a hazy evil puppet coming my way, has spurs on beneath his red robes. In my head, I imagine I can hear that old Western music they play during a showdown.

OooEeeOooEeeOooooh . . . Wah-wah-wah.

He seems to bob along the sidewalk in time with the soundtrack in my head, which makes the whole thing even more ridiculous.

What the heck is going on with his puppeteer, though? I can't see him at all. Did he shrink?

"Ada," says Cayden, "maybe we'd better go inside."

"No," I say, and now my voice seems stretched like taffy, as if time is slowing down. "No. If we run, he'll know it was us. Take a good look at the puppeteer. You should be able to see him if you really try."

I'm half expecting Whanslaw to be the bait in some elaborate trap. Right now, angry attack dogs should be jumping out at us from behind buildings, or something. But there's nothing. Just Whanslaw bobbing along in front of his mysteriously shorter puppeteer. Passing right by me without even slowing down, though he turns his head toward me and opens his mouth in his version of a smile. Then I see why. Behind him . . . behind him. Is Pearl.

They've got her hair styled in two neat puffs she'd think were babyish. She's wearing a plain black cotton dress and black Mary Janes. I glimpse a flash of gold at the back of her neck.

Her hands are working Whanslaw's controls like she's been doing it all her life. I don't think she has any idea we're even there. And she's wearing those shades, those horrible sunglasses. I have to see her eyes, see if they'll look back at me or be awful and vacant.

I don't realize I'm trying to get to her until I can't. Raymond's got me around the waist. I struggle to push his hands down and off me. I hit him in the face. But I'm not struggling like a smart girl who knows how to fight. I'm freaking out, shouting a name that doesn't mean anything to its owner anymore.

She doesn't look at me. She doesn't even pause.

The bells on the bakery door bang the glass as Badri comes rushing out, holding the door for Aunt Bets, who's back in her wheelchair. Whanslaw and Pearl are just passing them, and I hear my aunt's agonized groan as she hears my words and, looking, sees what I see. Badri's hands are twitching erratically, like he's seconds away from trying to grab Pearl. But there's nothing any of us can do.

This is my fault.

This is all my fault.

When I'm finished throwing up my bizcochitos in the bakery bathroom, I find Aunt Bets waiting outside the door. She rolls back a bit to let me pass.

"Guess you'll still have to get out of that contraption Badri made sometimes, huh?" I say. I wipe my nose.

Bets gives me a stare that says she isn't going to let me be fake okay. I guess carriers of that disease recognize the signs.

"I hoped you'd never have to see that," she says.

I'm so turned inside out with guilt that I can't even answer.

"Ada," she says, like she thinks my attention is wandering. "Ada. You saw. And I saw. But Mason didn't. Your mom didn't."

Now I'm looking right into her serious eyes.

"Where's Badri?" I ask. "Where are the boys?"

"Badri is walking the boys home, and they are having this same talk. Mason will be back from the co-op any minute. We have to pull ourselves together. Right now."

I let my jaw drop a little.

"That's it?" I ask. "That's all you've got?" I swear, I never used to be so rude to adults, but this is getting ridiculous.

"Young lady!" says Aunt Bets. She shuts her eyes for a second, breathes out slowly. "I don't like this any better than you do. But your mom is . . . fragile."

I know she is. Iknowsheis. I don't want to hear about it anymore.

I move to brush past Aunt Bets, but she grabs my arm in an iron grip.

"Ada." She waits until I look at her again. "Our family's lost enough."

"Do Mama and Daddy know how to see them?" I ask.

Bets sighs. "Yes."

I feel like the floor vanished, and I'm about to drop into the void beneath. All this time, they've known. I sounded brave earlier, but I want so much for my grown-ups to just HANDLE it. If they haven't already, it's not happening.

My aunt's still talking.

"We didn't want to get you and your mama's hopes up, but your daddy's been appealing to the WUT trying to get Pearl back—do not roll your eyes, young lady! He's doing his best, going through proper channels—"

"The puppets designed all the channels, Bets! Nothing's gonna change if we do it their way!"

Bets rubs her hands through her hair. "That may be, Ada. But we still have you and Mason to worry about. Even what little your daddy has done seems to have made the puppets angry."

Oh, please let that be true. Let what happened to Pearl be someone else's fault.

"He's going to be devastated, Ada. Promise me you'll keep this to yourself for now."

"Someone else will gossip," I say, but I look away before Bets does. I won't tell Daddy, and nobody will say a single word to Mama. That's just the way things work.

"Ada, promise."

I nod, but I couldn't be more shocked and hurt if Snooks jumped up and bit me. First my mama resigns from adulting, then Bets asks me to do it instead.

I walk out of this conversation, out of the back room, out of the bakery. Aunt Bets can lock up and collect Mason herself.

When I'm home, I head straight for the basement. I crash in a beanbag chair and pull an old blanket over me. Snooks was under the blanket, and he gets uppity and tries to yank it out of my hands, but I ignore him.

A few minutes later, I hear the back door rattle open, then shut with a bang, and my neighbor boy comes downstairs and joins me. Cayden doesn't say anything, just picks his own beanbag and sits there shredding a Full Bar. His parents found his cache and got upset that he's not eating them, so destroying the evidence is his latest hobby. NOW WITH NEW S'MORES ACTION! the wrapper blares. I think the cardboard-flavored foamy bits are supposed to be marshmallows.

We sit there in silence as I mull over the PC's obvious betrayals, and Aunt Bets's softer, subtler one.

If it's true that doubt is the beginning of wisdom, I'm going to end up a genius.

It's the third afternoon Cayden has spent in my basement. In theory, he's here to keep me company while I stare at the wall. But he eats a lot of sandwiches while he does it. I can't really blame him. Bets's sandwiches are approaching epic proportions now that she knows how hungry he is, and she's trying to apologize to me with food, too. I give Cayden mine.

Raymond's there, too, but everything is weird between us. I think that for him, "his" beanbag chair in my basement serves the same purpose as a hospital bed. Raymond's here for visiting hours.

I can't deal with him sitting there not looking at me for one more minute.

I load Nopes and pull up my post about the puppets. I haven't checked in for days, and it has a ton of replies. I scroll down, skimming as I go.

Sheesh.

The problem with Nopes is it's like a hydra, in the sense that it has no clue which head is in charge. And it has a lot of heads.

Some Nopesers are seizing the opportunity to say a bunch of really nasty stuff about puppets in general.

Others think the puppets are a figment of our imagination, the result of chemicals in our drinking water.

There's an argument going on about whether to demand the puppets' birth certificates, which is obviously pointless because of Oddiputians' long, proud tradition of feeding babies mush made from their birth certificates to keep them off the grid.

Then part of the conversation seizes my attention, and it's bad, bad news. My mouth goes dry as I realize what I've done.

"Nonono," I say.

Cayden leans over to see what I'm looking at.

"Ada, even I know not to read the comments."

I grab the front of his hoodie and pull him closer. I point at the screen.

"Look at that."

StringCan: *All I know is, there's been a lot less collusion around here since the puppets came to town.*

n00b: *What even is collusion? Does anybody know?*

AnonAnon: *I'm with the original poster. The members of*

the Protection Committee are not our friends. They're preda-
tors, and when they look at us, they see dinner.

SasquatchDude: *ZOMG, the puppets are cannibals?*

n00b: *If they were cannibals, they'd eat would.*

StringCan: *Wood they really?*

Anon-adon: *I did some checking, and I figured out what
kind of government we have. Do you know what a junta is? It's
a bunch of bullies who run off a community's rightful leaders
and take over. That's what we've got right here: a puppet junta.*

StringCan: *I don't care if it's a puppet jamboree, at least
they keep things orderly.*

AnonLebron: *Sure. And every now and then, they eat one
of us. NBD.*

StringCan: *So? It's not like Sparky was working on a cure
for cancer.*

SasquatchDude: *Still . . .*

AnonAnOnAnOn: *Only one way to solve this problem.
Somebody's got to destroy the puppet junta.*

I've never seen anyone dare to put something like that in
writing before. And instead of everyone freaking out and
swearing their undying loyalty to the PC, there's an anon-a-
thon of agreement. Then the conversation goes conspicuously
silent, and I strongly suspect we're about to have an epidemic
of collusion.

I whirl on Cayden and Raymond, not sure if I'm talking or
screaming.

"What are they talking about? Destroying the puppets
doesn't free the puppeteers. They just shut down! They die!"

Cayden looks as shocked as I feel, but it fades as he starts thinking things through.

"The Nopesers don't know that," he says. "We didn't put it in the post."

"What if someone's planning to do something tonight? We have to stop this right now!"

I start pounding keys, preparing to make another anonymous post so I can clear this up—and get only a gif of Whanslaw, shaking his head in grandfatherly disappointment, for my troubles.

Nopes is offline, and I just unleashed an anonymous army on Pearl.

"The hide-and-shack!" I say. "Someone could go out there to verify. We can tell them, and spread the word!"

I'm halfway up the stairs already, and I'm going with or without them, but it matters when they follow me even though I no longer deserve it.

I first get an inkling that something might be wronger than we thought when I detect a five-alarm smell for anyone who lives in the desert: smoke. Fire spreads so fast around here that there's no stopping it once it gets going. Raymond wrinkles his nose before I can say anything. He looks at me, not to tell me, but to see confirmation on my face. After all our disagreements, I'm glad to see that he still has confidence in me.

I see Cayden reach for his bag and pull out a recently

acquired slingshot. Something's different about the gesture. Less nerves, more readiness, I think. He's changing.

Part of me figured the cabin would be elsewhere and we'd have to sit around waiting for it to show up. But it's there. At least, what's left of it.

The shack is ablaze. As we arrive, one of the walls collapses inward with a crash. Another's a charred stub. The door is still there, but it's been kicked in.

I run to the wreckage. Cayden's right behind me. Then I realize that whoever burned it down could be watching, hoping to find Nopesers like we were, and I pull him down into the sagebrush instead. Raymond's already thought of this, of course. He skulks his way over to us, staying low.

Somewhere, the Blurmonster growls.

"I'm not wearing any BASH!" Cayden says, before I can ask. He looks around cautiously. "Do you think the Blurmonster did this?"

I shake my head. "If it was going to ram the shack, it would have done it when we were hiding. Also, the Blurmonster doesn't start fires."

"There are footprints all over the place," says Raymond. "Look."

Sure enough, there are.

And there are drag marks. Light ones, like from the edges of a robe.

I'm following them when I step around some brush and find myself mere cubits away from the Blurmonster.

It's not moving, really. Just sitting there, purring. We're

not wearing BASH! or hatching evil plots, and it's not hassling us.

The puppets have been lying like rugs about everything that matters. Maybe they lied about this.

"Whoa," says Raymond, coming up behind me. I hold a hand up to shush him.

Me and Raymond might not always agree, but the kid knows who he's dealing with. "Ada, what are you going to do?" he asks.

"I'm going to walk up to it and see what happens."

I'm so nervous as I move in the Blurmonster's direction that I imagine I can feel my body heading two ways at once. My steps are so cautious I bet I'm not even leaving prints. But I go. Closer, and closer. Its low rumble doesn't change tempo or volume. Closer. I hear Raymond and Cayden whisper-arguing behind me, but neither of them wants to make enough noise to break the stalemate.

Closer.

I extend my hand, fingers trembling.

Something shoots out of the sagebrush and runs smack into my ankles.

I about jump out of my sneakers. I don't scream, but I definitely emit a strangled squeal. The Blurmonster puffs in surprise, and the edges of it eddy upward, like it's bobbing its head in alarm. I freeze.

The critter that might have just sealed my fate goes bounding off, antlers held high, white rabbit tail flashing. I deserve it. I filled the co-op with them the last time Scoby advertised a special on free-range jackalope. I still think it honored the spirit of the ad. I shut my eyes, then open them when I realize how pointless it is to avoid looking at an invisible monster.

"Ada, come back," hisses Cayden, but I ignore him. The Blurmonster seems to have calmed. I want to say it's watching me, but of course I can't tell. Slowly, I edge my hand out toward it again. It takes a long time to work up the guts to step forward, but I do. Without getting any louder, its low, even rumble begins to fill the air, until everything around us—the air, the landscape, my own self—seems to vibrate. Closer . . . closer . . . and then my hand touches . . . something. It's warm. It's soft. Air puffs against my hand.

The Blurmonster makes a deep chuttering sound, and I jump a little. It snorts.

"Hey," I say softly. "This is all right. This is oooookay."

Once I've been there long enough to feel secure that it's accepting me and not just confused, I step away. Then I do the scariest thing of all. I turn my back on my blurry new friend and walk over to my startled old friends. Raymond stands out, dark against the late-day sky, and Cayden's eyes are wide behind the sweep of his hair.

"Sometimes," I say as I pass them, "a calculated risk pays off."

It follows us most of the way back before it slides off into the wild. I don't mind. Between the boys' silence and the voice in my head that won't stop shouting Pearl's in danger, I appreciate the company.

Chapter 28

Deserter

"Cayden?"

Mr. Mitchell collected the Sweepstakes canvassing forms today, and we were supposed to figure out what to do about the anonymous Nopesers after school, but something's not right at Cayden's house. Boxes of trash, a broken lamp, and a coffee table Xerple busted in a fit of enthusiasm are sitting out by the curb. A zombie rabbit is upside down in one of the boxes, feet flailing. Another one puts the lamp plug in his mouth, and the bulb lights up. I take the steps at a run, and find the front hallway cluttered with boxes and suitcases. I yell for Cayden, and he answers from upstairs.

I burst into his room. He's throwing his soccer cleats into his shiny wheelie suitcase, with the biggest frown on his face

I've ever seen—and I saw him during the fourth-period spider invasion.

"What the heck are you doing?"

I think he's been looking for someone to shout at. "What does it look like I'm doing? I'm packing."

I take a deep breath and try again. "Okay, never mind. WHY?"

He slams his suitcase shut half full, which is how I know he's doing it for effect.

"Remember what Xerple said about Signal Boost?"

I rack my brain. "The night we went . . . up there? About it being bad medicine?"

He shoves a stack of jeans into a duffel bag with great feeling. "Yeah, that. Turns out he was right."

"How do you know?"

"I switched out the labels, and replaced all my parents' Signal Boost with sodas from Bodega Bodega."

Uh-oh.

"It went badly?"

"My parents are back to their normal selves. Unfortunately, they've revised their opinion of our 'dog.' And our yard. And, you know, the town. They're demanding job transfers from Splint even as we speak."

"Can't you give them their Signal Boost back so they forget?"

He stares at me for a very long time. I guess it was kind of a selfish question.

"So that's it? You're just . . . leaving?"

"Oh, right. I forgot, I'm talking to Oddity's number one rebel turned double agent. My parents say we're leaving. And in the normal world, Ada, kids do what their parents say."

"Even if their parents call them Uncle Gunnar?"

"Right, except this messed-up town caused that problem, didn't it? Around here, evil grocery store owners drug people with old-fashioned sodas."

"You don't want to get to the bottom of why Greeley is doing that?"

"I bet I know why! Greeley and the puppets don't want my parents fixing the cell signal around here."

"And you're going to let them get away with it?"

"You know what? Yes! I want to go back to Chicago and go to baseball games, and eat deep-dish pizza, and do normal science homework and not Applied Bomb-Defusing Tactics."

I throw my hands up in the air. "Fine. Fine! But think about this: If you really want to leave so bad, why are you angry?"

I slam his door behind me before he can answer.

I end up on his back stoop, and to be honest, I'm a little numb. I ought to be thrilled. Without Cayden, I've got one less thing to worry about, right?

Except, in all fairness, he's shaped up a lot. When I've needed him, he's had my back. I might also be a little bit sappy over the way he's taken care of Xerple.

Right after this thought enters my head, someone sniffles. It's muffled, like the person's trying to be quiet, but he's about as subtle as a bear horn. I peer around the corner.

It's Xerple, of course. Poor little guy. He's on the other side of the house from the side yard, so he hasn't lost his mind completely, but still, being outside without us is taking his life in his . . . whatever.

I don't know how he's crying with no eyes, but he's doing it. Things are sploshy in the yard at his feet, and as I recall, we live in the desert. Mr. Mitchell said we're technically in grasslands and mixed conifer woodland, but whatever. I creep around the corner and say the little alien's name. He's so bummed out he doesn't even move.

"Hey, Ada," he says in a sad little voice. I reach out carefully and put a hand on top of his grape-shaped head, though I might get fouled out of his life for doing it. Instead, he leans into my palm. He's warm and pitiful.

"You heard, huh?"

"Yes." He takes a deep, shuddering breath. "Cayden is . . . l-leaving me."

Uh-oh. That's exactly how I feel. Like he's leaving *me*. But Xerple's getting a lot more left than I am. Even as the landlady, I'm not sure I can keep him safe if he has to walk through my yard to get in and out of the house. I'd better start thinking about who can take him.

I pat him a little. "Don't worry, Xerple. We'll find someplace safe for you to live."

He stands bolt upright all of a sudden, quivering with outrage.

"I do not want someplace to live! Places are easy! There are always more places. People are different. Finding the right person is HARD. And . . ." Here his bottom lip starts trembling, which is really alarming when you consider that it takes up roughly half his face. "Cayden is leaving!" He begins to sob. I sit with him until Daddy calls me in to dinner.

It takes me a long time to fall asleep, so I can't have been dreaming for long when I wake to a pattering noise I almost never hear: *rain*. The second I recognize it, I reach over, flip on my lamp, and look up at the water stains over my bed.

It must have gone on just long enough.

The vines curl down from the ceiling like they're curious, or reaching out to greet me after their long absence. I don't remember ever being afraid of them. They're covered, all over, with huge, bell-like paperwhite flowers. Some are as big as my head, and they're growing so fast they rustle as they unfurl. I always run to look for them if I'm home when it's raining, but they aren't fooled by ten-minute thundershowers that are bark and bite and nothing else. They wait for the longest rain of the year. They're one of the few things Pearl and I never argued about, too, which makes them even more perfect. I lie breathing in their faint scent, which reminds me of old letters scented with perfume so faded it's almost not there at all.

When I've gotten my fill of them, and the lowest one is brushing against the tip of my nose, I slide sideways out of bed and throw on my sneakers. It's time to initiate someone new into this little tradition of ours.

Mason wakes up right away when I shake his shoulder. I put a finger to my lips.

"Come on, kiddo."

He obeys without being told twice, sitting up and shoving his feet into shoes he keeps lined up by the bed, just like we taught him.

We creep downstairs. I make him wait in the hall while I check out the dining room windows to make sure there's nothing in the yard to worry about. Then I lead him outside.

I love the smell of rain on hot pavement. I don't think Mase has ever been out in the rain at night before, and his nose is twitching like a rabbit's. A real rabbit. But he doesn't see the best part until we round the corner of the house.

All across the side yard, they're coming up, the lucents. I don't know if they're fungi or flowers. They've always seemed like a little of both, really, with their tall, glowing stems and their globelike, beaming tops. They reflect in Mason's wide eyes. He squeezes my hand, and all of a sudden I'm in tears. I thought he was too big to do that anymore. I wish Pearl was here to hold his other hand while we watch.

I hear a tiny "Whoa!" I look over to see a zombie rabbit sleepily rubbing his eyes. More and more come to join him, peeking out of the landscaping in amazement, and then comes a true miracle: they're happy. They giggle, and whoop, and race in circles around the clusters of lucents.

I hear a gentle tap on glass, and glance at the house to find Daddy looking out the family room window. I figure I'm in for it, but instead he smiles at me as the gentle rain comes down, and down, and down, making pearls in our hair.

Chapter 29
Party Crasher

The problem with a town like Oddity is that there's nowhere to conspire. An unlimited amount of nowhere. Miles and miles of nowhere. And my legs are getting tired from hiking around the nowhere looking for the other anonymous Nopesers.

That's when it finally occurs to me. Collusion is hungry work. I don't have to search the nowhere. All I really need to do is find the best nowhere-adjacent restaurant.

Which is how I got where I am now.

The afternoon sun glares on the silver curves of Crash Diner (and the flying saucer sprouting from the roof). The bells on the door bang the glass as I push my way in. On the jukebox, Elvis is singing about how he's never lied to me. You know things are bad when I find that comforting.

It's busy, but not quite dinnertime yet, so I take a whole

booth without so much as a dirty look from Patsy. I down my Frito pie, then treat myself to Patsy's famous cactus float, which is fizzy pink heaven in a glass. As I sit there sipping and doodling on my place mat, I virtuously refrain from staring at one of the squid-chinned aliens. He's holding his red plastic basket of curly fries right up to his face, and it's totally fascinating because it's almost impossible to tell the fries from the tentacles.

As the level of float in my glass drops, I calculate my food-to-loitering ratio and figure I've got about fifteen minutes to spy on my fellow Oddiputians before I have to order something else.

Eavesdropping is not as exciting as it sounds. I quickly reach two conclusions: Oddiputians who eat early dinners have a lot of free time, and they mostly spend it complaining.

". . . and I told her, if you're not going to plunge the drains like I told you to, whatever comes up them when you're in the tub is your own problem to deal with. . . ."

"Oh, you don't have to tell me! Mine came downstairs this morning, and lo and behold, he's got a bump on his forehead. The Murphys just got over a spider infestation, so you know perfectly well that's what it is. If I've told him once, I've told him a thousand times, don't share hats! But no, he knows everything."

Just when I'm slurping my float as loud as I can in self-defense, someone across the aisle says, "Sweepstakes Day. It has to be then."

"But why? That's a terrible time. Everyone will be there."

"Exactly. Everyone will be there."

There's a pause. I lean over my doodling and sneak a peek. Two guys. One is my dad's age, with a mustache. The other is practically still a kid. He's got one of those neck tattoos that annoy me because I never know whether it's rude to read them, and the gauges in his earlobes are so big I want to give a zombie rabbit a Ping-Pong ball and send it over there to practice free throws. I immediately dub him YOLObes.

"Look," says Mustache, "if everyone sees it—"

"—we'll be killed," says YOLObes.

"Okay. Yes. Maybe. But it will be useful."

"Um . . . ," says YOLObes. "How?"

I hear Mustache shift in the booth. "I don't know how to do it yet. Maybe with smashing! Or an explosion. Or a car chase. But—"

"No, I mean how will being dead be useful? Like, will our great sacrifice destroy the . . . you know whos? Will it save lives?"

Another pause.

"Oh. Well. Not necessarily. I think it will be symbolically useful."

"Symbolically useful?"

"Yes. You see, what happens is, we try to kill them, and they kill us."

"Riiiiight," says YOLObes. "And then there's a revolution?"

"Not exactly," says Mustache. "But everyone learns an important lesson."

"What lesson is that?"

"They learn that you can stand up to . . . you know."

"If you want to get killed."

"Yes."

There's a long pause as YOLObes thinks about this. Finally, he says, "Or we could go play Winterhammer."

"Move over, Fred," says a woman, shoving her way roughly into Mustache's side of the booth.

"No names!" Mustache hisses. I can't see him anymore behind the newcomer's broad shoulders and her hair, which is so bed-head spiky it looks angry. Her head turns my way, and I instantly look back at my place mat, pretending to read an ad for insurance. NOW WITH ARMADUINO PROTECTION!

"What did I miss?" Angry Hair asks.

Duke, the skinny-jeaned server, blocks my view.

"Anything I can get?" he drawls.

Out of my way, but I can't say that out loud, so I order a soda instead, and he ambles off to get it. I crane my ears like satellite dishes to find out what I missed.

Angry Hair is talking. "If you want to be useful symbols, Godspeed, but I've got bigger fish to fry, like that big cod Lanches—"

"Shhhh!" hiss Mustache and YOLObes.

She lowers her voice in that way that suggests she has no clue how to whisper. "Look, Sparky was my mailman, and where is he now? We owe it to him and everyone else they took to wreck the junta. At least we can rescue the ones they're using now."

I startle in my seat because this is what I've been waiting

for. I need to go over there this second and tell them what's what.

Angry Hair gets up faster than I can, though, tossing cash down on the table to cover everybody.

"I'm not known for being soft-spoken," she says. "Let's get out of here so we can talk."

"Where are we going?" asks YOLObes.

"Nowhere."

Figures. I jump up to follow them.

"Djoo pay?" asks Duke, wandering over with my soda. I thrust money at him and hurry out the door. They're disappearing around the side of the diner. I'm rushing between the parked cars and the building, past a red bumper, when someone grabs my arm.

"Ada, I'm so glad you're here!" says Song. "Come help me with this."

"Song, I can't," I just about wail. "I have to go!"

"It's fast," she assures me. "Come on."

She's surprisingly strong. I let her drag me around the back of her car, craning my neck to track the Nopesers over my shoulder. She jams her key into her trunk lock and turns it. The hatch pops open.

"See?" she says, shoving me in front of her. "Right there."

Before I can react to the mannequin reaching for me, it's already pulled me in with it.

"Song!" I shout. "What are you—"

She slams the trunk shut behind me.

Chapter 30

Scoby

By the time I can have an actual conversation with Song again, I'm spitting mad. I'm also tied to a chair in the basement of her shop. Mannequins. You can kick and pinch them all day, but they don't care, and I don't have any matches on me, because Song took my backpack.

"Who keeps a mannequin in the trunk of a Ford Escort?" I demand.

"They're my roadside assistance plan. Mannequins are surprisingly good at changing flats."

"And kidnapping kids."

"Don't even try to play the victim card with me, Ada Roundtree! I know who you are. You're that anonymous user who's been fomenting rebellion on Nopes!"

"What even is *fomenting?* It sounds like something Scoby would do."

"Ada!"

I take a good look at Song, and it calms me down a little. I mean, obviously this is not how she should treat her independent contractors, but her forehead is glistening with sweat, and her hair's borderline disheveled.

"Song, why are you so upset?"

"Because you think you're invincible!" When I realize she's on the verge of tears, I finally get it.

I look down at myself in disbelief.

"Are you saying you tied me up for my own safety?"

"That's exactly what I'm saying! If I hadn't stopped you today, you'd have gone and . . . colluded with those Nopesers, wouldn't you? Everyone in the diner could hear them talking! Have you thought for one second about how fast that's going to get back to the Protection Committee?"

"Don't you mean the puppet junta?"

Song wipes her palms on her dress. It's white with black spots today, and I can't help but think of another one of Cayden's weirdo books, *Treasure Island*. Song's wearing hundreds of warnings. When she speaks again, though, her voice is quieter.

"Ada, I know things have been hard, but you have to stop behaving so recklessly. The police have been in twice asking me who bought sunglasses recently, did you know that? This is no time to start being all . . . death-defying."

Hey. I was defying death way before it was cool.

I sigh.

"I guess I understand why you're worried, and . . . it's nice that you care. But I swear I have reasons. You know about my sister—"

"Pearl."

Oh, I love Song. No one says her name anymore.

"Yeah. Pearl." I look Song straight in the eye, which I've been avoiding. "If you untie me, I'll tell you everything. I promise I won't try to run."

Then again, there are like fifty mannequins standing guard, so I guess it's a compliment that she tied me up in the first place.

Song weighs her options for a minute, then nods to a mannequin behind me. It unties the ropes, and I rub my wrists. Then she pulls up a stool and listens like she promised, her face serious. She does not interrupt me once. In the color and whirl of her shop or the diner, it's easy to miss how beautiful Song is—how she stands out from everything around her. Here, illuminated by a bare bulb in the dark of the basement, she's suddenly the only thing I see, and the idea of losing her friendship if she doesn't understand hurts almost as much as losing Pearl. Untouchy me gets touchy all over again, and I reach out to take her hands. Mine are scruffy, with dirt under the nails. Hers are smooth and perfect, with bright red, shiny nail polish.

"I believed so many lies, Song," I tell her when I'm finished. "Mike Hannagan wasn't a murderer; his store was in Greeley's way. I bet you anything the original mayor and

sheriff didn't commit arson, either. The puppets wanted to run things, so they framed them. I know—" I hesitate. No one talks about where new people come from, even if she had told me. "I know you came here from someplace bad. If the junta is allowed to keep using people as puppeteers, Oddity will be a bad place, too. So they have to be stopped. But I'm not colluding with anyone. I just can't sacrifice my sister if there's a chance I can save her. I need everybody to stay out of the way and let me try. Please?"

Song is always smiling, always moving. Only now, when she's so still, do I realize that being happy can be a way of hiding. I guess it's a better way than Mama's, but I think I'll see through it from now on. Her warm, tan face has gone almost gray, quiet enough for the dust motes twirling down through the harsh light to start seeming like they're making noise. Then she squeezes my hands.

"You could get hurt. Even killed."

"I'd rather be a dead person who tried than a live person who did nothing. Are you going to rat me out?"

She flinches, and her eyes widen in shock. "Ada, no!"

I try not to look relieved. "What are you going to do, then?"

"I'll be quiet if you be careful."

I squeeze her hands. "Deal."

So now I'm walking home for dinner. I totally lost the Nopesers, and I'm betting I'm not going to get a chance like that again. It's my own fault for not noticing I was being stalked while I was stalking them. I should tell Mr. Mitchell that I really get irony now.

The Sweepstakes is bearing down on me like a charging Blurmonster. I never canvassed half my route, though that probably doesn't matter now.

But because Song interfered, I still have the element of surprise. No one else knows I haven't given up, not even Raymond, not even Whanslaw. There has to be a way to put things back in balance, to save everyone, including Pearl. I just have to find it.

Then something that's been tugging at the edge of my attention for weeks finally connects, and I realize I have an idea who might know.

The store bell jangles as I enter the co-op, but the way the monstrosity in the jar on the counter is glaring at me, you'd think I'd pulled the fire alarm. I never, ever come in here, and he's the reason why.

Scoby.

Imagine a huge sun-tea jar, the kind with a spigot at the bottom, filled with a pale, bubbling liquid. Now imagine a yellowish-brown, flying saucer–shaped funguslike thing floating in it. Back in third grade, when Delmar puked on the floor in the middle of GMO Taste Testing Day, Ms. Burchett told us that another word for puking is *emesis*. Every time I see Scoby, I think about how the word *nemesis* has *emesis* right in it.

That can't be an accident.

There's a white five-gallon bucket on the floor under the

tap, to catch drips. On the counter next to the jar is a black sign with white lettering that reads TAP HARASSMENT WILL NOT BE TOLERATED. There are, in fact, a number of pretty cranky black-and-white signs around the co-op. SHUT THE FREEZER DOOR WHILE YOU THINK. UNATTENDED CHILDREN WILL BE CONSIDERED SOURCES OF FREE-RANGE MEAT. That kind of thing.

The first time Mama ever brought us to the co-op, we must have been three years old, because we were wearing our bike helmets and carrying wooden swords. We didn't understand Scoby was alive until we were right up by the counter. He slammed against the side of his jar and snickered when I screamed.

He made Pearl cry.

Nobody makes Pearl cry.

This is the first time I've come in here to do anything but wreak havoc in eight years.

I eye the little fungus.

"They're not here!" he shouts.

I roll my eyes. "Who isn't?"

"Anyone! Whoever you're here to see! I'm the only one here, ergo they're not! So get out!"

I fold my arms and do my best to look bratty.

"You're out of luck today, Scoby," I say. "I'm here to talk to you."

He ignores my oh-so-on-purpose mistake. "Like I have time."

I crane my neck to look pointedly around at the nothing that's happening in the co-op right now.

"I'm going to go ahead and talk," I say, "and if you don't like it, you can leave."

We both look down at the place where the jar meets the counter. He snarls, a nasty, bubbling sound, and spins around to face away from me.

Mad as he is, I don't think he'll . . . well, I was going to say run and tell the junta, and of course he's not going to do that, but I don't think he'll tell on me, is the point. I'm banking on the fact that Scoby hates . . . well, everybody.

"I have questions about the Protection Committee," I say.

"Why would I know anything about that?" he asks with another snarl.

"You've been here longer than anybody. In fact, I'm pretty sure you came to town with the original Greeley and the puppets." One good thing came from all that glitter torture. While redoing the cardboard caravan, I realized: That's not a bottle painted on the side. It's a jar.

Scoby rotates in his fizzy potion until he's facing me again.

"You filled the co-op with bees!"

"I did not!" I say. In my defense, it was an act of social justice. Me and the bees were liberating the honey.

"You're the one who taught the other children to call kombucha *Scoby-Doo*."

That was Pearl.

"I have nothing to say to you, you little germ!" he burbles. "Get out of my store!"

"It's not a store, it's a co-op, and you're being pretty unco-operative right now," I say.

He sneers. "Well, isn't that just too bad?"

I've had it with uppity mushrooms who replace the frosting in my sandwich cookies with toothpaste. I grab the spigot on his jar.

He freezes. I mean, not literally, I'm sure he's room temperature, but he stops moving.

"Don't you dare," he says.

"I do," I say. "I totally do dare. I am going to drain this jar dry if you don't start talking, Scoby, because I do not have time for your nonsense right now."

He locks stares with me, but I don't flinch. Finally, he . . . blinks, I guess, and says, "Ask your inane questions."

Slowly, I remove my hand from the tap.

"So . . . ," I say. "The puppets use puppeteers as, like, batteries, right?"

"As energy sources, yes," he says. He seems to puff up a bit as he speaks. "The puppets use the energy from the puppeteers' souls."

"I guess that makes sense," I say. "After all, a puppet wouldn't have a soul."

He snorts at me. Ew. That means there's Scoby snot in the kombucha. One more reason not to drink it.

"Shows what you know," he says. "Most puppets aren't alive, are they?"

"Of course not. But these puppets are different. You said so yourself. They're alive because they feed off people's souls," I say.

"I said no such thing!" he says. "How would they ever get

the idea to feed off people's souls if they weren't alive? Dead things don't get ideas."

What?

"That makes no sense," I say. "If they need souls to be alive, how were they alive before they had souls?"

His edges ripple a bit. It's interesting, watching a fungus be smug.

"Better ask yourself, 'How long have they been puppets?'"

Now that's interesting.

I widen my eyes to look extra curious. "How long, Scoby?"

He dips forward in the jar, like he's leaning my way. I step closer.

"That blue-faced fancy man and his fish-headed friend came to America with Cortés, the conquistador."

I'm insulted. "I know who Cortés is. But, um, their names are Whanslaw and Lanchester. That doesn't sound very Spanish."

"Haven't you ever heard of an alias, little girl? The point is, they came in their own skins."

It takes a minute for it to sink in.

"They were people, and they put themselves in puppet bodies on PURPOSE?" I ask.

He wibbles in a way that must be nodding.

"They have their own souls, and they're using ours ANYWAY?" I ask.

He wibbles again.

"Those jerks!" I say. "Why don't they use their own?"

"They last longer the less you use them," he says. "Here's a better question: Where do they keep them?"

That, I realize, is the ten-million-dollar question.

"Do you know?" I ask.

"Do you know?" he mimics. "No! How would I know?"

"I thought Kiyo might have told you."

"That wicked old thing? Why would she tell me something like that?" he asks.

This confuses me. "Well, I thought maybe you came to America together, since you come from the same country and everything."

He draws back, creating eddies in the liquid in his jar.

"Which country?" he asks.

Uh-oh. I hesitate. "Um . . . Japan?"

Scoby squishes all up. If he had hands, they'd be on his hips right now. "Japan."

Isn't kombucha Japanese? Like sushi?

"Right," I say. "Japan. Right?"

"Get out," says Scoby.

"Where are you from, then?"

"Get. Out."

"Korea?" I ask. "Is it Korea?" This is super embarrassing.

"GET OUT!" Scoby's kombucha foams wildly. His jar rocks and thumps on the counter.

I duck behind a rack of potato chips in case Scoby's jar explodes, and make my escape. But I make sure to slam the door when I go.

Chapter 31

Plotting

Though Nopes shows no sign of ever returning, the sunglasses continue to appear, and the junta doesn't take this little protest lying down. When taking all the dangling sunglass halves they can find doesn't work, they clear the unbroken ones from store shelves. They confiscate Song's supply.

Protestors spray-paint sunglasses on walls and sidewalks instead. It's not all kids anymore, either. Word is spreading.

Then the police start knocking on the doors of people who've been buying spray paint at the five-and-dime. Doesn't matter. People use chalk. There's no point confiscating that. After all, there are plenty of rocks around here that work just as well as chalk, as any kid who has ever been bored can tell you.

The junta can't watch everybody all the time, no matter

how much they might like to. Even the zombie rabbits and aliens get in on it, scrawling insults on every available surface, though they're really terrible spellers.

Even when the junta orders everyone to be inside by sunset.

Even when the secret police cruise the streets in black vans at all hours.

I'm sitting in bed going over and over the remaining holes in my plan when there's a thump low down on my door. I swing my feet out of bed and go to answer it, cautiously, in case it's Aunt Bets and she's traced all this trouble back to me.

Instead I find Snooks.

He's wearing one of my purple-striped leg warmers. All I can see are his toes and his head. It's like he's been swallowed by a predatory turtleneck.

"Raymond is climbing the house," he says, without bothering to greet me.

"I'm sorry, what now?"

"He's outside my window. It's okay. We needed someone to heckle. But I tell you so you know, in case we hurt his feelings and he leaves."

I'm not gonna even get into Snooks calling Pearl's window *his*. She can handle that mess when she gets back. I tiptoe down the hall.

"Make a little more noise," I tell Raymond from the relative safety of Pearl's . . . er, Snooks's window.

"Will you pull me up?" he asks. "These little punks are gonna wake the dead."

From below come the jeers of our tiny delinquent crew.

"You climb like a dog!"

"Dogs don't climb," he says.

"Right! You get it!"

"They like it when you argue," I say, hauling him up by the armpits. He turns sideways to sit on the sill, swinging his legs into the room, then shuts the window on the taunting below.

"Thanks. What's the trellis doing on this side of the house, anyhow?"

"Dad moved it so I couldn't use it to avoid punishment."

He nods. Dirtbag. He's got a ground-floor window.

Snooks is standing at the door like some sort of bizarre, purple-striped sentry. Raymond eyes him pointedly. I have a wild urge to pull out one of those old movie lines, like "Whatever you can say in front of me, you can say in front of Snooks," and a giggle rises up in my throat. I squash it.

"See you later, Snooks," I say so we can get on with things. He blinks.

"I will wait in your room." Right. Because that's what I meant. I'm going to be up late reading him bedtime stories from one of Cayden's weirdo books, I can just tell. I suppress an impatient sigh and turn to Raymond.

"Did Cayden tell you he's moving?"

"I'm trying not to think about it."

He bumps my shoulder with his. "Sorry."

"Me, too."

Finally, Raymond lets out a long breath. "You gonna do something on Sweepstakes Day?"

"Yeah. You gonna try and stop me?"

He doesn't answer right away, so I sit on Pearl's bed and stare at her poster of zombies fighting unicorns, waiting while he thinks.

I want to convince him, but what do I say? He doesn't trust me anymore. That's unlikely to improve if I tell him Song kidnapped me to stop me from getting busted for collusion, so . . . things are looking pretty lose-lose, Raymond-wise.

"What are you going to do?" he asks.

"I'm going to find the puppets' souls and turn them loose. If that wakes Pearl up, then we destroy the puppets." I explain what Scoby told me.

"How are we going to find their souls when we're supposed to be at the carnival?" he asks. He's poking holes, and a huge wave of relief sweeps over me. Criticizing means he's in. This is what we do, and it'll be a stronger plan because of it.

"I figure the thing to do is get seen at the carnival at times we choose. Then, even if we're gone for a while, everyone will assume we're lost in the crowd."

He nods. "I bet they'll know it, when their souls are free," he says.

I thought of that, too. "We're going to have to time it just right."

"We," he says, not like he's objecting, but like he's scoping out the right spot for a puzzle piece. "Where do I fit in?"

I need about a million more hands than I have. Then it hits me.

I give him my wickedest grin. "I've got an idea," I say.

The orange flappy-mouthed alien, the one we dubbed Bigmouth, blinks at me. "Regionals?"

I fold my arms. "Well, obviously. I mean, you're highly skilled, and that kind of talent pays off. Sweepstakes Day is the perfect time to take things to the next level."

After weighing my options, I decided to bank on the hope that punkball is so confusing because everyone's making up the rules as they go along. If they can do it, I can, too.

"Who would we be playing?" asks Bigmouth.

I scoff, shaming it for not knowing. "It's not about who's playing. It's about who gets there first."

Coral Brain and Jump-Rope Ears drift out of the bushes, followed by some of the other aliens. The zombie rabbits are bivouacked on the other side of the yard, thankfully. I'll get to them later.

Raising my voice slightly, I continue.

"See, regionals aren't so much a game as a quest. If you're really worthy, then your team will be the first to find them."

"Find what?" burbles Coral Brain.

"The trophies." There's muttering among the ranks of tiny aliens. I quell the urge to run for my front door. Conviction. Loads of eye contact.

"How many are there?" asks someone farther back in the mob.

That one's easy. "Four."

The greedy little boogers groan. "Only four?"

Jump-Rope Ears has a more practical concern. "We don't have a trophy case."

I bug my eyes at it like it's out of its mind.

"Good, because the last thing you'd want to do with a regional punkball trophy is display it for everyone to see!"

They're all confounded by this little tidbit.

"Don't tell me," I say, "that you don't know what to do with regional trophies!"

There's some scuffing of feet, but no one wants to admit they don't know.

I lean down and beckon. "Okay, I'll tell you. But you can't tell anyone where you got this information."

They scuttle forward to listen. The ones that have necks cock their heads.

"The thing about regional trophies," I say, "is that you have to destroy them as soon as you find them . . . *so no one else can get them.*"

"Ohhhhh," they say as one.

I figured that would work. They're mostly motivated by malice and paranoia.

"Where must we go on Sweepstakes Day?"

I lift my arm and point to where the puppet junta's house hulks on the hill like a constipated werewolf.

"There."

Chapter 32
Outburst

I remember how it felt to wake up to the music of the merry-go-round, the smell of fried rattlesnake, and the clattering alarm bells of the shooting galleries and know that today, somebody's whole life would change.

Today, I'm afraid it might be mine.

Even though I knew Sweepstakes Day was coming, even though I've got a knot in my stomach the size of the brain-coral alien, I've got to go see, like we've always done. Part of me thinks it would be bad luck not to.

I throw on jeans and my sailor blouse, tear down the stairs and out the front door, and run smack into Cayden.

"OW!" I yell, much louder than I need to, then glare around, waiting for a zombie rabbit to mess with me. Strangely, there aren't any in the yard. Just aliens, panting under the hedges.

Maybe they won, and all the rabbits are evicted. Why does that make me even madder?

"What did you think you were doing?" I ask, glaring at Cayden.

He's rubbing his forehead. "It's Sweepstakes Day. I thought you might want some company."

"Last I checked, you had one foot out the door. You couldn't wait to get back to Normal Land, where everyone douses themselves in BASH! and eats deep-dish pizza and . . ."

"Ada, shut UP!"

I'm so shocked that I do. He shoves his hair out of his face, which is now extremely red, and starts shouting at me.

"You know where you screwed up just now? You never asked me, 'Cayden, do you still want to leave?' No, you went off, like you always do. You are the most annoying person I've ever met!"

"You really want to stay?" I stare at nothing, thinking this over, calculating his potential to survive to adulthood. Surprisingly, it's gone up quite a bit. I look at his blotchy face. Should I apologize? But he's already talking again.

"Did you ever read those Narnia books I loaned you?"

I'm confused. "The Narnia books?"

"Talking lion? Magical world?"

"Yeah, yeah. I know what books you're talking about, but I don't get what that has to do with—"

"Remember Eustace Scrubb, in the third book?"

Ew. I do. He was a total whiner. I was waiting for him to get eaten for hundreds of pages, and then he didn't. Total missed opportunity, C. S. Lewis.

Cayden's watching me. "See? You hate him. Everyone hates him. He gets to go on this amazing, magical adventure, then he spends the entire time inventing buzzkill."

"So? He's made up!"

Cayden turns around and sits down on our front steps.

"But I'm not. And I don't want to be that guy who'd go home in the middle of the story if he got the chance. Aslan always *makes* the other kids go home at the end, remember? They don't *want* to. You're not supposed to want to."

I'm leaning against the railing, taking this in, when he looks at me.

"Do *you* want me to?"

I think of almost getting savaged by a leopard because of his slow reflexes, of getting chased by the Blurmonster because of his BASH! spray, of his parents pushing Signal Boost on me like drug dealers. I think of him coming with me to Whanslaw's basement, and I think of Xerple hiding behind his house to cry.

I sit down next to him on the steps. For a minute, the only sounds are the carnival music and the rush of the scrambler ride. I make a totally, completely selfish wish.

"I wish you could stay."

He sighs, and shoves me. "Me, too. At least let me help."

I side-eye him. "You sure? Because if you are, I have something you can do."

When I head down to the carnival for some early reconaissance, Aunt Bets is already there, with Mason and Badri.

She's testing out her new running blades. Her gait's different than it used to be, but she's really, truly walking around on actual legs—shiny black ones that curve at the ground to form "feet" with little spike pads attached to help with traction.

Badri's bakery coaster was such a win that Bets decided to research whether prosthetics could be made out of metal, too, and lo and behold, they could. Or something like metal, anyway. Carbon fiber, I think she said. Cayden heard that kind is super expensive to make. When I asked Bets how she did it, she said something about a forge, and an autoclave, and was my homework done yet and why didn't I just bring it downstairs so she could have a look? So I quit asking.

I watch from a distance as Mason cracks wise and she attempts to go after him, laughing. I can't tell if she's swaggering or just balancing, but either way she looks terrific. I'm careful to stay out of her sight line, though. I'm way too jumpy. She'd notice, for sure, and then who knows what would happen? She gets an unhealthy amount of pleasure out of telling us how she's going to be even faster on blades than she is in the wheelchair. If I were her, I'd pretend to be worse at walking than I really was, just to have surprise on my side the next time I had to dish out some justice.

Daddy always works the early part of Sweepstakes Day, because he catches a lot more illegal critters with a lot fewer casualties when there aren't screaming bystanders in the way. City Hall is closed for the holiday, so Mama's lying down, of course. For now, I'm on my own.

I wander over to For a Song, but Song's nowhere to be

found, and the store's locked up, so I go back home. I watch a little TV. I pretend to read a book. Finally, I drift aimlessly around the house until I find myself outside my parents' room. Through the doorway, I see the end of their bed, the wooden footboard with the round balls on top, and on the mattress, a pair of feet in brown, high-heeled shoes. It's like living in a funeral home. I've been sad, and mad, and jealous, and all of a sudden it all comes boiling up and I don't have one more minute of waiting in me.

"Mama!" She doesn't move. Her feet don't even twitch.

"MAMA!" I scream. I enter her room, like I never do anymore, and I slam the open door into the wall on purpose. She hates that. She ought to be hollering at me to be careful, but she doesn't say a single word. She's awake; her eyes are open, staring up at the ceiling. All I want is to shock her out of this stupor. Just this once.

I reach blindly for the top of her dresser, and for one second I see the two of us, little, in the rosy light from her lamp, giggling as she sprays us with perfume. I grab the first thing I touch, a ceramic jewelry box, and throw it at the far wall as hard as I can. It shatters, and earrings fly everywhere. She doesn't blink, which only makes me madder.

I'm her Stella-in-the-closet, but I'm going to learn from Stella's example. I'm not staying in there anymore. Mama's going to have to see me. I throw one precious thing at a time:

Perfume atomizers?

SMASH.

Old cut-crystal vases, filled with pencils and dried flowers?
SMASH.

I destroy each of them, one by one, until there's a jagged mess on the floor that looks like I feel.

There are so many things I want to say to her, but why? She was a good mama once, and a good mama ought to know without being told. I wipe my wet cheeks with the back of my hand, and slam the front door when I get there, for good measure.

Chapter 33

Inevitable Betrayal

The carnival's a lot busier by the time I get back. When I get to the corner by Bodega Bodega, the curb is wall-to-wall packed with parked cars, and there are still people cruising for a spot.

I dodge between the slow-moving, turn-signaling vehicles with Xerple and Snooks close on my heels, and work my way through the throngs of Oddiputians. I pass a booth staffed by a tall, gray, black-eyed alien named Zacharias Cavalcade, who tells fortunes by having people breathe into a whirring machine he holds in the palm of his long-fingered hand. The last time I tried it, he told me I had a 27 percent chance of being killed by an Oddity Bodkin, and that I should buy an Oddity Bodkin for protection. I call shenanigans.

Dewey is standing in front of Greeley's automatic doors,

name tag freshly Sharpied. He's waving people over, ushering them inside, talking up specials on everything from sleep-inducing Popsicles to take-and-bake pizza. That is, except when he isn't. The zombie rabbits are Dewey baiting. From what I see as I go by, they're hiding under food carts like sparrows eyeing crumbs. Every few minutes, one of them will run for the automatic doors. Sometimes he sees them and starts yelling. Other times someone will greet him or ask him a question, and a rabbit will dash forward and trigger the doors before he notices. They're not going in, just messing with him, but Dewey is a lot redder than usual.

Manager distraction can only work in my favor, so I give one rabbit that notices me going past a discreet thumbs-up, and mouth, "Marshmallows." He does some complicated sema-phore with his ears, which I have to assume means yes. I'm betting there'll be a zombie rabbit semaphore instructional sheet written with who knows what slid under my door if I survive this.

"Go on, Snooks," I say, and he runs to join the others, gathering them under the nearest car. I don't see the ensuing conference, but I hear creepy little giggles and some cheering, so I assume they're as stoked about "regionals" as the tiny aliens, who are hopefully even now trashing Whanslaw's house under Raymond's direction.

The temporary stage and mic are set up in front of the tent, like last year, and Greeley is already warming up the crowd. I come into range as the folks watching laugh appreciatively at some joke he made. He's flashing those big white teeth of his, running his finger along the brim of his straw boater hat. I shake my head. Greeleys have been doing this act since Gold Rush times, I realize. Before the puppets found Oddity, the one town where they didn't need to conceal themselves, was the show how they chose their prey? Did Greeley slip through the darkness late at night, snatching the puppets' chosen targets from their beds?

I spot Song, looking fresh as a daisy in spite of the wind and heat. She's wearing a white dress trimmed with black and covered in bright butterflies. She was talking to Badri and Bets, but when she sees me, she excuses herself. She must not say my name, because neither of them looks to see where she's going, and then Mason runs up to them with his hand out for money or tickets, distracting them. Song weaves through the crowd, frantically reaching for me. She bends down to speak into my ear so no one else will hear.

"Do you see them?"

"Who?" I ask.

"The Nopesers! There's one by the cotton candy machine."

I give a sidelong glance. Sure enough, Mustache is over there chowing on cotton candy. It makes it look like he has two mustaches and one of them's pink. He's staring at the stage as he chews. Scanning the crowd, I spot YOLObes by the Tilt-A-Whirl. His neck tattoo ripples as he swallows nervously.

Left to their own devices they'd have run out of steam by now, so Angry Hair must be here, too. I ignore the sinking feeling in my gut. Hopefully there's no time for the Nopesers to do any harm.

I glance up at the puppets' house crouching on the hill. It's hard to tell from this distance, but as I look, I could swear I see papers flying out of an upstairs window. Lucky for us everyone else is too glutted on the aliens' barbecue to notice.

"Ada!" I hadn't realized Song was still talking. I meet her eyes, surprised by the intensity of her expression. "What can I do to help?"

Is she serious? She was so scared before. Now that I'm paying attention, it's clear she still is. Her hands are shaking. But she's offering, and she means it. She'd put herself in danger to help.

Just as I'm about to completely lose my head and hug her in front of the entire town, a hush falls over the crowd, by which I mean that Greeley yells, "And a hush fell over the crowd!" and we all yell "HUSH." The so-called Protection Committee is ascending to the stage, each with a dark-clad puppeteer trailing behind.

I told myself I could handle it, but nothing takes away the sharp slice of pain when I see Pearl behind Whanslaw, working his controls. She's wearing that same black dress. No point investing in wardrobe changes, I guess, when they're just going to use her up. I understand the sunglasses so well now. If I could see her eyes, I'd never be able to stop myself from running to her, shaking her, trying anything I could to make her see me. There's that flash of gold at her throat again, and this time, it startles me. Finally, I take a good hard look.

It's the locket.

I think back to that horrible night in the pit house, and remember the tug as I let go of Pearl. Wheels start to turn in my brain, but before I can come to any conclusions, the announcement begins.

The members of the puppet junta turn to face the crowd. Whanslaw moves to stand in front, with glubby Lanchester and elegant Kiyo flanking him, and Maggie on his other side. Her button eyes stare right at me out of her newly replaced face, her vacant smile freshly painted.

Whanslaw steps up to the microphone, but he doesn't need it. Fear inspires most of the townspeople to silence. You could hear a tumblegeek cough. Besides, I remember how Pearl and I acted before her name was drawn. The sooner the ceremony was over, the sooner we could go back to eating deep-fried candy bars. Some things aren't real until they affect your family.

With no introduction, Whanslaw reads off the winners' names in his deep, theatrical voice. The change is obvious right away.

They're almost all kids.

Some of them I recognize but don't know, but others, like that Emuel kid, and Delmar, are from our class. The only adult in the bunch is Mr. Mitchell, so I guess we'll be getting another new teacher on Monday.

They all shuffle up the steps onto the stage. A few are grinning, excited to be there, but most are obviously Nopesers. Maybe this is even meant as punishment, and a warning to the rest of us.

One girl with frizzy brown curls starts crying. Mr. Mitchell's hangdog expression shows he knows what he's in for, but at least he won't have to grade all our dioramas this weekend, which is for the best. "The Cactus Rampage of 1930" is not my finest effort.

"And, last of all, a very special winner . . . Miss Ada Roundtree!"

Maggie giggles, loud and wild.

Chapter 34

Mama

My body feels numb in the oddest way, like each individual molecule decided it needed personal space. The puppets knew it was me all along. It really is my fault Pearl's a puppeteer. Getting rid of me too is a nice, tidy solution, one the town will accept with a minimum of fuss.

Except that things aren't quiet right now, even though no one has given the crowd the signal to engage in One Minute of Loud and Genuine Applause. There's muttering as the adults realize the stage is full of kids. I bet some people are thinking back to my daddy's pleas at that WUT meeting and finally seeing his point. Then someone starts yelling.

"No!"

It's coming from the street, but there are people being shoved out of the way left and right as the person carves a swath through the crowd toward the stage. I hold my breath, because there's no way it's who I think it is, and I'm not going to cry when it isn't.

But it is.

It's Mama.

She makes it almost all the way to me before Daddy catches up and grabs her. He must have stopped home to drag her out of bed so we wouldn't be violating the rules. He's still wearing his brown animal control uniform. I think Mama might be more than he can handle.

"You leave my baby alone!" she wildcat-screams at the stage.

Whanslaw's not about to waste his time on her. He turns his head, and Greeley vaults back up beside him like some old-timey actor, dripping with fake sympathy.

"Now, now, my good woman," he says, like that's a totally normal thing to say. "It's beneath you to show such jealousy. And of your own child!"

I've never seen so much of the whites of Mama's eyes at once.

"You think you can spread spin control all over this situation like peanut butter, you giant cartoon? I already lost one child, and I am not letting this one go. Ada, come here!" She'd come and get me, but Daddy is strong, and anyone can see he doesn't want to lose his only remaining daughter AND his wife in one day. The cords are standing out on his neck like he's going to cry, but he doesn't loosen his grip on Mama for one second.

Greeley removes his straw hat and clasps it regretfully to his broad, white-shirted chest, where GREELEY is embroidered across his pocket in red thread.

"Madam," he says, with more than the usual amount of woe, "I'm genuinely sorry to say I can't do that. The results of the Sweepstakes are final, and your daughter, much as you might wish to be in her shoes, is the one bound for glory, not you."

"I'm bound to kick your—"

Just for one second, she looks exactly like Aunt Bets, who appears behind her to clamp a hand over her mouth. Most of her is hidden behind our parents, but I can see her face. Unlike Daddy, she's not looking at Mama. She's looking at me. She has tears in her eyes, real tears. If I could make my mouth move, I'd tell her it's okay, it really is, because no matter what happens now, I'll know that Mama showed up for me.

For *me*.

I see Badri behind Bets, carrying Mason, and I'm glad, even though he's a little too old for that sort of thing. Glancing the other way, I see Song. I take a last look around at all of them.

This is not quite how I planned things, but it's going to have to do. I just hope Raymond and Cayden are in position in time. I head for the stairs up to the stage, where Kiyo is flashing her demon eyes at me and Maggie is bouncing up and down. I'm almost there when there's another shout from the far edge of the crowd. This time, it says:

"FIRE!"

My first reaction is a split second of being purely

disgusted with myself. I mean, sure, I'm about to have my soul sucked out by a bunch of malevolent puppets, but how could any fifth grader worth her salt miss the smell of a wildfire? Because there is it, bold as day, wafting in over the smell of grilled burgers and hot dogs: the spicy, acrid, unmistakable smell of burning scrubland.

The most level-headed citizens are already raising licked fingers to the sky, testing the wind, then pointing at the source of this latest crisis. I turn. The fire's coming in from the east. If I strain my eyes, I can see the curls of smoke, even in the white-hot sky. There's been nothing but dry heat and wind since the night the lucents bloomed. We should have expected it.

There are mutters from the crowd.

"Some fool with a cigarette—"

"—are we allowed to leave?"

"All five buckets, you hear me? Get 'em full, then start spraying the roof. I'll be there as soon as I've finished at your grandma's—"

Whanslaw's bullfrog croak rolls out, stifling the chatter of the alarmed Oddiputians.

"COUNTERMEASURES!" he shouts. "All to your stations!"

At once, order is restored. Grills are doused. Carnival rides groan to a halt. The crowd makes way for city personnel. Giving me one last agonized look, Daddy heads for animal control to load a water tank in the back of his pickup and fill it. Bets and Badri each take Mama by an arm, because she looks like she's about to make another run for the stage.

269

"—NOW, Veda," I hear my aunt say. "There won't be a home for anyone to come back to if it burns down. You're in charge of Mason, you hear? He's your nephew, and he needs you now."

Bets doesn't say that I'd usually be in charge of Mason, but my mama sees him look over his shoulder for me, and the focus of her agony shifts. She reaches for his hand like it's a lifeline, and he lets her take it when he'd usually protest.

My family leaves me. They pass Old Joe and his Curtis Clone, Young Joe, who are already hosing down Bodega Bodega. Way down at the other end of the street, I can hear Scoby burbling orders.

I turn to look at the smoke again, and realize it's gone from pale to black, which means some poor sap's outlying home is already on fire. We were so focused on the Sweepstakes that this new danger has taken us completely unawares.

Now it's barreling right down toward Greeley's, where the four members of the puppet junta stand in the nearly empty Greeley's parking lot like sitting ducks, with only a handful of Greeley's blue-shirts for protection.

I think that's my cue.

Chapter 35

Cavalry

I have to get Pearl out of here.

"I don't care what you say!" I shout. I start shoving around in the line of winners like I've forgotten how to get off the stage, creating pandemonium in the ranks. "There's a wildfire coming! I have to get to my post! This silly contest can wait!"

I've got no intention of getting away, of course. I'm getting this show back on the road. It works, too. Before I can blink, Greeley plucks me out of the crowd of winners with one meaty paw.

"You will make your way into the store," glubs Lanchester.

No one says another word. We march down the stage steps, past YOLObes, who's still loitering nervously in the parking lot, though I don't see the other two Nopesers anywhere. We head for the front entrance.

Either the junta's as nervous as we are, or they're extremely cocky. They haven't bound my wrists, or patted me down, or anything. I've still got my Oddity Bodkin in my right front pocket, and I'm lucky my shirt covers it where it's sticking out a bit. I don't know why girls' jeans have to have such eeny weeny pockets, anyway. As we approach the doors of Greeley's, Dewey reaches to unlock them, and actually salutes Greeley. I could not make this up. From the corner of my eye, I see Snooks's long, flowered ears flicking in the shadow of an SUV.

Here we go.

The doors whoosh open.

Greeley pushes me forward.

As we move out of the first door's sensor range and the second set of doors sweeps open, we're suddenly knee deep in a surf of zombie rabbits. They flow past us into the store, swarming up the side aisles. Greeley roars with consternation.

"Not again!"

"Never mind, Greeley," says Whanslaw, behind us.

"But, sir," he groans as we move up the center aisle, where they're already stocking anti-slip mats for Bath Safety Month even though it's months away, "they'll trash my store! I'm still sweeping up rice from the last time!"

Whanslaw is alongside me now, which means Pearl is behind me, next to Greeley. I crane my neck to see her, and once again catch a flash of the locket's chain. I wonder. . . .

"Trust to the plan, Greeley," says Whanslaw.

Before I have time to worry, I hear a chorus of groaning rabbits in the baking aisle.

"Hey! Where are the marshmallows?"

"Keep the ball in your eye!" shouts Snooks. "Think only of regionals!"

Bless his little weirdo heart.

Greeley pushes me ahead of Whanslaw again, and I just about open the swinging doors at the back of the deli with my face.

"Hey!" I object.

"Shaddup," advises Greeley. With Kiyo, Lanchester, Maggie, and all the other Sweepstakes winners and blue-shirts behind us, we march into the stockroom. There's another rush of zombie rabbits as, following Snooks, they storm the back of the store, just like I told them. I can see the freezer. It's open. Its lights are on. The tunnel door yawns darkly, waiting for us. The zombie rabbits stream toward it. And then—

"Ohhhhhhhhhh," the zombie rabbits intone.

As we reach the end of the rows of shelves, I see what got the rabbits' attention. Between us and the freezer, off to the right, is the biggest pile of marshmallows I have ever seen. It looks like Greeley and his blue-shirts emptied the store display, pulled out all their back stock, and ordered more marshmallows in, to boot.

Even punkball can't compete with that.

The rabbits break ranks, rushing the marshmallow mountain and throwing themselves at it like kids at a pile of leaves.

They scream with joy, pelting one another with marshmallows, stuffing their mouths with both tiny paws.

Snooks is fidgeting halfway between me and his villainous little crew, like he's not sure what to do. I'd like to make some suggestions, but Greeley is hustling me toward the tunnel double-time, fueled by his hatred of zombie rabbits.

There's no way I'm going to get away from four puppets and Greeley long enough to search the pit house by myself. The rabbits are totally crucial. What am I going to do?

A shout rolls through the stockroom, and Angry Hair appears, brandishing an enormous butcher knife and running straight at Lanchester. The Sweepstakes winners scatter, some screaming, others cheering. Two of them plow into Maggie in the confusion, and she and her puppeteer go down in a tangle of strings. Greeley leaps to unravel them.

Kiyo shrieks. Up come her horns, and her eyes flash yellow and red. She goes after the wide-eyed, backpedaling Angry Hair, ramming right into her and biting her arm with her rows of sharp, pointed teeth. Lanchester is pummeling at the Nopeser with his hands, fish-mouth gaping as he burbles in alarm.

But Angry Hair is one tough customer. Pulling Kiyo along with her, she swings her right arm, slicing and sawing her way through Lanchester's strings until he collapses to the floor. His puppeteer's hands fall limp at his sides, still holding the controls, as used up as a slowly deflating balloon.

Kiyo releases Angry Hair's arm and flies at her again, trying to take a bite out of her neck. As Angry Hair holds her back, she raises one booted foot and brings it down on Lanchester's head. Again, and again, she stomps, jumps with all her weight, until something cracks under her feet, and then she focuses her energy in that spot until it gives. Kiyo swoops at her again and again, biting anywhere she can reach, but Angry Hair doesn't stop until the whole side of Lanchester's head is caved in.

There's a horrible, ghastly silence. Maggie crawls across the floor toward the disaster that was Lanchester, elbows and knees akimbo, dragging her tottering puppeteer along behind her. When she realizes that the spiky-haired Nopeser is still standing on the ruins of Lanchester's head, she stops, cocking her head at a predatory angle. Now that Angry Hair's attention is undivided, Kiyo backs off, hovering out of reach of the knife.

Angry Hair's knife is at the ready, though she's bleeding from Kiyo's bites, but instead of taking revenge, she turns her head and locks eyes with Whanslaw.

I step between them.

"No," I say.

Angry Hair stares at me, and I realize she has no clue who I am or why she should listen to some random kid. Behind us, Whanslaw begins to laugh.

"Oh," he says. "I see. How sweet. You hope to save your sister."

The way he says it makes me feel small and sad, and so hopeless.

Kiyo and Maggie are prowling behind Angry Hair, ready to attack as soon as there's an opening.

"If you kill him, you'll kill my sister, too," I tell her. "Help me!"

She doesn't trust me, and I guess if I were her I wouldn't, either. The knife flashes as she shifts position. "Get out of the way."

"Heads up!"

Whoosh! Cayden runs toward us at top speed, making a hissing noise. There are startled cries as he cuts through the crowd of Sweepstakes winners and ducks under Greeley's ham-size arms.

"What was that?" screeches the frizzy-haired girl.

"Oh!" groans somebody. "What's that smell?"

It's BASH!

The hissing is coming from the extra-large cans in Cayden's hands. He sprays an enormous cloud at Angry Hair as he goes by, then attacks the marshmallow pile.

"Ew!" I hear from somewhere deep within the marshmallows. "Something smells like sweaty Viking!"

"It's the marshmallows!" shrieks another rabbit. "Abort! Abort!" Zombie rabbits scuttle away from the marshmallows like roaches. Snooks, still lurking around mallow mountain, brightens up like the whole thing was his idea. "This way!" he shouts, and zombie rabbits stream through the freezer and into the tunnel.

Angry Hair circles frantically, trying to keep Kiyo and Maggie at bay within the enormous cloud of stink. Then the swinging doors that lead to the front of the store fly open so hard that they slam against the wall, revealing an empty space that's dangerously out of focus. The Blurmonster has arrived.

I know my cue when I see one.

"It's a MONSTER!" My scream is totally B-movie spectacular. Cayden adds his voice to the bedlam, waving his arms over his head and loping through the crowd riling up my now-panicking fellow citizens, who must be seriously rethinking the word *winner*. Running blows his hair back. He's grinning as he dodges through the crowd and makes his way to me.

The Blurmonster knocks Angry Hair and Lanchester's puppeteer flying. The puppeteer rolls over and over, hands still at his sides, and comes to rest against the wall like a giant squeak toy. Angry Hair lands in the BASH!-soaked, half-eaten pile of marshmallows with a wet squelch. Then the Blurmonster turns its attention to the puppets, and their reaction is more than I dared to hope for.

Kiyo and Maggie are in full retreat. Their puppeteers sway backward, maneuvering them through the stampeding crowd, putting human bodies between them and the Blurmonster. People are shoving one another and slipping in marshmallow goo. The Blurmonster plows through them, single-mindedly pursuing the puppets.

And they're afraid of it.

I've never seen the puppets seem afraid of anything. They're the embodiment of power and control. The Blurmonster is . . . well, we don't know what it is. That's part of what makes it scary. And reports of them fighting it off seem to have been greatly exaggerated.

There's a shouty groan from the marshmallow swamp. Angry Hair is rising up out of the morass, coated in goo like she's the A-marsh-a-mallow Snowman. (They prefer the term *yeti*, but I think I can be forgiven for a little political incorrectness at this point.)

The Blurmonster turns, and at first I think it's being lured by the smell of marshmallow BASH!, but instead, the blur starts moving in this direction. I step to one side, and it heads straight for Whanslaw and my sister.

"Time to go," says Whanslaw, and I know just what he's going to do. He's going to pop back down the tunnel and pull the door shut behind him, separating me from Pearl.

"Cayden!" I yell, and dive for him.

Urged on by Whanslaw's thoughts, Pearl backs quickly into the freezer, which has been emptied for the occasion. Cayden and I scramble after her, and the Blurmonster bears down on all of us with a growling roar.

Whanslaw's hard wooden hand reaches for a handle on the inside of the tunnel door, and it moves so quickly, balanced far more lightly than I'd ever have guessed. It's more than halfway shut by the time we get to it, and I thrust my body into the gap, shoving at the door to make room for Cayden.

"Go, go!" he shouts, shoving me so hard that I land face-first on the dusty stone floor of the tunnel. The door slams shut, echoing heavily in the long, empty space. A second later, the Blurmonster crashes against it, making the wall shake. It clatters and roars its rage.

I roll over to see Cayden crouched, hands on knees, panting.

"You okay?" I ask.

"The door almost cut me in half," he says with a disbelieving laugh. I pull myself to my feet, ignoring my scrapes. If there's a door on the other end, and Pearl and Whanslaw reach it first, he'll lock us in here.

"Come on," I say, and work my way from a stagger to an all-out run. The lights along the tunnel are few and far between, but all I can do is run and hope I don't break my neck.

We luck out. The tunnel slopes gradually up, and even Whanslaw can't make working a puppet's controls faster than running with both hands free. By the time we reach stairs, carved into the rock of the hill itself, we've caught up to them. From here, we can hear shrill voices raised in glee and argument. Whanslaw, intent on this new disturbance, doesn't bother to acknowledge us. Cayden tugs my shirt.

"What do we do now?" he asks.

Once, he'd have asked that with his voice cracking so much I'd have checked to see if his pants were still dry. Now he sounds like an Oddity Middle kid. I'm his team leader, and he's waiting for orders. The kid actually makes me proud.

"Keep your eyes open," I say. "Anything could happen."

I really need that on a T-shirt.

Chapter 36

I Hate Puppets

As Whanslaw and Pearl reach the head of the stairs and step through the open tunnel door into the junta's basement, there's a sudden screech, and Pearl takes two swift steps backward into me. She leans against me, my hands holding her arms, her head on my shoulder. She's cold all over. The chain of the locket digs into my neck. A zombie rabbit charges past, holding a broom like he's jousting. I can't see his opponent, but I hear the crash as they connect.

Whanslaw gives a croak of anger and alarm and he sweeps out of the tunnel, taking my sister away with him. When we follow, I discover he's entered the workshop full of creepy puppet parts, where Sugar is supervising what appears to be the destruction of everything. Rabbits brandish chisels and rasps, bash wooden arms and legs on every available surface, and operate power tools without permission.

It's pretty great.

Whanslaw looks plenty distracted, but not upset enough for something as precious as a soul to be hidden here. He's not rushing off to any other room yet, either.

"You think he's realized his upstairs is full of aliens?" asks Cayden. He points at the stairs we came down on our first, ill-fated trip. There's a messy pile of leather-bound books at the bottom. A bossy little voice upstairs is yelling, "Hup! Hup! Hup!" and another book's arriving every few seconds.

I'm shaken up from touching Pearl. I want to go upstairs to find Raymond. A girl needs her bestie at a time like this. But searching the pit house is my job, and I don't know how long we have. Sooner or later, the mess we left at Greeley's will sort itself, and either the Blurmonster will head up here to kill Whanslaw, or Kiyo and Maggie will come to kill us. I doubt even Whanslaw will be able to stop them.

"Come on," I say.

The zombie rabbit with the broom salutes, as does his opponent, who has a Swiffer. It's like we have our own zany honor guard on either side of the entrance to the pit house.

Inside is more chaos.

I didn't think there was anything much in the pit house to smash, but it looks like the rabbits have found it all. Then I realize the aliens found the trapdoor and opened it. Everything from the study that isn't already on its way down the stairs is getting chucked through the hole. The rabbits are using wooden puppet limbs as baseball bats, trying to hit whatever comes down. Some of the aliens are hanging from the log ceiling like bats, and there's a lot of heckling on both sides.

"Hey, batta batta batta, sa-wing, batta!"

"You throw like a tumblegeek!"

"You catch like a slug!"

"Slugs don't have hands!"

"Exactly! You get it!"

Cayden shakes his head, marveling. "These guys are ridiculous. Look at that!" He points at the cells, where the rabbits appear to have opened the remaining prisoners' padlocks.

"How did you do that?" I demand of Snooks, who's hauling a tottering, dangerously skinny woman out of her cell.

He stares. I mean, he always looks like he's staring, but whatever.

"I turned the latch," he says. "Easy."

"The what?" I ask. "Show me." He bounces up onto the nearest barred metal door, which swings partway closed. He snaps the big metal padlock shut, then waggles his hands ceremoniously for our attention. As we watch, he shoves one ear in the padlock, wiggles it for a minute, then turns it. The lock snaps open.

"Nothing is safe," says Cayden in my ear. I nod, then help the lady nearest me to the hallway. The escaped prisoners head for the stairs.

Raymond thrusts his head down through the trapdoor.

"Hey," he hollers down. "You guys okay?"

"No," I yell back, "and neither are you." I summarize our situation regarding wildfires, evil puppets, and the A-marsh-a-mallow Snowman.

"You know they prefer the term *yeti*, right?" he asks.

I'd roll my eyes, but I doubt he can see them from here.

"Did you find anything?"

He shrugs. "I mean, I'm not sure how we'll know when we find them. We're smashing everything, though. That's a start, right?"

"Keep looking!"

He nods and vanishes.

"Where do we begin?" says Cayden, turning to survey the pit house.

I'm at a bit of a loss, which is bad, because sooner or later our troubles are going to catch up with us. The cells and the pit-in-a-pit. That's all there is to this place.

"Let's check along the walls. We'll go in opposite directions, and meet on the other side," I say.

He nods, and we start looking. I can't find anything, though. There aren't any more doors. There aren't any niches in the walls. There's a pile of buckets and stuff in one corner, but those are obviously just for dealing with the prisoners', um, needs. I wrinkle my nose at the smell. Poor Pearl. By the time I get to Cayden, my stomach is doing barrel rolls.

"Anything?" I ask.

"Not a thing," he says, shoving his hair back impatiently. "Maybe we should go help Raymond?"

"I don't want to get that far from Pearl . . . ," I begin, only now realizing that Whanslaw might have gone upstairs himself, when the lights flicker and go out. I put a hand on Cayden's arm, just to reassure myself he's there. Some very dim light is filtering down through the trapdoor, but that's it.

"Well, that's not good," says Cayden.

Just as I'm about to call him Captain Obvious, the lights cycle up again, and I hear the cough of a generator in the distance. It's officially the first time I'm pleased with the puppet junta's evil brilliance. I sigh with relief. Then—

"What's that long black thing?" says a small, wicked voice.

"I don't know. Let's eat it!"

There's a loud buzz, then a zapping noise. The lights go out again with great finality.

In the darkness, someone giggles.

"There you are, Maggie dear," says Whanslaw from the direction of the pit-house doorway, dashing my last hope that I'd imagined her.

"Puppets can see in the dark?" I say. "That stinks."

"I suppose it will be easier to surrender if you can see our faces," says Whanslaw. "We had an emergency kit here, with glow sticks, but it seems to be missing."

Three glowing zombie rabbits scuttle in from the hallway. One of them has the word SUGAR across his middle.

"Ah," says Whanslaw. "That explains it."

"Over here, guys," I say, and they group themselves around my feet, illuminating Whanslaw and Pearl, as well as Maggie and her puppeteer, who are smeared with marshmallow and soot. Cayden and I use the light of the glowing rabbits to keep our distance without falling in the pit.

"I think you're assuming a bit much if you think we're about to surrender," I say, acting braver than I feel. "From where I'm standing, your house is overrun with vermin, and you're the only two members of the junta still standing."

The glowing zombie rabbits are fist-bumping one another with verminous pride.

"It makes no difference whether we're standing or not," Whanslaw says. "We are far more easily repaired than you." Maggie giggles and capers in the half-light.

At that moment, there's an enormous, roaring shout, and Greeley falls through the trapdoor, making me jump. He fetches up about just above the pit, wriggling in midair, still wearing his porkpie hat, and thoroughly bound in—

"What is that?" I ask Cayden, who makes a disbelieving *idunno* noise.

"Electrical cord," calls Raymond, his silhouette edged with flickering light. "It was the aliens' idea, but I tied the knots."

At my feet, Sugar chortles.

"Look at hammy man! He looks like a worm on a hook!"

"Mmmmmm, worms," says another rabbit, off in the dark, and suddenly there's a mad rabbit rush to the pit. Some take the ladder, but most of them jump. I manage to grab Sugar before he joins them.

"Hey!" he protests as I hold him aloft by his ears, like a lantern.

"Oh no," I tell him. "You're not leaving me here in the dark."

From the pit, I can hear dozens and dozens of sets of creepy little baby teeth clacking, like the rabbits are actually tiny sharks. Serves Greeley right for his big fake "I'm your chum!" act. He's not a happy camper. He's screaming like a mermaid at her first voice lesson.

That's when I see Stella.

Or at least, I see her arriving. Mist curls from the locket around Pearl's neck. Pearl, of course, doesn't react to it at all, and since it's happening behind him, Whanslaw doesn't notice, either. As Stella coalesces, I can see her face reflected in Pearl's sunglasses. Then she turns to me.

I wore that locket for years, and it never sprouted a ghost before.

I am totally jealous.

Stella starts gesturing at me, but I can't tell what it means.

"Ada," calls Raymond, "the fire's coming up the hill pretty fast."

"Good to know." What else am I supposed to say? *I'm trash-talking these evil puppets as fast as I can?*

"Greeley, an update, please," says Whanslaw. Greeley is man-shrieking as the rabbits leap at him. He pulls it together for boss-puppet, though.

"Uh, sir, well, one of those conspirators we were looking for fought Miss Kiyo. Kiyo held her own, but she lost in the end, sorry to say." He grunts as he twists in his bonds, trying to avoid rabbit teeth.

"And the creature?"

"Ate both Miss Kiyo and Mr. Lanchester, sir. Darndest thing. Didn't even know it ate wood—OW!"

Right on the end of the nose. Cayden and I wince, but I'm thinking more about Kiyo's poor puppeteer than Greeley. What have I done?

"The humans?"

"Ran off, sir."

"Then there will be no cavalry," says Whanslaw, ignoring his employee's peril. "Excellent."

That's when everything goes sideways. Maggie makes a sudden lunge for Cayden. I try to stop her, but I can't do anything useful, because I've still got Sugar in one hand, and he's the only reason we can see. Cayden yells, and Stella gets right up in my face, which makes it even harder to see what's going on and help Cayden. Cayden's grappling with Maggie, and I'm trying unsuccessfully to stick my head through Stella, when out of the darkness, a round purple head with a big set of choppers appears, and bites Maggie's left hand clean off.

Xerple crunches it, which is a huge relief because the last thing we need is a creepy Maggie hand running around. He plants his little feet in defiance, and shouts:

"You leave my Cayden ALONE!" Then he charges again. Whanslaw was wrong. Xerple's the smallest cavalry I've ever seen, but he's here, and boy, I'm glad to dimly see him. Now that Cayden has help, I pull my head out of Stella and turn to see what she's trying to show me.

I was wrong. The trapdoor and incandescent rabbits weren't

the only sources of light in here. Over there on the wall, there's a patch of light. Which means there's an opening, and it goes to the surface. I don't even think. I start for it.

"Miss Roundtree."

I aim Sugar over my shoulder.

Whanslaw is holding his small silver pistol to Pearl's head. She's working the strings that allow him to do it. Watching her hurts. I freeze.

"You won't," I say. "If you kill your puppeteer, you're help-less." Still, I don't move. How can I? If I move, I might kill her. If I don't move, she'll die sooner or later, sucked drier than a chupacabra's juice box.

There's a whoosh, and Raymond slides down through the trapdoor on a second length of electrical cord. Mr. Bakshi, the gym teacher, would admire his free rappelling technique, but that's not something I should be thinking about right now. When he's level with the top of the pit, but a safe distance from the now whimper-sobbing Greeley, he swings his way over to the side and jumps off.

"Ada, go!" he shouts, running our way.

I'm paralyzed with indecision, and I never am, and I hate it. "I can't!"

Just then, Stella swoops in front of Whanslaw. I don't know who she startles, him or Pearl, if Pearl even can be startled, but his arm jerks. Raymond launches at him.

I know my cue when I see it.

"Don't kill them!" I shout; then I race for the light spot on the wall.

Chapter 37

Venting

It's some kind of vent. It angles up, and it's frighteningly narrow, but Whanslaw didn't want me near it, and we've trashed everything else. The souls must be up there.

I don't have time to trust in the zombie rabbits' destructive impulses. I have to do it myself. I drop Sugar.

"Finally!" he says, and I know he's about to join the others harassing Greeley. As I force head and shoulders up into the vent, I shout, "Sugar, go help Raymond! Don't let Whanslaw hurt my sister!"

"Oh!" says Sugar, startled. "That's nice. I thought she looked like you."

"GO!"

I hear the whine of a bullet, and feel a vibration in the wall. Maybe Raymond's got hold of Whanslaw's arm and he's shooting wild. Or maybe I'm about to get shot in the legs. I worm the rest of the way in, until I'm past the angle and more or less standing. Then I press my hands and knees against the front of the tunnel, and start worming my way up. The rock scrapes my hands, and the knees of my jeans are going to be gone in minutes.

The light above me seems so far away. It's flickering, and even down here I can smell smoke. I work my way up, and up. I don't know how I'm going to have the strength to get back down if I have to stop. Then, above me, I see an irregularity in the rock. Bracing myself as tightly as I can, I slide one hand up the rock wall. Above my head, almost beyond my reach, my fingertips slide over the lip of a ledge.

Please, oh please.

I can't find anything. I can't reach the back, either. I give up my grip on the ledge to shove myself a few inches higher, then try again.

Doggone it, where does this thing go, Tibet? Below me, I hear mass confusion. Above me, my town is on fire. Everyone I love is in mortal peril. I just need one little stroke of luck.

Then I hear a tiny grunt.

Way back on the ledge, something is scrabbling, and something else is being dragged. The tips of a pair of flowered ears come into view.

"These trophies are as heavy as beeves," complains Snooks.

He puts a stoppered clay jar into my hand.

I am going to read that little sack of rabbit all the bedtime stories. He doesn't need Pearl's room. He can have mine.

"Are there more?"

"Three."

"Bring the next one! Hurry!"

He chortles with competitive glee, and vanishes.

I turn the jar in my hand. It's not a jar after all, not really. It's a clay figure, with closed eyes and lobed ears that stick out on the sides. It has a cork in the back of its head. That's why I thought it was a jar. It's almost like—

"You hid your soul in a puppet? That's original," I mutter.

I look down the vent, between my knees. I can't see the bottom in the gloom. I don't dare drop this, though. If it doesn't smash on the angled surface at the bottom, it will roll right out of the vent, and anyone could get it. I cup it in the palm of my hand, draw my arm back as far as I can in the cramped space, and smash it against the side of the shaft.

I'm nose to nose with the darn thing when it breaks, and I get a face full of a red rageful light that I know at once is Kiyo. For one moment, I see the woman inside the wood. Her soul is so different from the flawless puppet. It's blotchy and bloodshot-eyed, like her anger is eating her from the inside out. She screams upward in a shower of red sparks, going off like fireworks as she exits the vent, and I'm left temporarily blinded in the dim light.

"Snooks!" I call. "I need another one."

It darn near hits me in the head as he rolls it off the edge. This one is squared-off, though still with a face. It makes it easier to smash.

It must be Lanchester, though it looks nothing like him.

Glimmering light reveals a dark-haired man, good-looking in his way, but with eyes just a little too wide, like he's trying to appear guileless. I have a sudden breathless sensation, as if I've been plunged underwater, then he, too, streaks away to the surface.

The smell of smoke is worsening, and I cough as Snooks hands me the third puppet jar. My legs are tired and starting to shake from bracing me against the walls of the shaft, and I feel sick from the hatred swirling around me. I smash the jar without looking.

At once, I feel nasty, grabby hands all over me. Poking, pinching. The shaft reverberates with the echo of wild giggles. But this soul doesn't go up. It scuttles away down the shaft like it's looking for something.

"Look out!" I yell. I don't know if anyone can hear me. I cough my throat raw, and try again. "Look *out!*"

Alarmed yells ring out below me. I have to get back down there.

"Snooks!" I say. "HURRY!"

"Okay, okay," he says crabbily. "Hold your forces."

He brings me a clay frog. I don't have to smash this one to know whose it is.

I lift my arm, ready to smash it as hard as I can.

Then the wall of the shaft crumbles under my left shoe, and I slip.

In my panic, my instinct is to preserve the frog when I should destroy it instead, so I don't use my right hand to stop myself from falling. Instead, my left leg drops, my other leg isn't enough to hold me up, and I slither and fall to the bottom of the shaft, so hard that I raise dust and my bones rattle.

Before I can recover, hard wooden hands are dragging me out into the pit house.

I'm coughing and choking on dust, and Whanslaw's face is looming over mine, his features edged by the light from the shaft.

I can't think fast enough. I don't know whether to roll over on the clay frog to stop him from taking it, or throw it, or slam it down on the ground, and before I can do any of those things he's got my wrist and is twisting it so viciously that I'm crying aloud.

He drags me to my feet.

Whanslaw tries to take the frog with his free hand, and I have just enough presence of mind to stumble into him. The frog falls from my overpowered fingers, but it doesn't break, just rolls clinking across the hard floor. Whanslaw is sandwiched between me and Pearl, but he's already shoving me away. As he releases my wrist, I have one moment of clarity, and shove both my hands through the center of his strings like I'm playing a life-or-death game of cat's cradle.

I have to slow him down, but I can't break his connection to my sister.

I grab for her hands, and hold them down on the controls.

He lunges for the frog jar, Pearl moving with him, and I throw myself down, gripping Pearl's hands just as tight as I can. We collapse on our sides on the floor.

Whanslaw is twisting and snarling, trying to get at me. Raymond and Cayden are shouting questions, trying to help.

"Get the frog!" I yell, but I don't know where Sugar got to, and it's so dark. They probably don't have a clue what I'm talking about.

Then I hear a delighted little voice exclaim, "A-ha!"

"NO!" booms Whanslaw, and then there's the loud smash of terra-cotta against the floor.

The air around Pearl and me pulsates with a shocked, roaring bullfrog croak, and Whanslaw's puppet arms and legs stick straight out, rigidly, tightening the strings painfully around my arms. I scream again.

Behind my back, something nasty scrabbles across me and squirms its way between me and Whanslaw. I cry out in disgust. Then the noise becomes muffled, as if it's coming from inside the puppet.

"Smash him!" I shout to the boys. "Smash him now!"

Raymond's boot comes down on the puppet. There's a splintering crash that shakes me all over again, and a final, maddened, strangling croak.

Greeley yells, "Boss! No!"

I hear businesslike snapping, like someone's sizing kindling.

Then I hear the only noise I care about. Pearl's voice, confused, but hers.

"Ada?"

"Hey, Pearl."

Whanslaw's strings are cutting into my skin as the boys

destroy him between us. My fingers cramp as I force them to let go of Pearl's hands. The wooden control bar whispers from her grip and clunks against the floor.

My head hurts.

"Ada?" says Snooks. "I smashed the trophy. We won regionals. Be excited."

I pass out.

Chapter 38

Splinters

"Xerple, stop! You're going to get splinters!" says Cayden.

The loud crunching must not have been in my head, then.

"So?" asks Xerple, crunching some more.

"It's bad for you!"

Xerple makes the noise he uses to shrug, since he doesn't have shoulders. "Is good for everyone else."

"You might as well drink Signal Boost to wash it down," Cayden grumbles.

I blink. My eyes are prickly, but my head is resting on something soft.

"I hate puppets," I croak.

"We need that on a T-shirt," says Raymond.

"Stop patting me on the head, Pearl," I say. "It's demeaning."

Wait.

I open my eyes all the way, and keep them open, even though it stings. The first thing I see is glowing green light. I turn my head toward it. The three glow-stick-eating rabbits are in an inverted pyramid formation, with Sugar on the bottom. He gives me a grin and a thumbs-up, and the whole trio wobbles dangerously.

Then something slides into view directly above me, and I turn my head to look straight at it. It's Pearl's head, upside down. My head must be resting on her lap.

"So, hi," she says. "You saved me from the evil puppets, but you couldn't save me from hair puffs?"

"Waah," I say. "You stole my locket, and suddenly it has a portable ghost. So unfair."

There's a loud crash overhead.

"Is that the aliens?" I ask. "Someone should tell them we found the trophies."

"I think it's the rest of the house falling down," says Raymond, like it's no big deal.

"I'm sorry, what?"

"The pit-house roof seems to be protecting us from the worst of it. The rabbits had to get out of the pit, though."

There's some grumbling off to one side.

I cough, then sit up, scooting so I can lean on Pearl in case she tries to vanish or something.

"What did you do with Greeley?" I ask.

Cayden shoves his hair out of his face, revealing some nasty scratches on his forehead. "One of the rabbits bit a knot by accident. Greeley got loose and climbed back up the cords right before the house started collapsing. I don't think he made it out in time."

I nod, and point at his poor bloody head.

"Maggie?" I ask.

"Yeah."

Xerple takes another big bite out of what I now see is a pile of red robes, black yarn, and puppet shrapnel. He chews with vicious satisfaction.

"I understand beavers now," he says. "Trees are jerks."

"Why are we still here?" I ask. I didn't save Pearl just to get her buried in a fiery grave.

"What were we supposed to do, carry you out on a travois made of evil puppet parts?" asks Pearl.

I shudder. "Okay. But we're leaving now." I stand up, and nothing wobbles but me, so that's good.

There's a carpet of zombie rabbits and tiny aliens all around us, stretching away into the dark beyond the rabbit lamp. The aliens must have retreated down here when the fire got bad. They look pretty dispirited to have lost regionals, but things are remarkably peaceful, aside from a bit of shoving in the ranks.

"We made them shake hands," says Raymond. "It took forever."

Coral Brain grunts. "Appendage-ist."

Raymond deflates a little. It has been a really long day.

Pearl pats him on the shoulder. "Come on, Mendez. Let's go see if the town burned down." Her hand trembles a little, and I think about how long it's been since she's been home.

"Hey," I say. "Pearl."

She turns to me, and I grab her and hug her as tight as I can. She hugs me back, right away, which makes me feel less ridiculous for doing this in front of everyone. This time, she's warm, like a sister is supposed to be. I lean my cheek against hers. We're still just the same size and shape. I may never let her out of my sight again.

"It'll be okay," I say. "Our family kicks all the butt."

"Yeah," she says, and I know she's smiling.

Over her shoulder, I notice how worried Cayden looks when I say that. He probably thinks his parents are roasting the town's remaining marshmallows in the oncoming flames while quaffing Signal Boost.

He might be right.

"Let's go," I say, letting go of my twin, and we limp out to the hallway with aliens and rabbits flowing around our knees.

"We're going to have to come back, you know," says Raymond. "We can't just leave the pit house here for someone else to use."

The log roof caves in behind us with a terrific crash. A shower of sparks rushes out into the hallway. Zombie rabbits everywhere beat out the flames on one another's pajamas with their ears.

"Or not," says Raymond.

The tunnel seems twice as long going back. The power's permanently out, so the glow-stick rabbits do their best to light the way, but there's a lot of stumbling and running into one another and complaining. I sure hope the Blurmonster didn't damage the other door too badly to open it, because the mood's going to go south in a hurry if we have to backtrack. Xerple snarls at anyone who gets too close to Cayden. When the flickering green glow lights them for a moment, I catch Cayden patting Xerple on the head.

It takes all of us to budge the door when we get there—the aliens and rabbits stack themselves in bizarre, swaying towers to help. It finally opens with a squeal, then falls off the hinges completely. It lands on the floor of the freezer with a groaning crash, rocking slightly on what's left of Whanslaw's sculpture's bashed-in nose.

We troop out of the freezer. I'm so tired, I'm zombie-walking, but I'm awake enough to remember to check for the Blurmonster, just in case it's still cranky. To my relief, the loading dock door has a Blurmonster-shaped hole in it, through which I can see a gorgeous New Mexico sunrise. I hear a distant chutter, so I figure we're probably safe.

Then, off to the left, I hear a shrill, whiny shriek.

"No! Absolutely not! No no no no no!"

It's Dewey.

If it weren't for the name tag pinned to his safety vest, he'd be unrecognizable. His hair is standing straight up, gelled with marshmallow. In fact, he's basically head-to-toe marshmallow, coated with soot. Despite his personal filth, he's running a floor buffer through the middle of the sea of melted marshmallows and BASH!

His eyes are bugging in a thoroughly irrational way. They're also fixed on us.

"No!" he screams again. I hold my hands up to show him we come in peace (this time).

"Whoa, Dewey. We were just—" I say, but he's having none of it.

"What?" he squeals. "Are you back to unleash a plague of locusts? Paint a mural on the front window with kale smoothies? Take a random dollar amount from each cash register right before shift change? When my uncle gets back, he's going to—"

"Dude," says Cayden, "I don't think he's coming back. The puppet junta's house sort of burned up and fell on him."

"Well that's just GREAT!" Dewey yells. "Now I have to close! And tomorrow I have to open! I have to CLOPEN!" He revs the buffer, and I realize he hasn't blinked in a really long time.

"We should go," I say, nodding like he's rational and I'm respecting his space. "We'll just . . . we'll go now." We all begin shuffling toward the front of the stockroom, trying not to turn our backs on him. The rabbits and aliens run ahead, bursting through the swinging door and whooping like kids coming back from Unstructured Outdoor Social Interaction.

I guess we don't move fast enough, because Dewey snorts like an angry bull.

"GET OUUUUUUT!" he rages, and it almost sounds like an honest-to-goodness Greeley roar. Dewey brandishes the buffer, sweeping it in wide arcs back and forth across the floor, then runs at us. "AAAAAAHHHHHHHH!" he yells.

"AAAAAHHHHHHHH!" we yell.

We run.

Chapter 39

In One Piece

As it turns out, Oddiputians didn't need the puppet junta near as much as they thought.

The town is filthy, but it's still here. Old Joe and Young Joe are in front of Bodega Bodega, handing out water bottles. They do a quadruple take when they see me and Pearl together, but we just thank them for the water, and guzzle it down.

Pearl looks at each building like an old friend. Through the co-op window, we see Scoby drifting, exhausted, in his jar. Outside, Raymond's mom is using a squeegee to clean the windows. Raymond gives each of us a shoulder squeeze or a slap on the back. Then he goes to hold her stepladder for her, because she's staring at me and Pearl, and her eyes are welling up, and it looks like she's about to fall off.

The bakery's in one piece, but locked.

"Wait'll you see what's new in there," I tell Pearl.

As we approach our street, Song steps outside her shop with a broom.

"Song!" I yell. I run to her and give her a hug, finishing the job of trashing the butterfly dress I found so pretty yesterday.

"Ada!" She gasps, and hugs me back hard. "How did you get away?"

"Oh," I say. "We overthrew the junta."

No one would dare to say something like that if it wasn't true, and she knows it. Her thousand-watt smile starts powering up and hits full brightness right as she looks up and sees Pearl. All of a sudden her eyes are sparkling with diamond tears.

"Hello, Pearl," she says.

Pearl smiles, but her attention's all focused on our street. She grabs for me, and we walk up the hill swinging our hands between us, Cayden and Xerple trailing behind us.

We crest the top of the hill just as Bets is stretching her back. I bet she's been on her new blades way too long. She looks sore. When she sees us, she loses her balance and just about falls over. Daddy steps out from behind the hedge and grabs her, steadying her. I can see her squeezing his arms, but she never takes her eyes off us.

"Sis?" Daddy asks.

She points. Daddy turns and looks at us, and he sways like a tree about to fall.

Then Mama walks around the side of the house with a

bucket. She spots us right away, but it's like she's all of a sudden stuck to the ground. I can see the water sloshing over the top of the bucket as it shakes in her grip.

Pearl squeezes my hand till it hurts.

"Dale?" says Mama.

"Yeah?" he says back, real soft.

"Are they really there?" Oh, my poor mama.

Daddy gives a bit of a sob. "Well, Veda," he says, "I don't know." He reaches a hand back to her. "How about we go and find out?"

She puts the bucket down slow, wiping her hands on her skirt. Then she walks over, takes Daddy's hand, and they come down the front steps together.

It's not real until Mama touches us. She reaches out to feel Pearl's sleeve, and when that turns out to exist, she puts one shaky hand on my left cheek, and the other on Pearl's right. She cups our faces together. I forgot how she did that. It must have looked strange to her when it was only me, like half of a valentine heart.

Daddy gives a great big sob behind Mama, and the next thing I know, he's hugging all three of us so hard we might get compressed into one person by the time he's done. He's kissing on all three of our heads, and I hear Bets yelling for Mason and Badri somewhere over his shoulder.

Cayden's mom hollers for him from their back porch, sounding much more like Aunt Bets than her recent, Signal Boost–addled self. Cayden takes off at a run, with Xerple loping behind.

Daddy finally loosens up on us a little, and my mama fingers Pearl's puffs.

"Your hair needs done," she says, like she can't think what else to say. "Come on inside, and I'll get it all fixed up."

She pulls us toward the house, but before I can go anywhere, my daddy takes me by the shoulder.

"Will they be coming for you girls?" he asks me, low. "Do we need to ready ourselves?"

I can see in his eyes that he means it. He'd take on the whole junta all by himself before he'd let us go again.

"No, Daddy. We took care of it." He cups my face like Mama did. Then, to my everlasting surprise, he picks me up like I'm a little girl, and hugs me tight.

"Just one more time," he says to me, "before you're running the show."

I guess that's okay with me.

Six months later

You would not believe how much chaos a bunch of fifth graders searching for pizza can cause. We won the end-of-year pizza party, of course. With Pearl back in class, how could we lose? We were unstoppable. We also (and this is key) convinced Mr. Bakshi and Principal Zimmerman that ordering from Ransom Pizza and hunting down our reward would be a good bonding exercise for the fifth grade. Raymond, Cayden, Pearl, and I have been planning today for months.

I sidle past the gym, where Myrtle is head down in a bin full of volleyballs. All I can see of her is her feet and her braids. There are clangs and screams coming from the cafeteria kitchen, where the trolls, Ralph and Delmar, are pillaging. I race around the corner undetected and join Raymond and Pearl, who are crammed into the water fountain nook outside the principal's office.

"Last one," I say, passing it to my sister.

"You didn't open it, did you?" Pearl demands, taking the greasy pizza box from me.

I scoff.

Cayden eases the office door open from the inside and waves us over. Raymond and I keep a lookout as Pearl passes Cayden the pizza. He disappears inside. He's back a minute later, empty-handed.

"They're so busy laughing at the security monitors I could have put one on Mrs. O'Halloran's lap," he says scornfully.

"This was a good idea," I say. "The grown-ups were getting a little too comfortable around here."

"Seriously," says Raymond. "How do they not realize we can avoid the surveillance cameras? Time check."

I glance at my phone. "Eight seconds . . . six . . . four . . . two . . ."

An enormous explosion rocks the main office. Tomato sauce and cheese hit the windows with a splatter so loud that I bet it's making janitors shudder ten miles away.

We can hear Mrs. O'Halloran having hysterics.

Pearl and I look at each other.

"I missed you so much," we say in unison, then laugh.

After school, the class crams into our yard to eat the non-exploding pizza we paid for by passing a hat around. Sending pictures of our pizza-coated teachers to literally everyone we know is not quite as good as a really great sneak, but it's a close second.

Later, when only the four of us are left, we lie on our backs in the patchy grass, tossing marshmallows in the air for the zombie rabbits.

The consequences of the fire are mostly dealt with now. Evil puppet mansion is a heap of rubble. Kids go up there on dares sometimes, but that's about it.

Cayden told his parents how Greeley had been drugging them and why. He took them to the co-op, where they talked to Raymond's mom (and Scoby, after some initial shock) about natural detox protocols. Now they drink kombucha instead of Signal Boost.

I'm not sure that's an actual improvement.

But it turns out that when they're not being drugged, Cayden's parents can be reasoned with. So Cayden gets to stay, Xerple gets to keep his person, and we definitely have more bars on our phones, as long as we're not calling long distance. We might even get high-speed Internet, if Cayden's parents can convince Splint to put them in charge of the project.

The other aliens have relocated to the Murphys' house, for the most part. There's an infestation of monkeys with type-writers over there, which they find amusing, and of course it's total chaos. The zombie rabbits have sort of adopted Xerple as one of their own, which makes everything much easier. Pearl and Snooks are still fighting for possession of her bedroom. He locks her out pretty regularly, so it's a good thing Daddy moved the trellis.

Last night, it was warm enough to sleep with my window open a little, and I thought I heard the Blurmonster growling in the distance, but I can't be sure.

Lying in the yard with my friends, my sister, and our toothy little minions, it's hard to worry about it.

I hear Badri's truck doors slam down on the street, and Mason comes bounding up. He grins at us, raising his arms over his head.

"BOOM! SPLAT!" he yells, obviously thrilled to be one degree of separation from Pizzapocalypse.

We cheer.

"You still running deliveries for me tomorrow?" Bets asks Cayden, as she and Badri arrive more slowly. Badri has his arm around my aunt's shoulder. She's got her capris rolled up, and her blades are as elegant as the legs of a crane.

"Bright and early," agrees Cayden. He eats a lot better, working for Bets. She makes sure of it.

"What's for dinner?" asks Pearl. It's Badri and Bets's turn to cook. I'm stuffed, but my sister is still making up for a year in the puppet junta pokey.

"What is for dinner?" repeats Badri, with great enthusiasm. "We are going to have some curry, and I am going to teach you amateurs to eat soor. Get on in here and roll up your sleeves.

I need sous chefs." He's still talking as he enters the house. I hear Bets and Mama calling out to each other, and Stella slamming my closet door in greeting.

"Curry sounds gooood," says Pearl, getting up and reaching down a hand for me. I grab it, and let her pull me to my feet.

Snooks makes a run for the house. "I'll be in my bedroom!" he shouts.

"Stay out of my hat pins!" Pearl says, taking off after him.

Down at the Murphys', there's an explosion. The tiny aliens cheer. The monkeys scream. A smoking typewriter lands in our yard with a crash.

It's going to be a great summer.

Acknowledgments

Just as *Oddity*'s strength lies in the bonds between members of its community, so, too, does mine. There are far more people to thank than I could ever name here, but I'll do my best.

To my agent, Brooks Sherman. You are exactly what I believed you'd be: my toughest critic and staunchest advocate. You impose order on my chaos while somehow managing to be utterly subversive the entire time. I'm forever grateful, super-agent. If we're someday attacked by zombies, I promise not to leave you . . . but I'll be watching you like a hawk.

To Holly West, editrix extraordinare, geeky fangirl, and cosplay goddess. Our very first conversation was a lightbulb moment for me, and I knew right then that you were the perfect editor for *Oddity*! Working with you is a delight. Thank you so much for making this dream a reality.

To the amazing team at Macmillan, including Ilana Worrell,

Melinda Ackell, and Liz Dresner. You put so much work into making this book shine (and had to ask some really weird clarifying questions, because . . . me). Thank you!

Thanks are due to both Bridget Smith and Laura Biagi, who may be surprised to discover they share a brain. I'm eternally grateful for your generous (and spookily similar) feedback.

Many thanks to the members of Working Title, my first and most precious critique group, to Katie Glover for bringing us together, and to Robots & Rogues/Main Street Books, for hosting. To my Midwest Writers family: thank you so much for our big, friendly clan, a gold mine of shared knowledge, and the opportunity to meet talented and savvy professionals, my agent included! Carmel-area writers, you give amazing shop talk and feedback, and are my favorite reward for writing.

In a household as bustling as mine, the best way to write is often to leave. And so, to Robin Raabe at the Tramontane Cafe, Colleen Mathews at Fuel Coffee, and all the good folks at Star City and Greyhouse, thank you for filling my cup, both literally and figuratively.

To all my Pitch Warriors, particularly the inimitable Brenda Drake, my mentors, Jaye Robin Brown and Cat Scully, and the Pitch Wars '14 crew (ToT). Your support and insight mean the world to me. To the many friends I've made as part of the 2017 Debuts: your pooled knowledge and enthusiasm have been so crucial to the transition from writer to author!

All my love to the writers who hold me up and keep me sane, especially Amy Reichert, Melissa Marino, Carla Cullen, Allison Pang, and Summer Heacock. To Chelsey Blair, a gimlet-eyed reader who did Oddity no end of good, and to those beloved friends who read Oddity and instantly "got it," especially Nina Moreno, Angie Thomas, and Jess Walton. (Kayla Whaley, you did me such a solid by introducing me to Jess!) To any readers not already named or alluded to: I would not be here today without you. Thank you.

To all the hipmamas and rebelmamas, the fierce, brilliant, rowdy tribe of women who've been there from the beginning. I love you all.

To the many writers on Twitter who take on the often thankless tasks of education and advocacy: I learn so much from you. And many thanks to the authors further down the path who've shown me so much kindness over the years, especially Sarah Prineas, who gave me some of the best advice I've gotten (during my biggest crisis of faith), Sage Blackwood, who always takes the time to have a care for my career, Heidi Schulz, who distributes reassurance and spiders in equal measure, the wonderfully collegial members of the #Bteam, the darling Stephanie Burgis, and the delightful Tiffany Trent.

To my Lancaster mamas, Katye, Melanie, Kym, and Diana. Diana, we'll miss you forever, and yes, this is the best day of my entire life.

Many thanks to my sisters and brothers (Jenny, Kate, Chrissie, Scott, Josh, John, and Matt), and to my parents and Bill's. In particular, I have to thank my mom, Beth, who knew I would do this even when I did not, and my mother-in-law, Cathy, who is always ready with all the straight talk about the "work" of prioritizing my work.

Most of all, I owe eternal gratitude to my husband, Bill, and our kids, Will, Rosemary, and Graeme. Our family's oddball sense of humor and general geekery underpin every word of this book, and it would never have been written without your unflagging support. You are the Swiss Army knife of families.